Thirst Hollow

A Work of Climate Fiction

Doug Jones

A lot of hard work went into this book., I hope you enjoy it and I sincerely thank you for reading.

1

The Riot

The crowd oscillated Pepper forward and back. Slowly like the ocean, but also as powerful. Pepper's feet were his anchor, so when he rose to his tiptoes the crowd swayed him harder, but his toes maintained contact with the earth.

Up high Pepper was able to get a good view of the rippling mass of people surrounding him. In every direction turbulent waves of people crashed, spraying noise like salty sea mist. Some individuals that made up the mass held slogans inscribed on home-made signs held high above their heads.

Water For Locals Not Casinos
Keep Vegas Water in Vegas
We're Thirsty

Spreading past the yelling protesters lay the quarter-mile long water fountain of the Bellagio Casino. Its idle rippling water sent flashes of the hot, dry desert sun into Pepper's eyes, so he turned away and faced the police barricade. Officers in riot gear stood in front of the crowd protecting the casino's entrance, a row of tinted black glass doors. Only a flimsy waist high metal barrier separated them from the crowd, and occasional shoving arms and swinging fists penetrated the boundary from both sides, some striking their target, some missing.

Riot helmets and tinted shades prevented Pepper from seeing the officers' faces, but he knew they were scared. Cornered and grossly outnumbered, their barrier was nothing more than a safety blanket. The crowd would rush the doors of the Bellagio whether or not they held their ground. But for the moment, the crowd was kept at bay.

Pepper sympathized with the police. He came to Las Vegas not to start trouble or to hurt anyone, but to try to help people in need of water.

Lake Mead was drying up, and Las Vegas, a city spawned from the harsh, dry desert, drew most of its drinking water from it. With a large portion of the water aggressively claimed by downstream cities like Los Angeles and Phoenix, Las Vegas couldn't simply take more water. Instead, they watched it flow through Hoover Dam, leaving a receding shoreline and a dirty bathtub ring reminiscent of a wetter time.

A week earlier the level of Lake Mead hit a historic low. Its surface fell below municipal water intakes, so household taps across Las Vegas went dry. People didn't have running water. No water to bathe with, no water to cook with, no water to drink.

FEMA reacted quickly by hauling tankers of water to Las Vegas, but the trucks were unreliable and insufficient, so the citizens of Las Vegas were drying out under the hot desert sun. Their plight drew sympathy from Pepper, but an even greater transgression put his feet in motion and brought him from his home in southwest Utah.

While the people of Las Vegas grew thirstier and thirstier, tourists visiting the strip enjoyed a normal vacation of water-filled pools, long showers, and iconic blasting jet streams of the Bellagio fountain. Using their status in the city legally or otherwise, the casinos made sure their supply of water, and therefore cash, continued uninterrupted.

The profits of corporations were paramount to the needs of the citizens. And to add to the injustice, many of those same people worked in the casinos, enabling the profits to continue. Maybe if those people quit, the casinos would be forced to reassess their actions, but how could they leave their jobs? If they quit, they wouldn't just be thirsty, they'd also be broke. They were trapped either by the corporations' design, or their indifference.

So the Las Vegans lived with the injustice, struggling to get by, until the nationwide environmental group Net Zero took notice and organized a protest in retaliation. Support spread the nation like wildfire and once Pepper caught wind of it, he drove down from his home in Utah to stand with the people of Las Vegas, against climate change, and against corporate oppression of the working class.

Pepper tried to convince his girlfriend Olivia – who he endearingly called Olive – to join, but she thought it was a bad idea.

"What if something happens to you?" she asked. "Is it really worth risking yourself for those people? You don't even know anyone in Las Vegas."

Pepper hardly registered Olive's arguments. He had heard similar objections from her a hundred times before, but she wasn't any more successful that day than any of the other times she tried to get him to consider their own needs before helping someone else. What Olive saw as an undesirable and persisting reality, Pepper always put others' needs before his own, and even hers.

Pepper understood Olive's instinct of self-preservation was pragmatic and a product of her difficult childhood, just like his own behavior was a product of his troubled past. But he couldn't ignore the needs of the Las Vegans, no matter how much Olive tried to persuade him otherwise. There was an instinct built deep into his anatomy, only differing from a fight-or-flight reaction in that it was acquired at twenty-three years old instead of at birth.

So when Pepper heard Las Vegas was struggling without water, he couldn't turn a blind eye. A sinking feeling in his gut paired with his anxious mind that looped nonstop, *You'd better go join the protest. They need help. If you don't help, and things get worse for them, it will be your fault. How will you forgive yourself if something bad happens out there knowing you could have done something about it?* Pepper couldn't take Olive's advice of self-preservation, no matter how strong her argument was.

Olive was well aware of Pepper's compulsion to help others, but she didn't fully understand the root of his behavior. In the time Olive had known Pepper, she saw a sudden shift in his personality – from young and selfish, to mature and compassionate – following a terrible accident while they both were wildland firefighters. But Olive never asked for details about what happened that day. Pepper carried a lot of pain and guilt because of it, and she didn't want to hurt Pepper more by digging up the past.

Instead, Olive tried to guide him away from his habits she viewed as self-destructive. But those attempts were ineffective, so she was forced to at least try to come to terms with Pepper's compulsion to help others. So Olive stayed back at their home in Utah lamenting Pepper's decision to leave for Las Vegas, while Pepper bobbed in a sea of angry protesters, restrained by a fragile dam of policemen that showed signs of breaching.

The day started as Pepper expected. They marched along the strip, holding signs and chanting. Camaraderie and hope radiated through the air. Pepper was happy to help, and basked in the sunshine and good vibes, but once the parade arrived at the front of the Bellagio, the atmosphere changed.

Blocked by the police, there was no more space to move forward, and the crowd crashed in behind Pepper. Like an avalanche settling, protestors cemented around him, forcing the air from his lungs and Pepper's panic set in. Pepper was pushed from behind, and with no space between him and the next person, the kinetic energy transferred forward.

"Sorry," Pepper said as his frantic eyes watched Newton's law demonstrated in real time. The equal and opposite reactions created a ripple of collisions, and the pulse traveled all the way to the police barrier. As it hit the blockade, the police were pushed toward the casino's doors and the crowd instantly consumed the relinquished space. A frightened policeman shouted for everyone to keep back, but just like Pepper's apology, the officer's voice was lost in the ambient angry shouting.

Deafening noise assailed Pepper from every direction. He was trapped, and the mass of bodies surrounding him, bumping into him, added to his panic. Pepper frantically wanted to get out, but there was no way. There was no room to move, much less escape. He was trapped at the mercy of the hundreds of people surrounding him, all of whom were also powerless to the collective mob, an entity whose will and direction had become autonomous, its power greater than the sum of its parts.

Then, *WOOSH*. A noise erupted, not necessarily louder, but so wildly different in character that it upstaged the crowd's yelling. Over the heads of the protestors, Pepper saw a series of cascading towers erupting into the sky. The white misty exteriors danced back and forth, up and down. A show that would have been beautiful if not for its medium, or worse, its timing. Whether it was a tragic accident, a misguided attempt at de-escalation, or a hubristic *fuck you* to the protesters, someone had initiated the Bellagio's iconic water fountain.

The fountain's terrible noise vanished as soon as it came, but not because it was shut off. Instead, enraged by the frivolous use of water, the crowd erupted into fiery chaos, drowning out the sound of the blasting columns. The crowd screamed and pushed and Pepper felt pressure from all sides, elbows jabbing and hands shoving.

Fuck. He thought. *I need to get out of here.*

Pepper's eyes darted, looking for a way out, but all that surrounded him was an unbroken mass of people. Like atoms forming a solid, each insignificant person joined together to create an impenetrable surface.

Far behind, Pepper saw a wave. From the back of the crowd, a pulse of energy traveled through a medium of people as one person crashed into the next. As it neared, Pepper tightened his shoulders to brace as it crested upon him. He leaned back in anticipation, but the enormous energy knocked him forward. Momentarily disoriented, Pepper only saw angry faces as he tried to recover his bearings.

Pepper looked forward just as the wave collided with the police line, blowing their bodies to the ground. A void momentarily opened at the front of the crowd, and the protestors instinctively heaved forward, running until they slammed against the shiny, black glass doors of the Bellagio. Around Pepper, people flew by, racing toward what they saw as their enemy. They wanted inside for either water or blood. But Pepper didn't follow. In the vacant space around him, Pepper saw his opportunity to flee.

Pepper turned about face and tried running the way he came, but the opposing current of running bodies was too strong. Desperate, Pepper looked right then left, and saw his way out. He turned and ran perpendicular to the flow of the crowd, running into people, and others slamming into him.

Somehow keeping his feet under him, Pepper finally reached the railing separating the raised entrance way from the Bellagio's fountain. Almost instantaneously bodies of protestors filled the empty space. Pepper could feel the air grow thin, diluted and poisoned with carbon dioxide. He was scared, but he was where he needed to be.

Pepper looked over the railing. His path to safety, his salvation, and the cause of the chaos around him were one in the same: the water fountain.

Five feet below him, the glinting surface of the water welcomed Pepper. He took one last look at the crowd, swung his legs over the railing, and fell into the cool sapphire water. For a moment, while floating weightlessly, the deafening yells of the crowd were muted. Underwater there was no noise, only peace.

Suspended, Pepper watched as an amorphous cellophane bubble floated past his face – a small volume of air Pepper brought with him into the water. The bubble raced upward and breached the shimmering membrane above, crossing the threshold into the world Pepper just left. Running low on breath Pepper kicked his legs and pumped his arms, pulling himself toward the water's surface not to rejoin the world as the bubble had, but to escape it.

Pepper's head surfaced, but his body stayed below the cool water as he swam, weighed down by his wet clothes and heavy shoes. The fountain continued to shoot powerful blasts of water into the air, and Pepper didn't dare submerge his head for fear of being struck. Instead, he doggie-paddled.

With his head up, Pepper was able to keep an eye on the peaceful protest turned violent mob. The transformation frightened Pepper, but he understood. They were thirsty and scared for their lives. They were angry the casinos diverted their water for frivolous use by tourists. It was unfair and he wanted to help, but his fear for his safety was greater than his want for justice.

Pepper swam until he was far enough from the protest's violent epicenter to feel safe. Treading along the edge of the fountain, Pepper found a maintenance ladder and climbed out. He was soaked to the bone, and his clothes hung heavily off his body, but even in his aqueous state, Pepper could feel the hot desert sun radiating heat onto his body. As he walked, small squirts of water came from his shoes – tiny replicas of the fountain that so quickly escalated the protest.

Other protestors passed, but Pepper was of little interest compared to the scene at the entrance of the Bellagio. The mob began using benches and metal ashtray towers as battering rams to gain access to the casino. Once the doors were compromised, they funneled into the casino like sand through an hourglass.

People passing by watched with fixed eyes, but Pepper didn't look back. He had had enough. He was there to make a positive change, to try to get what the people of Las Vegas deserved, but since his life became endangered, he had no interest in what was happening. Instead, he slogged back to his truck, leaving a dark, wet trail on the sidewalk behind him. The water sparkled in the hot, midday light, but quickly evaporated, leaving no trace of his presence.

Pepper walked for blocks and blocks before coming to where he left his truck. He didn't bother to try to dry off or remove his wet clothes before he got in. It was an old pickup, and a little water was the least of its problems.

As Pepper sat in the driver's seat for a moment, relieved he made it back, his hand went to his pocket where he felt his phone. Slowly he pulled the sleek, shiny iPhone out, pressing the home button in hopes the screen would light up, but only a reflection of his own face appeared on the dark, lifeless screen. Disappointed and a little mad at himself, Pepper tossed the waterlogged phone on the passenger side of the bench seat, not worried about its functionality, but more about his inability to call his Olive.

He knew she would be worrying as she checked the news about the protest and watched it escalate into chaos and violence. Unable to call and tell her he was okay, Pepper started the truck and guided it back to the interstate to get home and tell her in person. He didn't want her to keep her in the dark longer than necessary, and he worried her initial misgivings about him going to the protest would ferment into a stronger, more hostile feeling the longer he was gone. As he drove away, Pepper turned on the radio to NPR, the preset station, but quickly turned it off as it was live coverage of the protest. Pepper didn't need to be reminded of the chaos he just left.

On the edge of the sprawling Las Vegas metropolis, the city's orthogonal buildings dissolved into organic brown, rocky desert. Speckling the roadside stood the native residents of the area; creosote bushes, mesquite trees, and the occasional Joshua tree. These plants, unlike the local human population, were adapted for the tiny amount of rainfall endemic to the area. They didn't rely on water drawn from the dammed Colorado River like Las Vegas. Instead, they stood stoically, hoping they also could survive the megadrought plaguing the American west.

After leaving Nevada and barely grazing the northwest corner of Arizona, Pepper passed through the tight, winding Virgin River Gorge. On either side of him, gray limestone cliffs towered, cut by the lowly Virgin River which also supplied Pepper's municipal water back home. Pepper looked at the water tumbling over and around broken limestone cobbles, grateful it was his water source, and not the Colorado River like the poor souls in Las Vegas. Though the Virgin River wasn't without faults of its own. Its problem wasn't quantity, but quality.

Climate change increased the Virgin's water temperatures and promoted growth of a blue green algae and the release of a harmful neurotoxin which posed a serious risk to the potability of Pepper's drinking water. At the time, the water reservoirs were voluminous enough to dilute the toxin, but ever-increasing water temperatures forecasted a dire situation.

With the thoughts of the water-fueled riot still buzzing in the back of his mind, Pepper worried about his water supply. Far fewer people lived in southwest Utah than in the Las Vegas area, but he had seen earlier that day how dangerously desperate people could act.

Would his own neighbors become violent when water and other resources became scarce? Would they try to take what was his if they didn't have enough of their own?

Pepper and Olive had long discussed the impending consequences of climate change. They loved existing alongside the uncaring beauty of Utah's red rock desert, but knew it was an environment that even in the best of times provided humans with a precarious existence. Olive and Pepper had talked about moving elsewhere. Somewhere affordable where they could create a little homestead and live off the land. Somewhere with water and lushness. Somewhere they could live off the grid and grow their own food.

Pepper dreamed of a lifestyle that connected him to the seasons, the weather, and the Earth. One that would put him in harmonious synchronism with the rhythms of nature, and would not only reduce their carbon output, but through regenerative farming techniques actually sequester carbon from the atmosphere into their soil.

Olive thought all that sounded fine and good, but what attracted her most to the homesteading lifestyle was the idea of self-sufficiency. Learned early in life from her deadbeat father, Olive believed she couldn't count on others to take care of her needs, that only *she* had her best interest in mind. And the more time she was with Pepper – who she originally started dating because of his genuine generosity towards her and others – the more she felt she couldn't always count on him to put her needs first. So with the impending consequences of climate change, the idea controlling every single resource needed for her survival appealed to Olive.

Their homesteading dream was born years earlier, soon after Olive and Pepper started dating, and they tried to emulate a similar life in Utah. Pepper found a job at an organic farm to learn how to grow crops, and at home they grew a garden, baked sourdough bread, and canned food, but the desert climate and price of land didn't align with their goals. It was too expensive to find a plot large enough to support them that also was connected to irrigation water. To Pepper, the idea of buying a farm was always a distant hypothetical – something he deeply yearned for but didn't expect to happen anytime soon – but recently he had noticed a serious undertone in Olive's voice when she brought up the subject.

As Pepper drove, twisting around the jutting limestone canyon walls, with images of the protest in Las Vegas rattling around in his mind, the thought of starting a homestead began to sound less like an idealistic dream, and more like a necessary step to survive in an uncertain, changing world. Things were starting to get bad in the southwest. Even before the protest, record breaking heat waves swept southwest Utah, overloading the power grid by people trying to cool their houses and causing rolling blackouts.

Luckily power was always restored quickly, but seeing how people reacted to a lack of resources in Las Vegas made Pepper nervous about the future. Pepper thought that maybe it was foolish to ignore John Wesley Powell's words from over a hundred years ago that "there is not enough water to supply the land" and that moving someplace with water, somewhere he and Olive could homestead, was the only way forward.

As Pepper exited the gorge, the steep canyon walls dropped from his sides, revealing a vast landscape around him. Once again, only rocks and desert plants broke up the flat, sandy landscape, but far in the distance, soaring red buttes and the towering Pine Valley mountains gave the landscape dramatic topography. The tops of the Pine Valleys were white from a recent high elevation snowstorm, but from the seventy-degree weather five thousand feet below, snow seemed like an impossibility.

Pepper exited the interstate away from the mountains and towards his home, the town of Hurricane, pronounced *hur uh kin*, maybe because its desert dwellers were generations removed from anyone who had ever seen a real hurricane. The sun set behind him and cast a pink light on the red sandstone cliffs, making them glow as if the light came from within. Pepper was happy to be getting home before dark, and urged the throttle to carry him faster. He knew Olive was waiting and worried.

As Pepper pulled into the driveway and parked next to a shaded window, he saw Olive's silhouette rise and rush to the front of the house. Pepper walked from his truck to the front door, which swung open with all of Olive's force.

"Where the fuck were you? Why didn't you call?" Olive cried as she flew to Pepper and embraced him. She was shorter and weighed a lot less than Pepper, but her momentum forced him to take a step back. Mango, the couple's black lab-hound mix, rushed out of the house and jumped on Pepper to get his attention, but all of it was focused on Olive.

"I'm sorry, I wanted to but I broke my phone." Pepper squeezed her back to comfort himself as much to console her. "Let's go inside and I'll tell you what happened."

"Are you okay? I was so worried. The news was covering the protest and it got really bad. I thought you must have gotten arrested, or hurt, or something." Olive stepped back and Pepper saw tears streaking down her rosy cheeks.

"I know, I'm so sorry. I'm okay though."

"Why are you damp?" Olive asked as she touched his jeans, still not quite dry from earlier.

"I had to jump into the fountain at the Bellagio. It was crazy," Pepper said, reaching down to give Mango the attention she was not so patiently waiting for.

Olive's worried face softened into a smile, and slowly her stomach began to shake and laughter came from her mouth. "What? You were in the Bellagio's fountain?"

Pepper started laughing with Olive. "Yeah, it was crazy. Let's go inside so I can change, then I'll tell you about it."

The couple went into their small house and, after changing, Pepper described what happened in detail. He told her about the water erupting from the fountain, the crowd going crazy, and how he had to escape through the fountain. He told her about the desperation in the eyes of both the protesters and the police.

But mostly he told her about his fears. He feared the same despair and wildness would meet them. That if they stayed in Utah, they would run out of water, or wildfires would rage through, or some other disaster would wreck their home. He feared climate change was coming, and when it hit, the people in southwest Utah would become just as desperate as the people in Las Vegas. He told her that he feared for their lives.

2

The Water

The next morning Pepper woke first and without disturbing Olive crept to the kitchen. Trying to process the previous day's events, he stood at the window looking past the rocky desert of his yard, to the prolific greenness of his neighbor's field. Beyond the field, the sun peeked over the flat-topped mesas, igniting the hovering clouds a bright magenta. The grass reflected the warm light by means of a million tiny droplets laid by sprinklers spraying the field.

The water radiated out of sprinkler heads, elevated by metal wheels reminiscent of those on covered wagons. Pepper thought of the covered wagons that brought the Mormon settlers to that very place a century and a half before. They arrived to carve an existence out of an inhospitable desert, digging canals for miles through desert and bedrock to irrigate their fields and sustain their lives. Their settlement persisted to become the town Olive and Pepper lived in – a place in the modern age as delicate as when it was founded. Just as the Mormon pioneers drew water from the Virgin River, so did the sprinklers Pepper watched from his kitchen window.

"Morning." Olive's sweet voice came from behind.

Pepper turned and saw Olive still half asleep. She stood, her dark hair messy from the night's sleep, and her cheeks glowing with rest and elevated by her prominent cheekbones.

"Hey," Pepper smiled. "How'd you sleep?"

"Really good. I think I was exhausted from worrying all day, so my body just shut down when I hit the bed," Olive said and poured herself a large cup of coffee. She looked up and, through the window, noticed the sprinklers. With an edge of irritation she said, "God, it looks like the neighbor is watering again. It's not his day to use the water."

Due to the same drought plaguing Las Vegas, irrigation water was limited in Hurricane. To mitigate the shortage, properties with odd addresses were allowed to irrigate on odd dates, and even addresses on even dates.

But to Olive's annoyance, their neighbor used the irrigation water every day, odd or even. For the past few years, the irrigation reservoir ran dry by the middle of summer, so after that, there was no water for anyone. Olive and Pepper's garden would droop, and they would despondently try to supplement their water supply with rain catchment barrels.

And the neighbor was not the only one using irrigation water on prohibited days. Since the recent water shortages, many people subscribed to the philosophy of "get it while you can," and used as much water as quickly as they could. This exacerbated the shortage, so when the reservoir height was at a record low, people irrigated at record highs. The drought started before Pepper moved to Utah almost seven years ago, and he wondered how long-term the drought had to be before it was considered the new baseline.

Pepper looked out of the window, took a sip of his coffee and said, "Yeah, I guess he needs it," He wanted to defend the man though he knew he had to do it as gently as possible. Olive had strong feelings about the neighbor's water use, and he didn't want to start an argument, especially after what he put her through the day before.

Coming back from Las Vegas, Pepper stressed her out with hours of unresponsiveness, and Olive didn't even want him to go to the protest in the first place. What she wanted Pepper to do – not only in that situation but throughout all facets of his life – was to put his needs first, and by proxy her needs too. Pepper knew Olive saw his trip to Las Vegas as putting others' needs before his, and could sense her frustration with how it turned out. Pepper knew he had to tread lightly to keep from upsetting Olive further, though he just couldn't idly stand by while she badmouthed the neighbor's actions. Afterall, he was simply trying to take care of himself.

"I mean, we need that water too," Olive countered sharply. "I've been over there to explain the water restrictions. He knows, he just doesn't care."

"Well, maybe it's not that he doesn't care," Pepper said, trying to use a calm voice to keep the conservation from escalating. "Maybe, it's just that he really needs it. He lost his job last year."

Olive took a deep breath and sat down at the kitchen table, still facing Pepper. She forcefully clinked her spoon against her mug, stirring the sugar and cream into her coffee. Without looking up Olive asked in a calmer voice, "What does that have to do with it?"

"Well, he grows grass hay and sells it. I'm pretty sure that's his only income right now." Pepper felt tension settling in the room and he wanted nothing more than to lighten the mood. In an attempt to change the subject, Pepper asked over his shoulder, "Do you want some eggs?"

Olive looked up from her coffee. "Sure. Two is fine. Over medium please."

Pepper walked to the stove and lit the blue flame to heat a black cast iron skillet. He looked over at Olive who was staring into her coffee. He truly did love her, he just wished she wouldn't be so hard on everyone all the time. Pepper didn't understand why she couldn't cut the neighbor some slack for using some extra water, or more importantly, cut him some slack for going to Las Vegas. After all, he was just trying to help other people. Where was the crime in that?

After pulling a carton of eggs out of the fridge, Pepper hovered his hand over the skillet to test its heat. He stopped for a second to rethink the neighbor's water use. His neighbor wasn't the only one who used water when they weren't supposed to. In fact, since the water restrictions began, most people did.

But Pepper always obeyed the restrictions, and hated that his garden was never able to get enough water. It wasn't fair.

"I see what you mean," Olive said after mulling over Pepper's words. "I guess I would probably do the same thing if it was to support us. I would water the hell out of my fields," Olive laughed. "But I still don't like that he does it."

Pepper cracked an egg and watched it sizzle in the hot oil, then dropped three more, each into their own quadrant of the skillet. He was glad Olive was considering his point of view, but still felt they weren't quite lining up.

"I mean, I wouldn't use the water when I wasn't supposed to. I guess I just understand why he does, and don't hold it against him." Pepper said as he flipped the eggs, taking care not to break the yolks.

Olive's voice regained its edge. She wanted Pepper to start making decisions based on their needs. She wanted him to consider their best interest, after all, no one else was there to look out for them. Too many times Pepper helped others, leaving both of them in need because of it. "I guess I don't like him doing it for the same reason that I *would* do it. I want to protect what is ours. I want us to strive and survive, and I don't want anyone to get in the way of that. So, I don't like him using our water. That's *our* water, and we need it, but if I needed water to feed us, you bet your ass I'd be using the water when I wasn't allowed to."

"Yeah, I don't know," Pepper said. "If I used the water when I wasn't supposed to, I would just think about how it would affect everyone else. I would think about how other people wouldn't get enough, and worry if they needed it to support themselves or their family. I don't know. I don't think I could shake the guilt."

Olive let out a deep sigh letting Pepper know she was done with the discussion. Pepper knew Olive wanted him to change, but he also knew her frustration and criticisms came from a place of love. Olive wasn't the type of person to stay with someone unless she deeply cared for them. If she didn't love him, she would have written him off long ago.

So the fact that he was letting her down ate at Pepper. He didn't want to, but deep inside he felt helping others was the right thing to do. Years ago, Pepper neglected to help a few people, and because of that a terrible thing happened. That decision haunted Pepper so much that he wasn't sure if helping others was a decision he made, or an involuntary compulsion he couldn't control.

The couple finished their breakfast in a tense silence and Pepper gathered the plates and silverware, brought them to the sink, and started washing them.

With his back to Olive, Pepper spoke up over the sound of the faucet running and glasses clinking against each other. "So, I've been thinking about what happened in Vegas yesterday." He waited for Olive to respond but she didn't, so he continued. "You know how we've been wanting to buy some land and move back east? Seeing what happened in Las Vegas makes me think now is the time. I don't want us to get stuck in a situation like what I saw yesterday." Olive still didn't respond so Pepper turned from the dishes to gauge her reaction.

"Yeah," Olive stammered, caught off guard. "That would be great," They had been talking about starting a homestead for years, and though a recent windfall made purchasing land more feasible, she wasn't sure if Pepper was ready to make the move yet.

"Cool, well I guess let's just start looking and see what is out there. No need to rush it, but we might as well get a feel for the market."

"Okay, sure. Let's do it." Olive nodded eagerly as she stood up from the table and walked toward Pepper. "Do you need any help with the dishes?" Pepper's seemingly self-interested decision to protect themselves by moving back east appeared to alleviate Olive's frustration.

"No, I've got it."

"Oh, c'mon. Let me finish up, and you can go start looking at properties."

Pepper smiled at Olive. She wasn't mad at him anymore, and things were back to normal. He wished he could always please Olive and most of the time he knew how to. He just had to put their needs before others. But too often for Olive's, and even his own liking, he just wasn't able to follow through. Something deep within pushed him to do the opposite. But deciding he wanted to move back east pleased Olive, and doing that made Pepper feel good. He loved when they were on the same page.

"Okay, I'll go get the computer."

Pepper rushed out of the room, excited to start the hunt for their new home, and Olive took over at the sink. She quietly washed the dishes, rubbing the soapy water on the plates, and wiping away the sticky yolks. Water trickled down the sink's drain, and behind her in the neighbor's field, water continued to spray from the sprinklers, slowly being sucked into the thirsty desert ground below.

3

The Past

Finding a homestead was easier than Pepper and Olive expected. After a few weeks of scouring the internet, Pepper found a beautiful piece of land and a small cabin in a valley in southwest Virginia called Thirst Hollow. Since both Pepper and Olive grew up in Virginia, it was where they looked the hardest.

Pepper was raised in a well-to-do suburb outside of Washington DC. Both of his parents were corporate lawyers and hardcore capitalists. They loved the almighty dollar, prioritizing money and possessions over naive and lofty values like generosity and altruism. Because of this, Pepper never went without. In fact, he had much more than he needed.

Skating through high school on his natural intelligence and plagiarizing others' work, Pepper focused his energy on drinking and doing drugs, using the abundant money flowing from his parents to have what he thought was a good time. Nothing bothered him besides trivialities like which party to go to next, or which girl to chase, though he never worried much about those either.

He was popular. A large circle of people orbited him, though he couldn't truthfully call a single one a friend. They only saw him as a means to an end, but that was okay, he didn't care about them either. At the core of their relationships, each was simply using the other. Pepper was selfish, but he didn't see anything wrong with that. Self-indulgence and greed were what his parents taught him.

Pepper's indulgent behavior continued throughout his collegiate years. He attended a school in western Virginia which bore a reputation for stellar keg parties rather than academics. Barely skating by, Pepper performed the bare minimum to pass his classes, as long as they didn't interfere too much with his social life. But after six years – including two years of "victory laps" as he called them – Pepper finally graduated.

Then Pepper faced a crossroads. He didn't know what to do next. His parents extended him a nepotic offer for a position at their law firm, but Pepper didn't want to end the party that had endured since his adolescence. He wanted to continue to skirt responsibility, but his parents threatened to cut him off unless he found a job. They couldn't justify an unemployed some to the elite social circles they ran with, so after some cursory internet research, Pepper put in a few applications to become a wildland firefighter.

The job seemed exciting to Pepper, and even better, he would only have to work during fire season, which was about eight months. The rest of the year he could do as he pleased. Most of the other firefighters were his age, and the money was good, which Pepper didn't care about – he would still receive an allowance from his parents – but he figured that if there was a group of young guys making good money, they would undoubtedly be partying.

Since the west was experiencing hotter than average summertime temperatures, and consequently more catastrophic fire seasons, firefighters were in high demand. So despite Pepper's lack of experience and his poor work ethic, he landed a job on a fire crew in southwest Utah. When Pepper started, he found his assumption to be correct. The crew was full of young guys who liked to party. They had money to spend, and did exactly that. But unlike most of the crew, there was one who didn't indulge. That one was Olive.

Olive grew up in a completely different part of Virginia than Pepper. She was born and raised in the southeast part of the state, but what separated her from Pepper's world more than geography was her social class.

Olive lived alone with her father, but raised solely by herself. They didn't have much money, and what little they did, Olive's father gambled away. He was compulsive, spending every day, every night, and every dime gambling, often leaving Olive alone for long periods of time.

Olive's earliest memory was from when she was four years old. After being put to bed, Olive heard the front door open and close, then the car pull out of their small driveway. Olive knew where her father was going. It wasn't unusual for him to leave like that, in fact it was unusual for him not to. He was going to gamble.

Olive woke the next morning to find she was still alone. A situation she didn't like, but was familiar with. At least once a week, her father would gamble into the next day. So Olive got up and waited around until noon for her father to return. When her hunger grew too large, she poured herself a bowl of cereal and watched cartoons, already learning how to take care of herself.

Dinnertime came around, and with her father still not home, Olive began to fret. She had never been alone for an entire day before, and she worried that something may have happened to her father. But not having a phone number for him, Olive ate another meal of milk and cereal then put herself to bed, sleeping restlessly and hoping the sound of every car driving by was her father, though none were.

Her father didn't come home for another two days, and by then the food in the pantry was running low. Olive was dirty and hungry, and too young to understand the betrayal, she was ecstatic to see him.

Unfortunately that was not Olive's only memory of her father letting her down. Her father's negligence and selfishness persisted, and little by little Olive learned how to take care of herself, and not to trust anyone.

As soon as she was old enough, Olive began waitressing, making enough to feed herself and keep the electricity on and water running. Working as many hours as she could Olive tried to save, but between the bills, her father stealing from her, and paying her father's gambling debts when men came threatening violence, Olive never accumulated much.

In high school, Olive didn't have much of a social life. Not only was most of her time not in school spent working, but in her free time she just didn't want to be around other people. Sure she had a few friends, and she even occasionally allowed a boy to take her out, but she kept everyone at an arm's length. She didn't want to get stuck in her town by falling in love, and more importantly didn't want to let anyone close enough to hurt her. She had enough of that from her father.

Finally, Olive turned eighteen, and the day after her high school graduation she left, never to speak to her father again. Her departure was bittersweet. On one hand, she was free from the abuse and neglect. She would never waste another dollar on her father's addiction and could finally put her needs first.

But on the other hand, living with him wasn't all bad. There were few, but Olive did have good memories of her father. Every once in a while he would win big, and when he did he brought home presents. When she was young, he would shower her with stuffed animals and candy or take her to the store to pick out whichever toys she wanted. Later, when Olive was sixteen, he even bought her a car.

The car was later sold for gambling money, but Olive kept that detail in a separate compartment in her brain. Despite all of his shortcomings and failures, she loved her father. After all, he was the only one she had.

But Olive knew the good didn't outweigh the bad. Her father was bad for her. If she stayed, he would keep pulling her down, and she needed to take care of herself. The only way to do that was to leave. So with a heavy heart, Olive packed her few possessions into an old suitcase and stepped on a bus bound for Utah, headed to become a wildland firefighter.

Olive's motivation to be a firefighter was different from Pepper's. What attracted Olive was the opportunity to make an entire year's salary in eight months, then work another job during the off season to make more money. She would finally make enough to get ahead a little.

Unlike Pepper, Olive didn't care about partying. In fact, she hated it. She watched in restrained judgment as the rest of the crew, including Pepper, blew their entire paycheck at bars. They reminded her of her father, reckless and irresponsible, so she stayed away from them as much as possible, both annoyed by their immaturity and scared to let anyone close to her. The rest of the crew, including Pepper, thought Olive was unapproachable and a bit of a hardass, a perception that even passerbyers on the street shared.

So Olive and Pepper coexisted in different corners of the same crew for two full seasons without much interaction. Then, following a tragic accident, the two finally got to know each other, and eventually fell in love.

Early in their third season together, Olive and Pepper were on an assignment in California. A fast-moving fire tore through the forest, and their crew scrambled ahead to warn residents to evacuate.

The crew split up into pairs to cover more ground, but sooner than expected, the flames caught up. Everyone, including Olive, was able to flee to safety along their escape route, but the fire reached Pepper, his partner Blackwell, and the family they were evacuating too quickly. Pepper was able to survive the flame front by using a protective fire shelter, but Blackwell and the family didn't make it.

It was a tragedy for the whole crew. Each member felt the loss and guilt for not protecting the family and Blackwell, but Pepper was affected the most. He was allowed as much time off as he wanted, but Pepper returned in just a few weeks. And when he did, the crew barely recognized him.

Pepper wasn't the same selfish, party animal he was before, but now quieter and more reserved. With a newfound compassion, he stopped going out with the rest of the crew and instead focused on more altruistic activities. He helped others whenever he could, and even gave up eating meat.

In his free time, Pepper lined out contingency plans for every situation he could think of, and double then triple checked everyone's equipment to ensure everything was safe. He dropped everything he was doing whenever someone asked him for help, because that's what he wanted more than anything: help people.

Olive skeptically watched Pepper from a distance, waiting for him to revert back to his former self once the survivor's guilt wore off, but it never did, and Pepper even found opportunities to help her.

At first Olive rebuffed Pepper's attempts to help, but as more time passed Olive became more and more convinced in his sincerity. Gradually, Pepper's actions convinced Olive he had changed, that he was no longer self-absorbed and egotistical like he was before the accident, but now a kind, helpful person.

The more Olive got to know Pepper, the greater was her belief in his compassion, growing until she was persuaded that she had never met anyone who was as genuine in their passion for helping others. Soon, Olive started to feel an attraction to Pepper. And with Pepper's fresh perspective on life, he was able to see Olive in a whole new light.

By paying attention to her needs instead of living in a closed world of self-gratification, Pepper saw Olive wasn't an unapproachable hard ass. Instead, she was just a hurt little girl who had never gotten the love she needed or deserved. She wasn't cold and uptight, but funny, hardworking, and driven. She was filled with love and compassion, but kept those qualities close to her chest, only showing them to those she trusted. Soon, the two started dating.

Though they spent most of their time at work, the couple grew closer throughout the season, and Pepper continued to impress Olive with small acts of kindness and unadulterated care for her and others. Olive had never let her guard down before, too afraid of being hurt, but Pepper's authenticity finally allowed Olive to open up. Olive felt safe with Pepper. She thought she found the only person in the world who wouldn't let her down, and within a few months, they were in love.

Olive provided Pepper with a sense of closeness he had never experienced before. All of his previous relationships were based on what one could extract from the other, kind of like humankinds' relationship with the Earth. There was no genuine caring for each other, only self-interest driven transactions.

But with Olive, Pepper felt an authentic exchange of compassion and understanding. He wanted what was best for her, and she wanted what was best for him. Before the accident, Pepper's life had been a whirlwind of self-gratification. But Olive acted as an anchor. She was there to ground him, to keep him stable, preventing him from floating off to sea with no compass to guide him.

At the end of their fire season, Pepper confessed he didn't want to be a firefighter anymore. Olive suspected the trauma from the accident was too much for him, but she didn't know many details. The crew was debriefed about the incident so she was aware of what happened, but she never asked him for specifics. Pepper never said much, but Olive always suspected something more happened that day than he let on. Something bigger, more disturbing had to have happened to change him so drastically. Though Olive loved fighting fire, she had grown to love Pepper more, so she agreed to quit with him.

The couple rented a small house in the rural Hurricane Valley in southern Utah. Olive began working online as a government contractor, a position she would keep for years, but Pepper bounced between jobs often, trying to find where he fit.

Pepper wanted to work a job that felt meaningful. He wanted to do good in the world. Pepper worked for environmental non-profits, in a middle school teaching kids, in a treatment center for helping troubled youths, but none of them lived up to Pepper's ideals.

Although his employers' mission statements resonated with Pepper, the work never left him fulfilled. He didn't feel it actually contributed to the overall goal, or worse, the publicized mission was undercut by less noble causes, like earnings and profit. So Pepper bounced between jobs, yearning to find meaning and purpose in his work. And to compensate for the deficit left from unfulfilling professional pursuits, Pepper helped people he met in everyday life.

When meeting someone in need, Pepper dropped everything to help, offering his own time and money to fix the problem. At first, those sacrifices only affected Pepper, but as his relationship with Olive developed, they bled into Olive's realm.

At first, Olive fully supported Pepper's drive to help others. It reminded her of his generous character and how he loved to help her. But as he and Olive grew closer, Pepper began to view her possessions and time as an extension of his own. So when Pepper helped someone, he wouldn't only impose sacrifices on himself, but also force them upon Olive. And Olive felt betrayed by his overstepping.

In Pepper, she caught a glimpse of her father's negligence, and even feared he was taking advantage of her. Olive didn't want to live like how she did growing up – not being able to rely on anyone – so she wasn't shy about letting Pepper know when he crossed her boundaries.

But Pepper didn't intend to offend Olive. To him, the need to help others was self-evident, even if he did incur small inconveniences in doing so. He heard her complaints and tried to be mindful of her needs, but too many times he ended up hurting her anyway. Ever since the fire in California, he had no choice but to help, so he accepted the inevitability of arguments between him and Olive. But once Pepper discovered regenerative farming, his job started to satisfy his need to help others, and the clashes between him and Olive subsided.

As suggested by the name, regenerative farming is a form of agriculture focused on contributing to the health of the planet, rather than capitalizing its finite resources. Reminded of his own past of exploiting others to get what he wanted, the idea of working to nourish the Earth appealed to Pepper.

Since expanding his awareness after the fire in California, Pepper learned about widespread extinctions, heatwaves, droughts, and other indications of a struggling planetary ecosystem. The Earth's pain projected into Pepper's heart, so as he worked on the farm, he was filled with purpose and meaning.

Not only was he fighting climate change by improving the Earth's health, but he was providing people with healthy, nutritious food that carried a low carbon footprint. Finally, Pepper felt like he was making a difference. He was doing something good and worthwhile, and his need to help others somewhat subsided.

Pepper worked on the farm for two years, and gradually the idea of owning his own farm slipped into his brain. As disasters caused by climate change began to plague the news, he and Olive talked more and more about starting an operation of their own. They dreamed of living on a little piece of land, producing everything they needed in a sustainable way.

Olive liked the idea because she wouldn't have to rely on anyone else, or even the outside world, to take care of her needs, and Pepper wanted to farm so he could live without causing undue harm to the earth or other people, even though he worried the Earth had already endured too much irreparable damage.

But lacking the financial means, owning a homestead remained only a dream. It was only something they could talk about over dinner, planning the details of a fantasy neither thought could become a reality, that is until Pepper's parents passed away.

In the middle of Pepper's second year working on the farm, he got a call from an unknown number. When he answered, a Virginia State Trooper broke the news that his parents were in a car accident. Neither of them survived.

Pepper was instantly stricken with grief, but didn't have time to process what happened. He took the first plane back to Virginia and insisted on going alone. This concerned Olive. She wanted to be there to support him, and worried he would fall down the same dark hole he did after the wildfire accident in California.

But to Olive's surprise, Pepper was fine when he returned. Of course he was upset, but compared to his severe reaction following the deaths of Blackwell and the family in California, Pepper was doing great. Not wanting to be insensitive by asking why he was doing so well, Olive never brought it up. But even though he wasn't as close to his parents as he was with Blackwell, the differences in his reactions were enough for Olive to believe something more happened in California than Pepper previously communicated.

A few months after Pepper's parents passed away he got another call, this time from a lawyer explaining his inheritance. After settling all of their debts, Pepper's parents left him a few hundred thousand dollars. Pepper and Olive were floored. He hadn't even thought about an inheritance, and to him and Olive who didn't make much money, it was a fortune.

After Pepper's windfall, Olive started hinting more seriously about buying a homestead. Their dream was in sight, and she wanted it more than ever. But Olive kept her distance. After all, it wasn't her money, and she didn't have a say in how it was spent.

For a while, Pepper sat quietly on the money. Reluctant to make a decision, he waited in hesitation until he attended the protest in Las Vegas, which opened his eyes to the reality he was living in. Climate change was bearing down on them, and they had to get out of the desert.

So Pepper put an offer on a property in Virginia without a chance to visit in person, and within a month, it was theirs. He owned a homestead. All that was left was to pack up their house, and span the two thousand miles separating Olive and Pepper from their new home.

4

The Drive

In the whirlwind of the next few weeks, Olive and Pepper jam-packed a U-Haul truck full of their belongings, and loaded their 1995 Ford F150 pickup on a trailer behind. Early one morning the couple climbed into the cab of the U-Haul, Mango in tow, and said goodbye to their home in the desert. Pepper took the first shift driving, while Olive slept gently beside him, rocking back and forth in sync with the curves of the road.

Soon the U-Haul reached its first climb up a mountain pass, and despite flooring the gas pedal, they slowed to a painful crawl. Even tractor trailers zoomed past. Progress was slow but steady, and after a few hours they passed through the San Rafael Swell in central Utah. As the couple puttered down the interstate, gaining speed on downhills, then losing it on uphills, they passed under the shadows of soaring red and vermillion sandstone cliffs dwarfing them and all the other vehicles on the road.

Pepper almost wished they could drive faster. The trip was scheduled to take thirty hours, but at their snail's pace it was going to take much longer. Pepper was anxious to get to Virginia. He was excited to see the property and to start the million projects germinating in his brain. Pepper yearned for the cross country slog to be over, and for their new lives to start, but another part of him was grateful that his last moments in Utah were extended.

Watching the desolate, but peacefully beautiful Utahn landscape pass by, Pepper felt nostalgic for the time he had in Utah, and regretted it was coming to a close.

Surrounding him were the stoic red sandstone buttes and boundless blue skies that described a landscape more appropriate for a distant planet other than our humble Earth. There was something about Utah's topography that no matter where you were, you could see miles in every direction. For years, Utah's vast views offered Pepper not just aesthetic pleasure, but also perspective.

When Pepper first moved to Utah, he didn't even notice the views surrounding him. He was too focused on activities of self-gratification. Not until after his accident with the wildfire in California did Pepper literally broaden his horizons.

In the weeks and months after the fire, pain pulsed through Pepper's body, stemming from the knowledge he could have done more to save Blackwell and the family. Pepper looked for any escape from the memories running through his mind. But alcohol and drugs didn't appeal to him anymore. They were selfish cop outs, and he had enough of being selfish. He knew for reasons unknown to Olive or anyone else, that the tragedy wouldn't have been as tragic if he hadn't been so egocentric.

Pepper didn't want to alter his consciousness any longer, but he still needed an escape. So one day, in the depths of his misery, Pepper went for a walk. He dragged his depressed body up a hill familiar to him because his crew boss often made him and the rest of the crew run up it for exercise. He had been to the top of it hundreds of times, but that day was different. It was the first day that he wasn't focused on joking with the other guys, or planning his next weekend of debauchery in nearby Las Vegas. It was the first time Pepper simply sat and looked out at the view.

In every direction, sprawled out beneath him, lay the desolate desert landscape. Creosote and sage dotted the dusty ground, alongside imposing rocks and the occasional mesquite tree hanging twisted bean pods from wind-smoothed branches. The sun rose from his left, casting long shadows over the bare, sandy ground. Far in the distance lay the soaring white and pink flattened sandstone domes of Zion National Park, and somewhere south, outside his vision lay the mammoth gash of the Grand Canyon.

As Pepper gazed out, his eyes carried him tens of miles away, far away from his problems. Away from the sadness and guilt of his blood-stained hands. The long view forced a change in Pepper's perspective. Instead of suffocating himself with problems lying directly ahead, Pepper's awareness shifted outward. He saw the Earth didn't care about his problems. The desert didn't care. It just stood unmoving. Changing, but at a pace imperceptible to the human eye. Pepper felt small and insignificant. Unimportant, not in a demeaning way, but in a way that freed him and gave him clarity.

Contemplating the landscape unfurling beneath him, Pepper saw the world wasn't limited to what was right in front of him. It wasn't only composed of his problems, but was vast beyond comprehension. Pepper saw that his life was just a small part of a hugely complex and beautiful system and felt the weight of his worries melt away. He realized he couldn't change the past. He couldn't bring back to life Blackwell or the family, no matter how much he thought about it, or how depressed he was. It was done. They were gone.

But the world was big and there were many other people in need. Pepper could be the one to help them, he just had to go out and do it. He couldn't remain selfish, acting the way he had during the fire. He had to change.

In the following days, Pepper realized that he was greeted and comforted by incredible views everywhere he went in Utah. Those views were special to Pepper, and in the years following he found much clarity or guidance through them. They always offered him something, usually the ability to find that the answer he searched for already lay within him.

So moving to Virginia – a land Pepper knew was limited in its vistas – made him nervous. Back east, stifling green vegetation and trees blocked line of sight from all angles making it almost impossible to see farther than a mere hundred yards, unless of course standing on a football field. Pepper worried that when he moved back east, his view of the world would disappear, along with his perspective on life.

So as he, Olive, Mango and the U-Haul puttered down the highway, Pepper wasn't too bothered that they were moving slowly. At least he could enjoy a few extra minutes of the Utahn views he loved. And Pepper knew that once they arrived in the temperate rainforest of the east, he wouldn't have views constantly surrounding him, but a suffocating green curtain, blocking his views in every direction.

But soon the red sandstone cliffs of Utah morphed into the snowy mountains of Colorado, which flattened out into the plain planes of the Midwest. Though nostalgic, Pepper also felt relief putting the drought-stricken desert behind as the landscape greened around him. Back east, with forty-plus inches of annual rainfall, water would hopefully no longer be a stressor for the couple.

The days passed slowly as Pepper and Olive took turns driving, laughing with nervous excitement, talking about anything, and listening to podcasts in between. They cooked meals on a propane stove at rest stops to save money, and got off the interstate before sunset to search for a place to camp. Sleeping on the mattress that they stuffed into the bed of the pickup, they watched the stars twinkle above as they fell asleep. After two days of drab midwestern plains, the flat ground began to ripple as the Appalachian Mountains emerged. It was Olive's shift to drive when they passed over the Ohio River into Louisville, Kentucky.

"I have to pee," Olive declared over the noises of the U-Haul and the interstate. "I'm going to get off." Olive guided the hulking vehicle down the off-ramp and into a large gas station. "Lock the car if you get out," Olive said urgently as she hurried, unbuckling her seatbelt and sliding down from the raised cab. She slammed the door behind her and half walked, half jogged into the gas station.

Thinking Mango may need to pee, Pepper secured her leash and stepped down from the U-Haul. Immediately, Mango began sniffing the ground, absorbing the million smells offered by the strip of grass bordering the gas station, and hoping to find a half-eaten sandwich, or even a lonely potato chip.

The grass was too saturated with smells of trash and other dogs for Mango to focus on peeing, so Pepper led her to the vacant lot adjacent to the gas station, hoping for less distractions and for Mango to focus on the assigned task. As Mango slowly led Pepper around the empty lot, he noticed a man headed directly at him, walking with nervous purpose.

The man wore a blue knit beanie, a large coat bulging at the zipper from restraining many layers of clothes beneath, and well used camo cargo pants, each pocket stuffed near its capacity. Tangled tufts of dark brown hair escaped from under his beanie, and a short, messy beard covered his hard, deeply wrinkled face. Pepper didn't like to make assumptions, but his first impression was that the man was homeless. After noticing the man, Pepper trained his eyes on the ground, making sure not to lift them again until he was sure the man was walking toward him.

"Howdy!" Pepper greeted the man, more loudly than he intended. When talking to people who were down on their luck, Pepper often felt guilty for his own good fortune in life and overcompensated with enthusiasm.

"Mornin'," the man said in a low scratchy voice and a Kentucky accent. His eyes met Pepper's, but quickly fell to the ground. In one uninterrupted breath, the man spewed, "I hope you are having a nice day. My name is Victor. I am a Vietnam veteran. I am homeless and hungry. Can you spare a few dollars so I can buy some food this morning? Anything helps." The man's speech was quick, forced, and over rehearsed, a spiel given so many times, the words had lost meaning to him. The man's eyes peeked from the ground to gauge Pepper's reaction.

"Well, thank you for your service," Pepper said, again with enthusiasm though he wasn't convinced the man actually served in Vietnam. However, Pepper was sure that almost no one would beg for money unless they were in a bad situation, so Pepper wanted to help.

He always gave money to those who asked. At least he did when Olive wasn't around. If she saw Pepper giving even spare change away, she would remind him of the things they needed to buy, or wanted to but didn't have enough money. Olive couldn't understand why Pepper would rather help someone than use the money to improve their lives. And seeing Pepper give it away hurt Olive. She felt betrayed that her needs were less important than some random person.

But Pepper knew the person begging appreciated the money more than he or Olive would. Sure, neither of them was rich, but they were a long way from relying on other people's generosity to get by. So if Pepper could make another person's life a little better with a few dollars, he was happy to.

"And of course I can help you out," Pepper continued. "My wallet's in our U-Haul."

"Oh, thank you. God bless," the man said as Pepper turned to walk to the U-Haul. The man followed on his side, a half step behind, and Mango frantically smelled the ground, worried she had missed her chance to pee, or worse, to find food.

"No problem, I'm happy to help. And you kind of remind me of someone I used to know anyway."

Pepper opened the passenger door of the U-Haul, and rummaged around the messy floor looking for his wallet. After only a few days driving, it was impressive how messy the inside of the U-Haul had become. Finally, Pepper caught a glimpse of his wallet underneath a lone sandal and looked inside.

Pepper rarely used cash, and because of this, five twenty-dollar bills presented themselves, just as straight and crisp as they were when they came out of the ATM. He hesitated a moment. Twenty dollars was more than he wanted to give, and after buying their new property, money was tight. Pepper considered telling the man he couldn't help, that he thought he had smaller bills, but the thought of letting the man down invoked a visceral feeling of anxiety throughout his body.

What if the man really needs the money? What if something bad happens to the man because I didn't help?

Pepper slowly slid one of the twenties from his wallet, away from its companions, then glanced over his shoulder to see if Olive was in sight.

"Here you go," Pepper said and he held the stiff, new twenty toward the man. Pepper's anxious feeling that something bad would happen to the man subsided, only to be replaced by financial worries.

The man looked at the twenty and hesitated. He looked from the bill to Pepper's eyes, and slowly took the money.

"Wow, thank you so much. God bless." He took the bill, smiled, then beelined to the gas station.

Pepper watched him walk away and saw Olive come out of the gas station, a sight that made Pepper's heart drop. As the man hustled past, Olive gave him a funny look, not seen by the man but noted with regret by Pepper.

"Who was that guy?" Olive asked Pepper as she approached the U-Haul.

"Oh, just a guy asking for money," Pepper said nonchalantly, hoping to avoid the conversation he knew was coming. "He was hungry."

"And you gave him some didn't you?" Olive asked, trying to keep a docile tone, but coming off as critical.

"Yeah, I did." Pepper said, then paused, knowing that Olive wanted to know how much he had given the man. He reluctantly admitted, "I gave him a twenty."

"A twenty?" Olive's eyebrows lifted in disbelief.

Pepper responded with silence. He knew Olive was upset, but didn't see the big deal. Sure, they were tight on money, but twenty dollars wasn't going to break them. They wouldn't even notice it was gone, but it could make a huge difference to the homeless man. And if Pepper didn't help, something bad could happen to the man, and that would only add weight to Pepper's already heavy conscience. He and Olive stood in an uncomfortable silence, and to his relief, after a few moments, Olive changed the subject.

"Did Mango pee?" Olive asked, still with an edge in her voice, but deciding her annoyance didn't warrant an argument.

"No, not yet. I walked her around, but she won't go," Pepper said, shaking his head.

"Okay, let's do another lap and see what happens."

Pepper nodded, and he, Olive, and Mango started walking in the strip of grass. They walked slowly, letting Mango sniff to her heart's desire. The grass led them behind the gas station to another vacant lot. They meandered until Mango finally stopped, squatted, and released a long, deep yellow stream.

As the drop fell to the ground, Pepper noticed a man strode joyfully around the corner of the gas station. In one hand he had a small bottle of brown whiskey, and in his right a plastic bag sagging heavily with malt liquor bottles. Pepper's heart dropped. It was the man he gave money to.

The man looked up from his content stupor and saw Pepper. Hastily, he turned about-face and disappeared around the gas station.

"That was him. That was the guy you gave money to," Olive whispered accusingly, angry the man took advantage of them. He reminded her of her father – weak, dishonest, full of vices.

"Yeah, I know," Pepper conceded. Defeated, he turned and started leading Mango back to the U-Haul, temporarily delaying the imminent argument he thought he avoided earlier. Olive stormed ahead and forced herself into the passenger side of the U-Haul. When Pepper caught up, he got into the driver's seat. Without a choice, it became his turn to drive.

Olive waited until they were back on the highway, cruising in the far-right lane before letting loose.

"He bought alcohol," Olive said over the noises of the highway, almost astonished. "Didn't you say he was hungry? What an asshole. Fucking typical, spending all his money on booze."

"Oh, c'mon," Pepper said, half defending the man, half defending himself. "It doesn't matter." He didn't want a fight, but he wanted Olive to be fair.

"What do you mean *it doesn't matter*?" asked Olive, tilting her chin in and raising her eyebrows. "He's not hungry. He's probably not even homeless. I bet he has a family that he's not feeding because he's buying beer, and can't keep a job because he's drinking it."

"C'mon," Pepper pleaded. "You don't know that."

"Well, I do know he lied about what he was going to use the money for."

"Yeah," Pepper admitted, "but it doesn't really matter." He put on his blinker to pass an old Buick moving even slower than they were. Since the fight was unavoidable, he doubled down to defend himself. "Why should we care what he used the money for? Maybe he bought what he needed."

"No one *needs* to buy whiskey," retorted Olive flatly.

"Well, I don't care. I gave him the money. He's an adult. He can choose what he wants to spend it on. I'd rather give someone money who doesn't need it, than to not give money to someone who does."

"But you know how tight money is right now. We need those twenty dollars."

Pepper glanced from the highway to Olive and felt a twinge of guilt. Pepper wasn't sorry for helping the man, but Olive was genuinely worried about the money, and for that he felt remorse.

"Okay. You're right, I know we're trying to save. I'm sorry." Pepper paused as he changed back into the far-right lane, in front of the old, slow Buick. "But it was only twenty dollars. We can spare that. It was a good deed to help that guy, regardless of what he spent the money on. Next time, I'll try to give less, but I still think it's good to be generous."

Olive didn't respond, but stared out the windshield at the white dashed lines rushing by the U-Haul, wondering how many they had passed since leaving Utah. She knew Pepper had a compulsion to help others. She didn't know what exactly happened to make him that way, but she understood that's how he was, and, to some degree, she had to accept it, even if she wasn't happy about it.

Olive sat and let their differences simmer over her. She didn't know what to do. Why Pepper didn't realize that his actions not only affected him, but also her? They shared a bank account, so it wasn't just his money, it was also theirs. Being generous was fine and good, but when Pepper was so generous that it affected her without her consent, that crossed a line. At that point it was no longer generosity. It was neglect. It was exploitation. It was an indifference to her needs.

Olive worried they wouldn't be able to find a common ground and that it was her fault as much as it was his. Her communication skills weren't the best. She had trouble staying calm and saying what was actually going on with her. Instead, her emotions came out as anger or annoyance, when in reality they were pain and hurt. So how was Pepper to know what was really going on with her? He probably just thought she was being unreasonable. After all, he was right, it was only twenty dollars.

Olive didn't know what to do. She feared Pepper's need to help was going to continue to drive a wedge between them, and though she wanted Pepper to stop doing things that hurt her, she loved him. She couldn't imagine a life without him. But she also couldn't imagine living a life like she had when she was a child. Ignored, abandoned, forgotten. Olive escaped that once before and was determined not to go back. Olive adjusted herself in her seat and faced out the window as the U-Haul slowly, but surely, carried her to Virginia. She hoped things would be different there, that Pepper would learn to prioritize their welfare over others, but deep down she knew that was unlikely.

5

The Arrival

Olive and Pepper finished driving that day with the cab filled by an uncomfortable silence. But Pepper found a nice wooded area to camp in, and the next morning the tension had mostly dissipated, though a slight uneasiness lingered. Trumping the tension was restrained excitement. They were close to the end of their journey, and the beginning of their new life. Only a few hours of driving remained until they reached their new home.

Soon, Pepper and Olive exited the interstate and neared their destination. After passing through a series of increasingly small towns, and smaller, windier roads, they turned onto Thirst Run Drive.

The road followed a small creek, named Thirst Run, up the small valley of Thirst Hollow. The water in Thirst Run flowed year-round, cascading over limestone outcroppings and between white sandstone boulders, carving deep pools where lazy trout awaited passing morsels of food. The couple followed the road for a few miles until they saw a wood post with an address painted on.

"Thirty Thirst Run Drive," cried Olive, "That's us!" The excitement of seeing their property made her forget their argument and her trepidation.

The final lingering remnants of tension dissolve from the cab, and Pepper shot a big smile at Olive. She smiled back as Pepper slowed the U-Haul and turned down the gravel driveway, passing first through a wall of trees which gave way to an open field of grass, a quaint log cabin, and a steep ridge dotted with white sandstone outcroppings rising behind it all. Pepper and Olive had seen pictures of the property, and their realtor even sent a video, but the couple was seeing the property for the first time in person.

"We made it!" Pepper shouted as they stepped out of the U-Haul into the crisp late evening air.

"It's beautiful. I don't even recognize it from the photos."

"Yeah, it's even better than I imagined," Pepper said, his worries about a lack of views forgotten as he looked around the property.

In front of the two stood their new cabin. The exterior was made of pine logs stained red, and topped with a corrugated tin roof that gleamed with a slight patina in the sunlight. The south side of the roof was covered in solar panels, providing the cabin its meager supply of electricity. The chimney was made of white sandstone, same as the outcroppings on the ridge behind the house.

Hidden in the chimney's bricks were gastropod and crinoid fossils, hinting at the ancient sea that once drowned that very spot. A covered porch lined the entire width of the front of the house and was enclosed by wooden railing. Two red Adirondack chairs sat on the porch, making the cabin feel like home, even before they walked in. The front door and window frames were painted a deep forest green that contrasted with the red stain of the rest of the house.

"It's so cozy. I love it," Olive said as she stared at the house. "I have to pee, but then let's walk around before it gets too dark."

"Sounds good," Pepper smiled as he followed Olive inside, Mango close behind.

Once inside, Mango immediately went to sniffing, trying to familiarize herself with her new environment. Olive slowly walked around the small house, looking in every door. The inside of the house was divided into just three rooms. The kitchen, dining room, and living room were all one open space only divided by a countertop peninsula. In the corner of the large room sat a small wood-burning stove to provide heat, and even cooking if needed.

The bedroom was just large enough for a queen bed and space to walk around it, and a small closet for their clothes. Finally, there was the bathroom. Crowded near its entrance was a small vanity and toilet, and on the far wall was a large clawfoot cast iron tub. Since the house wasn't connected to municipal water or sewage, the toilet and other wastewater fed to a buried septic tank, and their drinking water was drawn from a well.

In the kitchen area there was a large stainless-steel sink, a small refrigerator, an electric stove and oven, and some counter space. The refrigerator, and the rest of the appliances ran from electricity generated from the solar panels, and if necessary, a propane generator.

Adjacent to the kitchen was a walk-in pantry, the walls of which were lined with unfinished wooden shelves spanning the floor up to the ceiling. Pepper hoped to start filling these shelves with canned vegetables and fruit from the gardens as soon as possible. After inspecting the house, Olive finally went to use the bathroom.

"It's beautiful in here," Olive said optimistically as she walked out of the bathroom. The house really wasn't much, especially without furniture, but it was theirs, and she loved it. "Let's go walk around."

The two stepped back out onto the front porch and looked out. The property sloped gently south away from the house, towards the road they drove in on. In front of the house was a large cleared area that took up over half of their four acres. It looked like it had once been farmed, but had long since been neglected and overgrown. This is where Pepper hoped to produce enough food to sustain himself and Olive.

Farther south, away from the house and past the cleared fields, was a grove of trees that blocked the view of the house from the road. In the grove were large maples, oaks, and pines, and a shrubby understory so thick it looked impossible to walk through. Past the road was Thirst Run, and though the stream wasn't visible, the ridge that bounded the opposite side of Thirst Hollow was, and its rippling edges provided a nice view from the front porch. As Olive and Pepper looked out, the sun was sinking close to the horizon created by that ridge.

The couple, loosely followed by Mango, walked down the three wooden steps from the porch and around the back of the house. Behind were a few outbuildings for storage, a large chicken coop, and a small orchard of eight apple trees that backed up to a steep slope that rose to a ridge, the top of which was the boundary of Thirst Hollow. Its angle jutted abruptly from the near flatness of Pepper and Olive's land, and the ridge's thick, green vegetative continuity was sporadically interrupted by small sandstone outcrops. At the ridge's base, a small spring surfaced, trickling pure, clear water from deep within.

"Wow, I can't believe this is all ours. We have so much more space than we did in Utah," Olive said, still smiling.

"Yeah, we can't even see any neighbors here, much less see them watering on days they shouldn't be," Pepper teased.

Though the sun hadn't set, it disappeared behind the ridge, blanketing Thirst Hollow in an airy purgatorial shadow. So together, hand in hand, they walked to the U-Haul to get their toothbrushes, food and utensils to cook, and their sleeping pads and sleeping bags. They were tired from a full day of driving, and decided to relax for the night, starting the long chore of unpacking in the morning.

After getting the essentials inside, Pepper and Olive walked back onto the porch just as, like a wildfire, the sky was lit ablaze by the sun setting somewhere beneath the ridge. They stood, hand in hand, leaning on the wooden railing. The clouds were outlined in a brilliant orange that contrasted with the pale blue color of the sky. They complimented each other, following laws so fundamental to be described by the color wheel, as if nature was designed to please humans' senses.

As Pepper looked across their new property, he thought of all the work ahead: unpacking, getting the house set up, restoring the coop and getting chickens, and planting the fields. The amount of work was daunting.

He was overwhelmed, but as he stood on the front porch, looking across Thirst Hollow, a sense of contentment flowing over his body counterbalanced his anxiety. The tranquility started inside his chest at his heart, then radiated out towards his extremities. It warmed his chest, arms, and legs, and as it spread, he could feel it in his ears, toes, and finally the hand that embraced Olive's.

Pepper was relieved, not only to finally arrive at their new home and find it more beautiful than imagined, but because he was able to share it with Olive. Pepper couldn't imagine taking on such an endeavor without her by his side. After he stopped filling his life with drugs, alcohol, and people who he didn't trust, and who didn't trust him, Pepper only wanted people in his life who he truly and deeply cared about. Of course he cared about everyone – that was one reason he felt the need to help anyone who asked – but there was a tender spot in his heart reserved for people he truly trusted and loved. A spot for people he could spend every moment with and still wish he could spend more. A spot in his heart that ached for how much he loved them. And that spot was only occupied by one person: Olive.

Pepper and Olive stood, hand in hand, until the colors of the sunset began to fade, and the warmth receded out of Thirst Hollow as more and more of the rotating earth separated them from the sun. Slowly Pepper turned, followed by Olive, and went back inside to spend their first night in their new house, sleeping on a mattress strewn diagonally across their living room, a million things to do, but nonetheless content.

6

Thirst Hollow

Fueled by excitement, and necessity, Pepper and Olive hit the ground running. After one day, the U-Haul was unloaded and returned to Faverburg, the closest large town about two hours away. After another two days, all of the couple's things were unpacked and organized. And by the end of the weekend the satellite internet was up and running, and the solar panel array and battery system was figured out, ensuring Olive would be able to work the following Monday.

Since Olive worked online, she was able to keep her job when they moved to Virginia. Though she was worried about money, Pepper convinced her to let him forgo finding a job and instead focus on getting the homestead up and running. He argued that the more work they put in up front, the quicker they would be able to achieve their goal of sustainability.

And once they were self-sufficient, they would be their own bosses and never again have to work a job they didn't want. It would be good for the planet, and also safer in case something happened near them like what happened in Las Vegas with the water shortage. Olive reluctantly agreed to Pepper focusing on the homestead, but with the contingency he would at least look for part time work.

So Olive was stuck working until they were in a position to support themselves. She had taken a week off of work to move, but the time had already come for her to start back up.

Monday morning came, and the internet was chugging away. Olive was Zooming into meetings, working on reports, and doing whatever else she did at her job, and since they were finished unpacking, Pepper was free to start work on their homestead.

Excited to begin, but unsure where to start, Pepper went outside to familiarize himself with the land. He walked the border of their property, corner to corner, then investigated the contents of each outbuilding, looking behind piles of wood, and in old forgotten toolboxes.

In the small orchard, he eyed the branches of the apple trees and their emerging buds, a suggestion of future bounty. Pepper turned from the trees and looked up at the steep ridge jutting from the back of their property. He walked to its base, where the slope and trees began abruptly and looked up the wild face. It called to him.

From his house, Pepper had a nice view of Thirst Hollow, but couldn't see anything outside of their small valley. He wished he could see more, but living at the bottom of a valley severely limited his line of sight. Looking up at the high point on the ridge rising above him, Pepper thought maybe it could offer a visual escape.

He badly wanted to climb to the top, maybe desiring some perspective, but he knew he shouldn't. Olive was working inside to support him financially, so going for a hike while she worked wouldn't be fair. There were a million things to do around the farm, so he decided to get to work and save the ridge as a reward, or refuge, for another day.

Pepper turned back to the valley, looking for something productive to do, when he heard a truck engine rumble to life somewhere in Thirst Hollow. Contrasting sharply with the soft sounds of nature, he stopped to listen. The truck crunched over gravel up the Thirst Hollow valley, then quieted as it reached pavement, but grew louder again as it turned up Olive and Pepper's gravel driveway.

Realizing the truck was coming to his house, Pepper's legs started moving, hurrying to meet his guests. Olive was already standing out front when he emerged, and Pepper slipped Olive's hand into his and gave it a small squeeze as they watched the pickup roll down the last bit of their driveway.

An old red Chevy, marred with dents and dings on the body, a little bit of rust in the wheel wells, and two border collies in the bed drove confidently toward them. Inside sat a man and a woman. The woman smiled at Pepper and Olive, while the man's eyes were fixed ahead, focused on driving. The truck passed the fields and parked in front of the house, next to Pepper and Olive's truck.

Out of the truck stepped an elderly, but fit, woman with curly white hair and faded blue jeans pulled up to her rib cage, and a tall, lanky, slightly hunched older man with a well-groomed mustache, a sharp nose and eyes to match. The two border collies paced excitedly in the bed of the truck, though their gait seemed to indicate old age, as did the gait of their owners.

"Good morning," Pepper welcomed them once they rounded the front of the old Chevy.

"Mornin'," they said in unison, though the woman's voice rang more enthusiastically than the man's.

"I'm Barb Burdette, and this is my husband, Tom. We are your neighbors over that way." The woman gestured up-valley toward an area from where Pepper had heard bleating cries of impatient goats and grazing sheep.

"Nice to meet you," Pepper smiled. He felt an instant bond with the Burdettes. Mrs. Burdette exuded an uncommon kindness, and though Mr. Burdette appeared a little less affable, Pepper sensed he was a solid, honest man.

"Must've been a long drive all the way from Utah," Mr. Burdette said as he nodded to the back of Olive and Pepper's truck, which had a Utah license plate hanging crookedly by one screw.

"Yeah, it was quite the haul. We're glad to finally be here," Olive said.

"Y'all get here on Wednesday, didn't you? I think we heard you drive in." Mrs. Burdette's voice chimed in with the cheer and expressiveness lacking in Mr. Burdette's. They both spoke with a friendly, welcoming southern accent, though their flavors hit Pepper's palette with a striking difference.

"Yep, just a few days ago," Pepper responded.

"Oh isn't that just wonderful!" Mrs. Burdette smiled, bending forward slightly, as if the joy was a bit too much for her aging back. "I don't mean to be nosey, but y'all will learn that you can hear most everything in this valley. It's nice privacy from the rest of the world, but not as much between those all who live here," she explained. "Shoot, I almost forgot! Tom, can you grab those jars from the truck? We just have a little housewarming present for you, it's really nothing."

Mr. Burdette turned and walked slowly to the passenger side of the old Chevy, reached in, and pulled out three mason jars full of peaches in a thick, amber syrup.

"They're from last summer, and they are so sweet, my goodness! The summers have been hot as Hades the past few years which is just awful to bear, but the heat sure has been a blessing for our peaches," Mrs. Burdette smiled.

"Wow, thanks so much," Pepper said as Mr. Burdette handed him the jars.

"Sure," said Mr. Burdette, the single syllable escaping his mouth with a slight downward nod.

There was a break in conversation, but no one made a move to end the interaction. Everyone, except perhaps Mr. Burdette, still wanted to get to know their new neighbors a little better.

"So when we bought this place, I saw that there are two other properties here in Thirst Hollow," Pepper said, breaking the silence.

"Oh yes," Mrs. Burdette explained excitedly. "Down-valley from here," she gestured, like before but in the opposite direction, "is the Robinsons' old place. They passed away, God bless their souls, about fifteen years ago now." Mr. Burdette shifted his gaze again to the ground as she said this, and a slight wrinkle appeared on his brow. "Their old stone house is still there, but their children and grandchildren haven't taken much interest in it and it's sat empty ever since."

"They were good people, the Robinsons." Mr. Burdette stated in a low voice, eyes still fixed down on the gray limestone gravel of the driveway.

"The entire other side of the valley, across the main road," Mrs. Burdette continued after nodding in agreement with her husband, "is the lawyer's property. It used to be ours, but about ten years ago, we sold it off to settle some debts. A lawyer that lives up in Washington D.C. bought it to hunt whitetail, but I don't think he has been back once since we showed it to him."

"Hm," Pepper responded, nodding his head with the corners of his mouth slightly downturned.

"And your land used to be part of our property too," Mrs. Burdette said with raised eyebrows. "We gave it to Barry, one of our sons, as a wedding present. Years ago he built this little house with his wife, Sharon. But Sharon got pregnant and had a few kids, and Barry got a good job in Tennessee, so they sold the house and moved away."

"Okay," Pepper said. "I don't think I ever spoke with him, but I remember seeing a Barry Burdette signature a few times during the back and forth with the real estate agents."

"That's our Barry! We miss him all the way down in Tennessee, but we are sure glad to see his house is in good hands." Pepper and Olive glowed from the compliment and Mrs. Burdette went on. "Then you probably know, behind our properties and up where the road turns to gravel is all National

Forest land. So, you two, and me and Tom are the only residents of Thirst Hollow."

"Well, I'm glad we have good neighbors," Olive smiled. "It's really nice meeting you two."

"The pleasure is all ours!" Mrs. Burdette smiled. "And just one more thing before I let y'all get back to your day, I started smoking a brisket this morning, so if y'all don't have any plans for dinner, we would love to have you over."

Pepper's mind swirled. The Burdettes' invitation was very kind and Pepper wanted more than anything to start building a relationship with them, but one thing held him back. Pepper was vegetarian.

He didn't want to offend them by not going, but was also acutely aware that some people have preconceived notions of vegetarians, and Pepper didn't want to come off as weird to his new neighbors.

"That sounds great," Pepper responded. "One thing though. I don't eat meat. I'm a vegetarian."

He paused, his back on fire with embarrassment.

"Vegetarian, huh?" Mr. Burdette said in his deep voice, lifting his eyes from the gravel driveway.

"Oh, that's no problem at all!" Mrs. Burdette chimed in, cutting off her husband. "We will have plenty of veggies for you. How does six o'clock sound?"

"That's perfect," Pepper replied, relieved Mrs. Burdette was accommodating, even though one of Pepper's pet peeves was people assuming vegetarians only eat vegetables. Or veggie burgers.

"Perfect. Well, I'd better get back to that brisket, and I'm sure you two have a hundred things to do, but we will see you tonight," Mrs. Burdette said.

The couple said their goodbyes and the Burdettes turned and walked back to their truck with their elderly gait.

The old Chevy started with a roar and some dark smoke expelled from the exhaust pipe. The two border collies' bodies poked out of the truck's bed, propped up by their front legs on the wheel wells to get a better view. The Burdettes slowly drove down the long, gravel driveway, past the trees and onto the main road. Pepper and Olive stood listening and could hear the truck driving the entire way back to the Burdettes' house.

Once they heard the engine stop running, Pepper looked at Olive and said, "It was really nice of the Burdettes to invite us over for dinner. They seem so kind."

"Yeah, and I bet they know a lot about farming. I'm excited to get to know them better," Olive replied, then paused. "Anyways, how's it going out here?"

"Oh, pretty good. I've just been checking out the farm trying to sort out what needs to be done. It's really incredible out there, but Mrs. Burdette was right, I do have a lot of work to do, so I guess I'm going to get to it. I'll come back in a bit and we can have lunch."

"Okay, sounds good, don't work too hard," Olive smiled. She gave Pepper a quick kiss, then walked back into the house.

Pepper turned back to face the fields. He stood for a moment envisioning the farm complete, full of vegetables growing tall and colorful, chickens foraging happily and laying eggs, and apple tree branches sagging heavily with fruit. He wanted it so badly it made his stomachache. He yearned for self-sufficiency and a connection to the earth. The overgrown fields were just a blank canvas, and he couldn't wait to paint the picture living in his mind. Pepper walked into the fields, not knowing exactly what to do, but searching for something to bring his dream closer to reality.

7

The Shed

In Thirst Hollow, Olive and Pepper were separated from the rest of the world, though the isolation wasn't as jarring as it may have been to many others since neither of them weren't particularly social in their pre-homestead lives. Olive didn't have any close relationships, having always kept people at an arm's distance in fear of being hurt, and after Pepper's accident and subsequent personality shift, he lost touch with most of his "friends" from his old life. Neither of them even had families to talk to. Pepper's parents had passed away, and Olive hadn't spoken to her deadbeat gambling father for over a decade.

But the backwoods of Virginia were more secluded than small town Utah. In Utah, the couple was at least peripherally around people, but in Virginia, they were isolated. Unless they went into town, they rarely saw, or even heard anyone. This took a little getting used to, though dinners with the Burdettes provided some social interaction, easing their transition into a more solitary life. After the Burdettes invited the couple to dinner the first time, the two couples made a habit of eating together once a week and quickly became good friends.

At their communal dinners, Olive and Pepper learned that before Mr. Burdette retired, he worked as a logger while Mrs. Burdette stayed home raising their five sons. Even with their hands full working and rearing a family, they found time to raise goats and sheep, keep horses, grow vegetables, tend to their small peach orchard, and even utilize the small stream running through their property to make moonshine. They did these things because they grew up doing them. Their parents did them, and their parents' parents also. The Burdettes were very self-reliant simply following the only lifestyle they knew.

This fascinated Pepper. The Burdettes seemed to have stumbled into self-sufficiency – not from dumb luck, but without the explicit intention of doing so. He and Olive on the other hand put so much effort into this goal that they moved across the country and devoted their lives to something that came almost instinctively to the Burdettes.

Their advice drew from a well of generational knowledge that many millennials, including Pepper and Olive, missed out on. Passing on an esoteric understanding of how to make moonshine, when to plant peas, or a favorite pickling recipe was lost to the age of Google searches and internet recipes. Even the Burdettes' children, growing up in an environment conducive to learning these skills, chose to leave Thirst Hollow in search of more "traditional" lives in urban areas.

But Olive and Pepper were eager to learn from the Burdettes' wealth of knowledge. During every meal eaten together, Pepper and Olive described their most recent set of problems, and invariably the Burdettes gave good advice. And their help wasn't limited to once a week. When either one of the Burdettes found time during the day, they would come check on the couple and counsel them on what worked for them in the past.

With all the time spent together, Pepper and Olive became very close with the Burdettes. And the couple enjoyed their company not only for the utility of their advice, but also for their personalities. Mrs. Burdette was easy to love. Sweet, caring, motherly, there probably wasn't a single person in all of southwestern Virginia who had met Mrs. Burdette and didn't like her. Mr.

Burdette, on the other hand, took a little warming up to. He was harder to understand, but underneath his gruffness was a kind man willing to do anything for his neighbor, and wished them nothing but success.

Though the Burdettes came around often, most of the time Olive and Pepper were alone on their farm. They embraced the isolation Thirst Hollow provided, waking each morning to the sound of birds singing and trees lightly brushing against each other in the dawn's breeze. Pepper worked all day transforming their fields into life-sustaining ecosystems, and Olive worked inside to make sure they had enough money to make it happen. They fell into a rhythm, isolated by the geography and their own decisions.

But Pepper felt vaguely selfish to completely shut himself off in their little valley. In the short time after leaving Utah, it seemed that something of a tipping point had been reached. The world was in its climate change adolescence, and Pepper didn't want to ignore the growing pains of people in more vulnerable areas of the globe. He felt he should at least stay informed on the state of the world, and to do so he and Olive tuned into a small, battery powered radio that sat on their kitchen counter.

Since they wanted to enhance their connection with their land, the couple opted not to get a television, and replaced their smartphones with a single flip phone for use in emergencies. The radio was Olive and Pepper's main connection to the rest of the world.

Each morning while eating breakfast, the two would try to listen to the news on a staticky NPR station. Depending on weather and the temperament of the radio, reception was highly variable, but every day that signal triumphed over static, Olive and Pepper listened in.

When they did, the radio told of the chaos that was mainstream American living: government shutdowns, Net Zero climate protests, riots, and natural disasters. Water shortages swept over communities in southern California, and powerful hurricanes damaged flooded cities and left millions of people without heat in their homes. Protests spread as people were ignored by their government. Uncertainty in the economy plunged stock prices, predicting an upcoming recession.

Nothing new. Only escalation. Change almost imperceptible if watched constantly and without intention, like parents only noticing their children's growth after seeing old photos. One storm only slightly larger than the last, another protest with a few more people, a continuing drought. Nothing earth shaking, but if measured closely as scientists were, or viewed once in a while remembering the past as Olive and Pepper did, the change was apparent and disturbing.

Olive and Pepper sometimes got so wrapped up in their rural lives that outside troubles felt foreign and distant to them. But the grimness of the news brought the world's problems to the forefront of their minds.

Olive and Pepper left Utah to avoid the effects of climate change. They thought they escaped the danger, but climate change wasn't content staying in the desert. It was infiltrating the rest of the world and closing in around them. Their safe little bubble didn't feel as safe as they hoped. While the radio was on, they worried. They could picture and even feel the reality it described.

But once they were done with breakfast, the couple would turn the radio off, and just like that, the rest of the world disappeared. All that remained was the serenity of Thirst Hollow, and Pepper and Olive returned to their peaceful existence. Olive would log on to her work computer, and Pepper would start laboring in the fields.

One morning, that happened to be NPR-less, Pepper came back into the house after a few hours of working. Pepper was antsy to start planting the fields, but the wet winter and cool weather left the ground too saturated to till. So Pepper built some raised beds to plant some radishes and carrots until the ground was ready to work.

"How's it going out there?" Olive asked. She had a look of longing in her eyes. Pepper suspected she was a little jealous that he got to work outside all day, while she was stuck in front of her computer.

In an attempt to shield Olive's feelings, Pepper tried not to make it too apparent he was having the time of his life. As he watched the farm slowly come to fruition, Pepper only wished he could work harder or that time would move faster so he could see the finished product – if a complete farm was even possible. Pepper was working his tail off, but he was happy to do so. It was a labor of love, and he did it not only for his own needs, but also for Olive.

"It's good," Pepper responded. "I'm planting some radishes in the raised bed, but I ran out of seeds." Pepper noticed that Olive's face was long and sad. "What's up? Are you okay?"

"I don't know. My boss is being kind of weird, but it's probably nothing. It just stresses me out because of all the layoffs."

Olive's employer, a government contractor, was struggling to get contracts due to a recent government-wide shut down. Members of congress couldn't agree on a funding bill. Democrats wanted money to address people affected by drought, sea level rise, and extreme weather events, while Republicans wanted money to bail out large corporations struggling from the recent economic downturn, and to fund the National Guard to police the growing civil and climate protests around the country. The federal government had been unfunded and shut down for over a month with no end in sight.

"Oh man, I'm sorry," Pepper said.

"It's okay. I'm probably worrying over nothing."

Olive went silent as she looked back at her laptop, her face glowing a cadaverous blue. Pepper waited for her to look back up, but the screen had swallowed her concentration.

"Well," Pepper said to get her attention, "I ran out of radish seeds, so I'm going to run into town. Do you need anything?"

"No, I'm okay," Olive said, barely looking up to give Pepper a quick peck on the lips. "Be safe."

"Thanks," Pepper said, then rushed out the door, excited to make more progress on the homestead.

Pepper hopped in the truck and started off toward Plomari, the closest town to Thirst Hollow. Plomari was small, only about five hundred people, but had everything the couple needed day to day. There was a small grocery store, a hardware store, and a gas station. Because of frequent trips required by his projects, Pepper became familiar with the locals.

After a quick stop at the hardware store for radish seeds, Pepper went to the gas station to fill up and decided to say hello to the morning gas station gang.

The gas station, named "Fill Up Eat Up," served hot food and had some tables and chairs for people to sit and enjoy their greasy food. Every morning five or six older men with gray hair sat at the two tables and ate breakfast and drank coffee. They wore mesh-backed trucker hats one size too big, and suspenders that pulled the top of their pants taught against the base of their overflowing pot bellies.

They were the type of folk who during turkey season talked about how they couldn't wait to hunt whitetail, and during whitetail season, how they couldn't wait to hunt turkey, and all year talked about high school football.

"While we may not have many rising seniors this year, we do have a lot of good talent coming up. As long as they work hard this summer, I really think we have a shot at regionals." They repeated this same analysis the day before, and the day before that.

After he finished pumping gas, Pepper walked in to hear the normal chatter.

"Three or four yards a play, that's all you need to move the chains. This is high school, not the NFL. A strong running game *IS* the name of the game."

"Mornin' fellas," Pepper greeted as he walked over.

"Mornin'," the group of men replied, almost in unison, some peering over their shoulders to see who they were greeting.

If only three or four of the men showed up for the morning powwow, they would all sit on one side of the table, facing the door so everyone was able to watch the coming and goings of the gas station. But that day, the turnout was good, and both sides of the table were filled with cheery, cheeky old men.

"How's the new house coming along?" asked a man who Pepper was pretty sure was named Jim.

"Oh, it's comin'," Pepper replied, knowing that these men ate clichés with their breakfast sandwiches and gas station coffee, so he made an effort to match their rhetoric. "I think I'll be able to get some plants in the ground soon. It's warming up around here a helluva lot faster than I was expecting."

"Oh, yeah. Mm hmm," the group murmured in agreement.

One man piped in, Pepper wasn't sure of his name, "Been here fifty-two years and I've never seen spring come so early."

Together the group nodded, adding words of affirmation.

"Maybe it'll give the deer a bit more time to put on some weight before hunting season," another man said, and a few chuckled at his upshot.

"Oh," interjected a man who Pepper was pretty sure was named Joel, "did you hear about the fire up by Castle Dale?"

"Nuh uh," Pepper said, shaking his head.

"Well, there's a forest fire about five miles northwest of there. It started from a lightning strike, and last I heard, it's burnt up almost seven hundred acres."

"Wow," Pepper muttered in disbelief.

Back in Utah, he had grown used to wildfires. In fact, one got so close to his house that he frantically bought renters insurance and loaded his possessions into the truck as black smoke darkened the sky above him. Fires were common back west, but during the entire twenty-two years Pepper lived in Virginia, he could only recall one fire, and though seven hundred acres wasn't large for the west, any fire in Virginia was surprising for Pepper.

"It's strange that they're happening in the summer now. We used to only get them in the winter when the humidity drops, but now with more heat, and less rain, it's anyone's guess when they'll come. And this one is even bigger than the one we had last summer," Joel continued emphatically as he sensed Pepper's interest. "That one only burned three hundred acres before they put it out."

Slightly shocked, Pepper raised his eyebrows matching the pitch of his voice, "There was a fire around here last summer too? Where abouts?"

Knowing Pepper was hooked, Joel strung him along for his and the rest of the group's amusement. "Oh sure, you didn't hear about it? Well I guess last year you were all the way back in...Arizona, was it?"

"Utah," Pepper stated matter-of-factly, knowing he was about to be taken for a ride. He hadn't been around these men long, but he knew that they loved to chat, and when they could leverage information, they would.

"Right, Utah," Joel smiled a bit and looked around at the other men sitting around him. None of them were actively eating their breakfasts anymore. They were all strapped in with grins spreading across their faces. "That's where they got the Grand Canyon isn't it?"

"No, that's in Arizona," the words came out of Pepper's mouth with a bit of an edge. Knowing that he wasn't any closer to getting his question answered, he was getting annoyed. So Pepper took a breath and changed his tone, deciding to play along. "Utah's got Arches National Park."

"Ohh, that's right. All them red rocks. Never been out there," Joel mused, "Seems hot."

"Yeah, it is hot, but it's not humid like around here," Pepper said, and the silent crew nodded in solidarity, thinking of the wet, sticky summer to come. "Anyways," Pepper took the opportunity to segue, "where abouts did you say that fire was last year?"

Reluctantly, Joel gave in. "Right, that fire was up near Kramer Gap in Shenandoah National Park, so even farther north than the one that's burning now, but we did get a little bit of smoke blowing our way during that one."

"Wow, that sounds nasty," Pepper empathized. There were times in Utah when the smoke choked the valley he lived in. His lungs would burn as they worked to filter out the particulate matter from the air, and the hot sun overhead would blaze an unsettling red color. "Do you think y'all have been getting more fires around here lately?" Pepper asked. "When I went to school up around here, I only remember seeing one the whole time."

"Oh, yeah. Seems like in the past what, five years, we've had at least one every year. I don't think any of us remember that many before," Joel responded for the group.

A few men nodded, but most had started to lose interest once Pepper was freed from Joel's wild ride. Their attention shifted back to their breakfast sandwiches and they began chatting among themselves.

"Welp, I'd better get going then," Pepper said, taking advantage of the break in conversation. "It's been real nice chatting with you all."

"Sure thing, and if you ever see that Tommy Burdette, ask him where the hell he's been and if he is ever going to come down and eat breakfast with us again," Joel said to the amusement of the rest of the breakfast crew. The group said their brief farewells as Pepper walked out the gas station doors and the men promptly went back to their philosophical argument on the merits of a strong running game in high school football.

Pepper walked back to his truck, lost in thought. *Two fires in two years. Utah has way more than that, but that's a lot for Virginia. I moved to escape the effects of climate change, but what's going on? Are they following me?*

Pepper thought he would be safer from climate impacts in Virginia, but maybe it didn't matter where he was. Maybe climate change would wrap its tendrils around anything in reach. He hoped that he and Olive made the right decision by moving to Virginia.

As Pepper climbed back into the truck, mind still racing, he heard a voice calling from behind.

"Pepper! Hey, Pepper!"

Pepper poked his head out of the open door to look. Walking with the longest strides that his short, little legs could manage was one of the men from the gas station crew. Pepper held the truck door open and waited for the man to catch up.

"Hey Pepper," the man repeated again as he approached the truck door. His name was Bill, a regular with the gas station breakfast crew and the owner of Plomari's only grocery store. He was a short, stout man, with a clean-shaven face and puffy red cheeks. Once Bill caught up to Pepper, he asked slightly out of breath, "Hey, what are you doing today?"

Pepper adjusted his body in the bench seat to face the man. "I was going to go finish sowing some seeds. Why, what's up?"

"Well, I'm in the middle of building a shed behind my house, and it sure would go a lot smoother with two people. If you're not too busy, how would you like to come help? I can pay you."

"Dang, I was hoping to get some seeds planted today," Pepper said. After hearing about the fires he really wanted to go home and work on the farm. With climate change bearing down, he and Olive needed to become self-sustainable, and the quicker the better. Even planting some radish seeds was taking a step in the right direction.

Part of Pepper wanted to say no, but there wasn't much of a question in his mind that he would help. Ever since the accident in California Pepper knew the importance of helping when asked, because if he didn't, bad things could happen. But as Pepper paused, Bill misunderstood the silence as hesitation, and chimed in.

"Are you sure? I can give you a hundred dollars and we should be done by this afternoon. That'll give you enough time to plant your seeds. How about you follow me back to my place? I'm just on the other side of Plomari. Real close."

"Okay, sure. Sounds good," Pepper agreed. Though Pepper was disappointed he couldn't work on the farm until later, he knew helping was the right thing to do. Also, Olive would be pleased if he brought home a little extra cash. Pepper still hadn't been able to find a part time job, and his prospects looked bleak. With the government shut down, and the country sliding into a recession, people just weren't hiring.

Pepper followed Bill to his house, and though on the opposite side of Plomari, it was just a few blocks away since the town was only a few blocks wide. They immediately got to work framing the shed and putting on wooden siding. Pepper didn't have much experience in construction, so he was happy to learn, though thoughts of encroaching wildfires smoldered in the back of his mind.

But the work made the time pass, and lunchtime came quickly. Bill disappeared into the house and brought Pepper a peanut butter sandwich and chips, after Pepper declined the original offer of ham and cheese.

"Vegetarian? You mean you only eat vegetables?" Bill asked in disbelief.

"Well, no, I just don't eat meat," Pepper explained, then specified, "or chicken or fish."

"Hm," Bill said as he disappeared into the house to fix lunch. Pepper wasn't sure if Bill's grunt was a result of judgment or contemplation. Either way, Bill fixed him a peanut butter and jelly sandwich.

The two men sat on Bill's back porch and ate, watching bright yellow goldfinches bicker over access to the hanging bird feeders. It made Pepper a little sad that the birds didn't realize how lucky they were. Bill would simply refill the feeder when it became empty. Their fighting was pointless.

"So why are you a vegetarian?" asked Bill as he took a bite of his ham and cheese sandwich, spilling a little mayonnaise from between the pieces of white bread.

Pepper, while chewing a large bite of sandwich, debated which answer to give Bill. Being vegetarian for years, Pepper had been posed this question many times. So depending on who the inquisitor was Pepper responded from a few pre-made answers, each different in both content and volume.

Sometimes the answer would be brief and diplomatic, hoping to avoid an argument with an obviously cantankerous carnivore. Pepper would simply state he thought it was better not to eat meat and leave it at that. This answer was true, and its brevity meant to convey his unwillingness for further discussion.

Pepper had encountered many meat eaters who were determined to prove his diet wrong, so rather than arguing, he chose not to engage with them. But Pepper decided Bill was unbiased and genuinely curious, so he decided to give the friendlier version of his answer.

"Well, I think there are a lot of reasons to not eat meat." Pepper would often say *not eat meat* instead of *be vegetarian* in an attempt to step away from the negative connotations of the word.

Pepper continued, "One of which is environmental. It takes way more resources to produce meat than it does vegetables. Just like y'all were saying about the fires, this whole climate change thing is coming fast. Maybe it's too late for it to matter much, but maybe not. Not eating meat is an effective way for just about anyone to reduce their impact, and who knows, maybe it will help save the earth.

"The second main reason I don't eat meat is that there are just other things to eat. All lives, including animals', have value, so if I have something else to eat, I'll just eat that and an animal doesn't have to die." Pepper looked over at Bill who was chewing a mouthful of his ham sandwich, but listening closely. "I guess it's kind of a respect thing. Sure, I would value a human life over an animal life, but that doesn't mean I can't value them both. I think animals' lives are worth enough to not eat them when it's easy enough for me to just eat something else."

Pepper's answer may have been succinct and informative, but he was passionate about his decision. There was so much suffering in the world, from warehouses full of sick cattle never seeing the light of day, to people going thirsty and dying from the effects of climate change.

If not eating meat held a possibility to reduce some of that pain, Pepper was enthusiastic to do so. Since the accident in California, he hated the thought of needless suffering, so it was a no-brainer to him. But Pepper knew other people had different views, so he made sure to add a disclaimer at the end of his speech.

"But ultimately, I think a person's diet is a really personal choice, so I don't judge anyone for what they choose to eat, or choose not to eat. There are enough things tearing this world apart right now, your ham and cheese sandwich doesn't have to be another one."

"Hm, okay," Bill said as he pushed away his empty plate. He sat in silent contemplation for a few seconds before saying, "Well, I guess we might as well get back at it. It's already one, so I'll let you get on your way at three. How does that sound?"

"Perfect," Pepper said. He appreciated Bill listening, and as far as Pepper could tell, he seemed to seriously consider Pepper's point of view.

The two worked on the shed for another couple hours, until Bill stopped to check his watch.

"Well, I guess you'd better be getting along, it's getting late. Thanks for all your help."

"Are you sure you don't want me to help you finish it up?" Pepper asked. The shed was almost complete, and he hated to leave when they were so close.

"Oh no, I think I can get it from here. And you need to get home to finish what you were working on. Let me get you your money," Bill said as he reached into the back pocket of his faded jeans. "Shoot," he said as he opened the leather wallet, shiny from years of abrasion against the inside of his denim pocket. "I forgot, I spent all my cash on the lumber this morning," he said as he looked up to Pepper's face. "Shoot," he repeated, "I'm so sorry. I can run to the gas station and use their ATM."

"No, it's okay. I need to get back home so I'll just get it from you next time I'm in town," Pepper said with a smile.

"You sure?" Bill asked, confirming Pepper wasn't just being polite.

"Yeah, it's no problem. I'm happy to help anyway," Pepper said, still smiling. "I'd better get going though, I'll catch you around next time."

"Sure thing," Bill said, nodding his head vigorously. "I'll keep a hundred-dollar bill waiting in my wallet for you. Thanks again so much."

"No problem, I'll see you then," Pepper said as he turned and walked around the house and got back in his truck.

Pepper drove down the windy road back to Thirst Hollow, initially feeling good about helping Bill. Though anxious to get the homestead ready for the summer, his heart was full from doing a good deed. It wasn't until Pepper thought more about the money that he began to feel a light panic.

When he got home, Olive would ask if he had gotten paid for his work, and he would have to tell her that he hadn't. Pepper knew Olive would be upset. She had been badgering him to find part time work to ease her financial worries, so when she found out that he worked without getting the money owed to him, Olive would be annoyed.

In Pepper's mind, Olive would be upset over the money, but in reality what bothered her was his pattern of helping people without regard for Olive's needs. She wanted him to stand up for himself and do what was best for him, and her. Olive knew he wouldn't assert himself and follow up with Bill to get paid. The debt would go uncollected, and Pepper would act like nothing happened. It would be just another example of Pepper putting others' needs before his, and what bothered Olive more, putting their needs before hers.

Pepper's head hung low as he pulled up to their house, an impending fight looming over him.

He got out of the truck and was greeted by Mango who was so excited to see him, she wagged not just her tail, but her whole body. After giving Mango the attention she wanted, and delaying imminent confrontation with Olive a few more minutes, Pepper walked inside.

Usually Olive sat at a small desk looking out one of the side windows of the house. But when Pepper walked in, she was sitting at the kitchen table, leaning forward with her elbows on the table and her face in her hands. Pepper stopped with the door still ajar behind him, sensing her pain, and forgetting about his fears of a tiff about money.

"What's wrong? Are you okay?"

Olive looked up at him, and with a tear-streaked face and puffy red eyes said, "I got fired."

Pepper rushed over, and sitting in the chair next to her, leaned over and put his arms around her. Olive rarely showed vulnerability, so when she did, Pepper knew she was struggling. He held her for a minute, letting the silent vibrations of her crying shake him too. The shaking released sadness and tears from Olive's body, and Pepper was more than willing to receive that energy from her. Though Olive often came off as tough and affectless, she was human too. Instead of being vulnerable, she held onto things, letting them pile until they inevitably came tumbling down.

Pepper was always there for her when this happened. Not necessarily to fix the problem, but to help Olive find the confidence to do it herself. So Pepper patiently waited while Olive let the sadness flow out of her, and she sorted her thoughts. After a few minutes Olive's shaking subsided and she leaned back, signaling Pepper to release his embrace.

"I think I'm going to lay down," Olive said with red, puffy eyes.

"Okay, do you want me to get you anything? Some tea maybe?"

"No, I'm fine. I just want to lay down."

"Okay. Let me know if you need anything."

Olive stood up and walked feebly to the bedroom. Pepper sat at the kitchen table swimming though his cloudy thoughts. He stayed until he heard a light snoring from Olive in the bedroom. She was so exhausted from worrying and crying that she fell asleep. Pepper quietly put on his boots and went outside to walk around the farm, hoping to clear his head.

The weight of the situation hit harder once Pepper saw the condition of the farm from their new position of not having any income. There was so much that needed to be done. Build a chicken coop, till and plant the fields, fix up the outbuildings, start seedlings. So much to do, and all of it required money. Pepper felt a wave of anxiety crash into his body as he looked around. Through tunnel vision, Pepper focused on the expensive projects needed to get the farm functioning. He frantically scanned the farm until he saw the ridge, and he stopped. His eyes looked up at it and his vision widened.

In front of him loomed the steep ridge. Pepper's eyes followed the thickly vegetated slope to where it met the sky. He longed to be on top of it, to look out on the surrounding country and get some perspective on his situation. He missed Utah, with its boundless views and the clarity that went with them. Maybe the top of the ridge would offer him some insight on his situation. So Pepper started hiking.

He walked along the base of the ridge, searching for a path or a game trail to follow, but with no luck he turned and forged straight up. His feet pressed, then slipped on years of decayed leaves and loose soil. Saplings and bushes resisted his movement, but eventually Pepper fought his way to the top. At the summit, Pepper's heart raced and he was out of breath, but as he looked out at the world below him, he forgot about his burning lungs. He forgot about Olive losing her job, and the subsequent financial worries. Instead, all that filled his mind was the landscape around him.

The view was expansive. Through the leafless branches of the ridge's trees, Pepper saw the entire valley of Thirst Hollow carved by Thirst Run over countless years. Rock by rock, sand grain by sand grain, the small flow of water excavated a trench, a drainage, a hollow Olive and Pepper called home.

But vista extended over the opposite ridge, past the limits of Thirst Hollow. A succession of blue rolling ridges and hills, each a little lighter tint of blue than the last, finally yielded into the flat Shenandoah Valley. In the valley, the tracts of farmland were distinguishable by different shades of jade, like a mosaic of sea glass – broken bottles smoothed and frosted by the continuous pounding of the ocean, fit back together to create the valley floor.

On the far side of the Shenandoah Valley, painted the faintest blue almost indiscernible from the color of the sky, rose the ancient Blue Ridge Mountains. Once as mighty as the Himalayas, over millions of years erosion chipped away at the Blue Ridge until they were as Pepper saw them, a faint undulating line on the horizon.

Pepper stood and took in the view. He let it permeate into his eyes, barely believing what he saw was real, and that he let so much time pass before visiting that sacred space.

Pepper let the landscape diffuse through his consciousness, and his mind went blank until eventually thoughts of his current predicament crept back.

Pepper and Olive were already running through their savings faster than they anticipated. Starting the farm was more expensive than they thought it would be, and they still had a lot of work to do. Work that would be expensive to accomplish.

Now they would have even less money since Olive lost her job. And finding a new one didn't seem feasible. Pepper had been looking for work since they moved to Virginia with no luck. With the economy deteriorating, Olive probably wouldn't be able to find a job either.

He refocused on the boundless view in front of him. It reminded him that the world was greater than just Thirst Hollow. This was easy to forget since living in the bottom of the valley, his entire visible world was Thirst Hollow.

But with the vast landscape laid out in front of him, Pepper felt uplifted and a thought came to him.

Maybe Olive losing her job is for the best. Changes are happening in the rest of the world right now, ones that are making it hard for everyone to survive. Maybe money isn't what we need right now. Maybe what we need is to get the farm going. And with Olive's help, we can do that twice as quickly. If we can produce everything we need here, it won't matter if we have money. Sure, at first we will need some to get everything up and running, but we have savings, and we can be frugal. Maybe this is a good thing. Maybe it's just what we need.

Pepper looked one more time at the scene in front of him, then set out down the ridge. He was determined to make their homestead work. And with no income, they were putting all their eggs in one basket. They had to make it work. There was no other choice.

8

The First Summer

Throughout the summer, Pepper and Olive worked their hands to the bone. Without the couple having a specific discussion about it, Olive understood the importance of getting the farm up and running. She knew they didn't have a safety net, that they needed to succeed.

So they toiled through the hot, humid Virginia summer, slowly changing the farm from a cabin in an overgrown field, to something resembling a homestead. The couple was passionate in their work, though for most of the summer, a literal presence loomed over the valley.

Several wildfires blazed across the region, and though they were never close enough for Pepper and Olive to worry of an imminent danger, thick smoke choked Thirst Hollow and turned the sky an unsettling yellow.

Spending long days mindlessly laboring under sulfuric skies gave Pepper a lot of time to think, often leading him down a rabbit hole.

Is climate change closing in on us? Was moving to Virginia the wrong decision? Maybe Vermont would have been better. Somewhere farther north. Somewhere cooler, with less fires. Maybe Canada. But I don't think they are letting people immigrate there. What if there is a drought over the summer? Then there will be even more fires, and how would the crops survive without rain? What if we run out of money and the farm isn't ready? How will we survive?

To fool themselves into believing they had some power over uncontrollable circumstances, Pepper and Olive tuned to NPR every morning for updates on the nearby fire. Due to lack of government funding, there was a massive shortage of firefighters, so it slowly smoldered for months, plaguing the air with smoke.

Though the yellow smoke screened the sun, filtering out valuable photosynthetic light, the couple's farm was productive. They were proud of what they grew and were able to make meals of their produce, supplemented with some staples bought from the grocery store.

Despite their many accomplishments, Pepper worried about their reliance on the grocery store. The couple's hope of producing enough food to live off was far from being realized, especially taking into account the amount of food needed to get them through winter and early spring when there would be no crops.

Olive and Pepper were able to preserve some food at the end of their growing season, but Pepper knew it wasn't enough to keep them fed through winter. At a cursory glance, the rows of mason jars in their pantry looked like a lot, but considering how many months they would have to sustain the couple if they weren't able to get food from the store, it was wildly insufficient. Pepper worried about how far they were from achieving self-sustainability, not only because of their food production, but also because of the state of the world.

During their daily radio tune-in, Olive and Pepper listened as apocalyptic stories flowed out of the little black box, confirming their belief that self-sufficiency would be a requirement in the near future. In addition to fires local to Virginia, record setting droughts and heat waves caused huge wildfires in the west. Then, late in the summer when rains finally came, huge debris flows and landslides buried entire towns.

People were displaced from their homes and relocated to FEMA camps. The droughts threatened food shortages and high prices, and the stock market was in a deep recession due to low confidence in the federal government, causing inflation rates not seen in almost a century. Hungry, desperate people went to the streets to protest, reminding Pepper of Las Vegas.

When the federal government finally reopened late in the summer, policy debates in Congress provided little hope they could agree on any sort of measure to help. Some politicians pushed for social support and increased firefighting efforts, others spoke about the need to lower federal spending to address the impending debt ceiling, and a few congressmen, soon to be ostracized, pushed for strict cuts in carbon emissions, which they believed to be the root of the nation's problems. To the couple listening in a distant numb horror, it seemed no one in the government, or elsewhere, could agree on anything.

The public split into two factions aligning with polar-opposite groups: Net Zero and We the People. The liberals who associated with Net Zero thought immediate, drastic action was needed to address climate change and their opponents were literally killing the future of humanity. The We the People crowd thought the Net Zero ideology exaggerated the severity of climate change, was ruining the economy, and directly attacked Christian American ideals.

Net Zero had long been protesting government policy and individual corporations, but with an increase of natural disasters and an ineffectual government, their protests grew in size, number, and intensity. As the summer went on, protests escalated from mostly peaceful demonstrations, to violent, anger-filled torrents. The violence partially stemmed from frustration about the government not taking action, but another reason was the counter-protesting by AR15-bearing We the People members.

We the People started showing up at Net Zero's protests, and the two groups would harass and antagonize each other until violence broke out. Police and the National Guard had trouble containing these clashes, and the conflicts would escalate sometimes to the point that they consumed entire cities.

The conflict was intense in the United States, but the nation was only a microcosm of the rest of the world. Activist groups bore different names in other countries, but their viewpoints, and the conflicts between them, were shockingly similar to those in the US.

Environmentalists versus conservatives, both thinking the other side was ruining the world, all the while climate change ruined it for everyone. The entire globe was in turmoil while Olive and Pepper sat and listened in from their small protected homestead. Though separated from the suffering world, Pepper felt the need to help.

A part of him wanted to go out and protest with the rest of the Net Zero crowd. After all, they were only a four-hour drive from Washington DC, a hotbed for activity from both sides. However, another part of him, possibly the voice of Olive echoing in his head, wanted to simply turn off the radio, ignore the problem, and focus on homesteading efforts. Pepper tried to convince himself he was doing his part to abate climate change by managing the homestead – that it was enough to work toward self-sustainability and have a small carbon footprint.

Though on a deeper level, a part of himself he wasn't completely conscious of, Pepper suspected his reason for separating from the rest of the world was selfish in nature. Actions speak louder than words, and Pepper was ignoring the implications of his inaction. Instead of heading to the streets to protest, Pepper stayed in Thirst Hollow and went along with his life, working to create a safety net for himself and Olive.

Both Olive and Pepper were working their hardest to make their lives self-sustainable, but since they still weren't producing enough food to support themselves, they made weekly trips to buy food in Plomari.

On the way to town, Pepper dreaded seeing Bill, the owner of the grocery store and the man who Pepper helped build a shed. Bill never paid Pepper for his work, and didn't appear to have any memory of the debt. Olive would invariably remind Pepper of the owed money and pressure Pepper to ask Bill for it.

"We need the money, this guy is such an asshole," Olive would say. "No one 'just forgets' they owe someone a hundred dollars."

"Oh c'mon, it's not much money. We don't need it that bad," Pepper would retort, wishing she would just drop the whole thing. He had done a good deed by helping Bill and felt payment wasn't necessary. "Also, I don't think that the grocery store is doing so well with all the food shortages."

Olive would interrupt, "Yeah, and we're the ones paying for it. Did you see how much cooking oil cost last week? Crazy."

These little arguments never went anywhere. Most of the time Bill wasn't at the grocery store, so Pepper was let off the hook, and the few times Bill was present, Pepper would neglect to bring up the debt and pay the price on the drive home. Olive would be upset for a while, not necessarily because they needed the hundred dollars, but because she was fundamentally against letting anyone take the slightest advantage of her, and by extension, Pepper.

Pepper had provided a service and Bill owed him, no matter how much or how little. A man was only as good as his word, and that's how she knew her father wasn't worth anything. A part of Pepper wished he was the person Olive wanted him to be. He knew that his relationship would be better if he did. Pepper wanted to make Olive happy, but his past just wouldn't allow him to make the change she wanted.

Pepper knew sometimes he helped too much and would get burned. But he was used to that, and if it only affected him, he was okay with it. Helping was the right thing to do, so that's what he would do.

But his generous personality didn't only affect him. It affected Olive too. He had begun to see that, even if Olive was unaware of his insight. But Pepper didn't know what to do. He couldn't stop helping people, but he didn't want to hurt Olive either.

The two sides of Pepper, like the two opposing political groups, couldn't come to any sort of agreement, but instead violently battled, destroying what both sides were trying to protect. When Pepper upset Olive, he would normally just wait out Olive's frustration. He wished he had a better solution, but he just didn't know what else to do. Eventually, the tension would dissipate as the enormous amount of work they faced distracted Olive.

So they worked all summer, ignoring problems until they culminated into an explosion. They would fight and animosity would concentrate around them. Nothing would be resolved from the arguing, but the negative energy would slowly dissipate into the surroundings, much like carbon emissions into the atmosphere. And just like those emissions, the tension wasn't really gone. It accumulated invisibly around them, imperceptible to the naked eye, but slowly building towards a breaking point.

Olive and Pepper didn't have much time to think about their problems though. They toiled through the hot summer, frantically harvesting all they could until fall emerged and the harvest slowed.

In the midst of it, Pepper and Olive didn't think they would ever finish plucking tomatoes or digging up potatoes, but one day they did. At first it was strange not to have crops to tend to, but they quickly found things to fill their time. The apples ripened, and firewood needed to be collected, then split. Homesteading was a full-time job, even in the off season.

Though Olive and Pepper hadn't reached self-sustainability that first summer, they learned a lot through experience and advice from the Burdettes, and had many ideas of how to improve the next year. They were still busy, but as autumn started to look like winter, they were able to breathe a little bit. Pepper and Olive no longer felt like they were treading water, and were able to catch up on long neglected chores. They hoped to take the cold season to get ready and start strong in the spring.

With their somewhat relaxed schedules, Pepper and Olive spent a little more time listening to the news on the radio, which became more dire with each passing day. The couple worried that any assistance from the outside world may soon be unreliable. They worried they would soon be on their own, that they wouldn't be able to buy gas or groceries from Plomari. Olive and Pepper knew they were extremely green at farming and homesteading, but they hoped that they learned enough in one growing season to get them through the next, even if they didn't have the outside world to rely on.

9

The Moonshine

It was late November when Olive and Pepper woke to their fields covered in millions of tiny ice crystals sparkling in the rising sun's light. Cold weather had been hitting hard, so in the mornings Olive and Pepper made excuses to stay inside as long as they could, finding small chores to do around the house. But that morning they had an even better excuse to stay inside. It was Thanksgiving Day, and the Burdettes invited them over for an early dinner.

Despite Mrs. Burdette's insistence that they didn't need to bring anything, Olive and Pepper were baking a dessert. The couple used the last of their fresh apples to bake a pie, and the house felt extra cozy with warmth radiating from the oven and the smell of apples and cinnamon in the air. As the dessert baked, Olive and Pepper sat at the kitchen table and played a few hands of gin rummy, joking about how the other was a sore winner or a sore loser depending on the outcome of the hand.

Both of them were enjoying a reprieve from the constant pressure they put on themselves to be productive. They accepted nothing was going to get done that day, and their normal stresses were put on hold until later. Instead they relaxed and laughed with each other, pretending that everything was okay. Pretending that the world wasn't crumbling outside of their little valley.

Olive took the pie out of the oven around two-thirty, and let it cool while she and Pepper put on their nicest clothes – though "nice clothes" consisted of a thick, blue plaid flannel for Pepper, much like his other ones but without tears or stains, and a knit sweater for Olive. Once dressed, they slid the pie into a cardboard box, and got ready to head out. Feeling indulgent because it was a holiday, Olive and Pepper decided to avoid the frigid wind and drive, not walk, to the Burdettes' house.

Though Olive warned Mango she wasn't allowed in the Burdettes' house, she wanted to come anyway. Mango hopped in the bed of the truck and wouldn't get out, so Pepper let her catch a ride. As Pepper parked in front of the Burdettes' house, Mango leaped out of the bed and dashed up the porch as if she thought if she got to the Burdettes' house first, maybe she could sneak inside.

Mango was right. As Pepper and Olive walked to the Burdettes' porch, the front door opened and Mango slipped past the legs of Mr. and Mrs. Burdette, who stood and welcomed Pepper and Olive.

"Happy Thanksgiving!" Mrs. Burdette greeted.

"Happy Thanksgiving!" Olive and Pepper responded in unison. Mr. Burdette wore a half smile under his mustache and nodded his head toward them.

"What's in the box?" Mrs. Burdette cried. "I told y'all not to bring anything!"

"It's an apple pie," Olive laughed. "We just couldn't help it. We still had some apples from our trees and they were starting to go."

"Well, you'd better come on in before that pie gets cold!" Mrs. Burdette said as she waved them inside.

As Olive and Pepper stepped inside, a hundred different smells hit them instantly. Butter in the mashed potatoes, marshmallows in the yams, garlic on the asparagus, and the smell that trumped the rest, the turkey in the oven. Olive and Pepper hadn't eaten since breakfast, so the aromas made their empty stomachs yearn for the source of the savory, salty, buttery, sweet, sweet smells.

"Oh my gosh, it smells delicious," Olive said. "Do you need help with anything?"

"Well, if you want to help make the salad, that would be great," Mrs. Burdette said as she gestured through the doorway toward a pile of misshapen, home-grown carrots of orange, white, and purple scattered on a scarred wooden cutting board.

"Anything I can help with?" Pepper asked.

"Oh, no. That kitchen is already too full with two people. If there were three, none of us would be able to get anything done. Why don't you just relax with Tom at the table? Dinner's almost ready anyway."

Olive walked into the kitchen and Pepper sat down across the table from Mr. Burdette. He was also dressed to a T, wearing a dark blue Pendleton shirt with contrasting white pearly snaps, and a fresh pair of blue jeans held up by a belt and a large brass buckle engraved with a black bear standing among tall pine trees.

Mr. Burdette sat in silence while Pepper tried to think of something to say. Since it was winter, there were no crops in the fields, and Pepper didn't have any problems that needed solving, at least none he thought Mr. Burdette could help with. Pepper knew if he wanted anything besides silence, he would have to do the legwork. As Pepper scanned his brain for ways to break the ice, Mrs. Burdette emerged from the kitchen carrying two glasses of a rich amber drink, and one large mason jar filled with clear liquid.

"I hope you like apple cider!" Mrs. Burdette said as she set one glass in front of Pepper, one in front of Mr. Burdette. Then she placed the mason jar in the center of the table next to the cornucopia centerpiece. "We also have some wine, Budweiser, grape juice…" Mrs. Burdette said, trailing off as she waited for Pepper to respond.

"Oh no, the apple cider looks great, thanks so much," Pepper smiled as he reached for the glass and took a sip. The sweet and tangy liquid cooled Pepper's throat and it traveled down.

"It's from the apples that y'all gave us," Mrs. Burdette explained.

"Really? Then why is it so much better than the cider that we made?" Pepper demanded with a smile.

Mrs. Burdette laughed and offered to share her process for pressing apples as she excused herself back to the kitchen. Mrs. Burdette may have thought he was joking, but Pepper really didn't think the apple cider he made held a candle to theirs. Pepper turned back to Mr. Burdette's stern face, reminded he still didn't have anything to say. But to Pepper's surprise, Mr. Burdette spoke up.

"Do you want a nip of whiskey in your cider?" Mr. Burdette asked as his eyes glanced to the mason jar of clear liquid.

"Whiskey?" Pepper was confused. He wasn't a big drinker, but when he heard whiskey, the color he thought of was brown.

"Well, corn whiskey," he said, but sensed Pepper still wasn't following, so he further explained, "Moonshine."

Pepper smiled. He knew what moonshine was, he had just never heard it called whiskey before. Pepper hadn't had moonshine since he was in high school, but from what he remembered, "the clear" was pretty harsh. The moonshine that had blackberries or cherries in it was pretty good, but Pepper had always stayed away from the clear.

"I make it here. I have a still in my shed out back. Ain't no better water for making moonshine than Thirst Hollow water," Mr. Burdette said proudly as he took the quart size mason jar, unscrewed the lid, and gently poured a small amount into his apple cider. He closed the lid, and placed the jar back in the middle of the table. Pepper followed suit, though the moonshine poured out quicker than he anticipated and he feared he added a bit too much.

"Well, happy Thanksgiving," Pepper said, raising his glass.

"Happy Thanksgiving," Mr. Burdette responded as their glasses connected. The two men relaxed back into their wooden seats and enjoyed their cider. No more words needed to be said.

By the time Mrs. Burdette announced dinner was ready, the moonshine had Pepper feeling warm and fuzzy. He stood and helped transfer the dishes from the kitchen to the table on shaky legs while Mr. Burdette got up to feed the stove with more wood. Soon, everyone settled down into their seats.

"Okay, let's say grace," Mrs. Burdette said pleasantly. She took her husband's hand and Olive's hand in hers. Pepper did the same, taking Olive's hand, and with a little apprehension, Mr. Burdette's which felt dry and cracked, hard with the calluses of many years' work.

Mrs. Burdette bowed her head and started, "Dear Lord, thank you for all the food you have bestowed on us today. To have such a meal is a blessing. Another blessing we have on this Thanksgiving is to share our bounty with our neighbors. It is a beautiful thing in this world to share what you have with others, whether you have a lot or a little."

Pepper felt a small smile come across his lips and gently squeezed Olive's hand.

"While in this life, we have never had a whole lot, we have always had enough. And we have had enough to share what we have with others. We are grateful for all that was given to us, and grateful to share those gifts with our loved ones. While our family is scattered around the country this Thanksgiving, and there is much turmoil in the world, I hope our loved ones are having as nice a day as we are, and that blessings fall on the rest of the world. In Jesus' name, amen."

"Amen," the rest of the table said in unison, then slowly raised their heads and opened their eyes, readjusting to the spread in front of them.

"Would you like to do the honors?" Mrs. Burdette asked Pepper, holding a carving knife out for him to take.

Pepper had never carved a turkey before and wasn't about to start then. "Well, I don't know if I am the most qualified for that," Pepper said, his voice trailing off.

"Oh shoot! I'm sorry, I always forget. Vegetarian," Mrs. Burdette apologized. She turned to Mr. Burdette and asked, "Tom, could you carve the turkey?" as she handed Mr. Burdette the wooden handle of the long, serrated, carving knife.

Mr. Burdette silently took the knife and went to work on the bird, only pausing once to pick out a shotgun pellet – the projectile responsible for the bird resting on the table instead of roaming happily through the woods. Mr. Burdette used the shotgun resting in the nearby gun case to harvest the bird for the occasion.

Once the turkey was sliced up the table began to eat, passing the sides around as everyone took a share. Mrs. Burdette was right when she said that there would be plenty of veggies. Pepper loaded his plate with creamed corn, Brussels sprouts, salad, scalloped potatoes, candied yams, and asparagus.

Mrs. Burdette and Pepper were the main drivers in keeping the conversation lively. There was laughing and the jar of moonshine made its way around a few times keeping the drinks lively as well. Seconds were had, then thirds, and when everyone was too full to take another bite, Mrs. Burdette brought out the desserts.

Olive and Pepper's apple pie had been adorned with a red porcelain dish, and came out alongside two beautiful strawberry rhubarb and pumpkin pies. As Mrs. Burdette cut a piece of everyone's choice, Mr. Burdette began coughing into his handkerchief. Mrs. Burdette paused and gave him a concerned look that deepened as his coughing continued.

The room was frozen except for the rhythmic hacking by Mr. Burdette. Pepper and Olive weren't comfortable eating their pie, or saying anything, so they sat awkwardly, unsure where to look or what to do. Eventually, still coughing, Mr. Burdette got up from the table and walked into the bedroom, closely trailed by Mrs. Burdette who shut the door behind. Olive and Pepper sat silently in a room that was suddenly drained of its cheer.

They looked at each other and Pepper asked in a hushed voice, "Should we do something?"

"I don't know," Olive responded shortly, and the two sat in silence, listening to Mr. Burdette hacking behind the closed door.

After what felt like an eternity, the coughing stopped, but Mr. and Mrs. Burdette didn't come back to the dining table. Though Olive and Pepper couldn't make out the words, they could hear muffled voices arguing in the bedroom.

The words were unclear, but the tone of the conversation wasn't. They were angry with each other. The muted back and forth endured until Mrs. Burdette raised her voice, revealing the first words audible to Olive and Pepper.

"Damnit Tom, you're bleeding!"

Olive and Pepper shared a wide-eyed glance with each other. Mrs. Burdette's words were quickly rebutted with unintelligible, deep grumbles from Mr. Burdette. There were a few more rounds of back and forth before their voices softened until Pepper and Olive could no longer hear anything.

A few moments passed before Pepper realized the Burdettes were probably going to come out soon, and Pepper panicked, feeling uncomfortable and almost guilty for witnessing such a private moment between Mr. and Mrs. Burdette. Pepper tried to search for a solution, but it was too late. The Burdette's filed back into the dining room, Mrs. Burdette leading and Mr. Burdette behind, head hanging slightly like a child being led to the principal.

"Tom isn't feeling well. I'm going to drive him to the hospital in Faverburg," Mrs. Burdette explained in a small, shaky voice. "I'm so sorry about this, please finish your dessert and help yourselves to whatever else you need."

Pepper averted his eyes to his untouched piece of pie, not sure what to do. He instinctively wanted to help, but didn't want to impose. The Burdettes' were very kind, but also very reserved, and Pepper didn't want to overstep. But before he could decide what to do, Olive spoke up.

"Please let us drive you there. It's a long way and you shouldn't go alone," she said.

Olive's sudden generosity surprised Pepper. She rarely offered to help others, but she had grown close to the Burdettes. Maybe Olive had grown a soft spot for them, and considered them part of her "in-group" – those who she was willing to help, even if doing so put her out. And that group was small. As far as Pepper could tell, prior to the apparent admission of Mr. and Mrs. Burdette, he was the only member.

Mrs. Burdette simply nodded and said, "Okay, thank you."

Mr. Burdette coughed once into his handkerchief, removed his coat from its hook, and stepped outside. His pride hurt, but he was humble enough to know to take help when he needed it. The rest of the party gathered their coats and met him outside.

The late November air chilled Pepper's cheeks and the tip of his nose. He realized his movements were still being affected by the moonshine, and discretely told Olive she should drive.

Mrs. Burdette and Pepper pulled themselves onto the small bench seat in the back of the cab, allowing Mr. Burdette to relax in the front. Olive started the truck, turned around, and headed down the gravel driveway towards the paved road, leaving Mango and the Burdettes' two border collies behind. Faverburg was a two-hour drive, and Pepper was crammed in the backseat. But more uncomfortable than the meager legroom were the thoughts swirling in his head.

Pepper was worried about Mr. Burdette's health. He had grown attached to Mr. Burdette's gruff, but kind personality. Pepper didn't want anything bad to happen to him, but what had him most nervous was going into the city.

Pepper hadn't made the journey to Faverburg since first moving to Virginia. It wasn't a big city by any means, but with a population of about thirty-five thousand, including the local university's students, it was a metropolis compared to Thirst Hollow, and even Plomari.

Isolated from most civilization, and being bombarded by the radio of terrible things happening in cities around the world, Pepper had caught a touch of agoraphobia. Though his fears were mostly unfounded since none of the civil unrest spoken about on the radio was set in Faverburg, anything outside of Thirst Hollow had started to feel unsafe. He felt the cortisol pumping through his veins as they drew closer.

But it was too late to change course now. Pepper looked out the small rear truck window, and watched trees blur past. He was anxious, but he needed to help the Burdettes. They had already helped him so much, it was the least he could do.

10

The Gas Station

The drive to Faverburg was quiet. Olive made good time, eyes glued to the road, pushing the speed limit when she could. Most of the drive Pepper gazed out the window, not knowing where else to look. He worried about Mr. Burdette, and wasn't sure what was wrong with him, or even why they were going to the hospital. Back at the house, Mrs. Burdette was intent on going, so Pepper didn't ask questions. Pepper only wanted to know because he cared about Mr. Burdette, but didn't dare to ask. Mr. Burdette was a private man, and Pepper felt like he was prying just by being in the car.

During the drive, Pepper ventured short glances away from the window and saw Mrs. Burdette with concerned wrinkles etched in her forehead, nervously kneading her hands into each other. He could see Mr. Burdette in the passenger side mirror, sitting slightly reclined, head leaned back on the headrest. His eyes were closed, but his face wasn't relaxed or tired. It was firm, as if made of granite.

Pepper wasn't sure if Mr. Burdette's uneasy posture was because he wasn't feeling well, or from embarrassment from being taken care of. There weren't any more coughing fits on the drive, but Pepper could sense something was wrong. Olive slowed the truck as they entered Faverburg just over an hour and a half after leaving, and Pepper fixed his eyes back to the world scrolling past his window.

Faverburg wasn't a large city by any means. It had a permanent population of about thirty thousand, and an ebb of additional five thousand university students in the fall. Olive and Pepper only visited Faverburg once to return the U-Haul when they first moved, so they weren't very familiar with the town, but driving down Main Street the second time, the town felt different.

The liberal arts college was on the south side of town, so it was the first part of Faverburg they drove through. In front of many houses Pepper noticed signs in support of the climate group Net Zero. The university students were proud to show their support of drastic action to combat climate change. But as they drove farther into town, away from the university, Pepper saw the signs fade from blue to red in support of the anti-environmental group We the People.

Faverburg locals were opposed to measures against climate change because they believed the economy would be negatively impacted, and their Christian values defiled. The liberal students and the conservative locals were in conflict with each other, and their signs displayed aggressive animosity.

Destroy Climate Change Before We Destroy You!

Warming is a Warning, Don't Make Me Warn You Twice!

The Only Thing I'll Change in This Climate is the Safety on My Gun

Whoever not Found Written in the Book of Life was Cast into the Lake of Fire: Revelations 20:15

Witnessing suggestions of the strife, Pepper's fears were validated. The nation's troubles weren't a distant hypothetical. They weren't just words coming through the radio, and they didn't stay put when he left Utah. They were real and conflict was near. Though his home was safe for the moment,

Pepper was scared into believing that it was only a matter of time before Thirst Hollow was hit by the troubles that plagued the rest of the country.

As the four rolled through the politically segregated town, the sun finished setting beneath the distant mountains, and the streetlights flickered on. The mixture of natural and artificial light was insufficient to fully illuminate anything, bright enough to outshine the streetlights but dim enough to blur the edges of everything. Pepper was unsure where one thing ended and the next began. He gazed fuzzy eyed at the ethereal setting until suddenly, the twilight was shattered by a glaring imposition of artificial red and white.

Blinding head and taillights jolted Pepper to reality. He first thought they hit a traffic light, but soon saw the idling cars were overflowing from a gas station as they waited to fill their tanks. Pepper had heard of gas shortages, but this was his first time witnessing their effects. Olive carefully redirected into the oncoming traffic lane to bypass the jam and continued to the hospital.

She pulled into the hospital's parking lot and gently stopped the truck. Pepper got out and opened the passenger side door for Mr. Burdette, receiving an annoyed glare from Mr. Burdette in exchange for his efforts, though no protestations.

Mrs. Burdette circled the truck, took her husband by the arm, which he promptly withdrew, then escorted him to the emergency room entrance. Pepper, not knowing whether to follow or wait outside, looked to Olive for guidance, but seeing her as lost in the situation as he was, Pepper spoke up as the Burdettes slowly shuffled away.

"Unless you want us to come in with you, I was thinking of going to get some gas."

"Oh sure. We will be fine. Thank you so much for driving and coming with us, but I think we will be okay," responded Mrs. Burdette, turning halfway towards Pepper.

"No problem," Olive said. "I'm glad we could help."

Mrs. Burdette forced a small smile then continued towards the automatic sliding glass doors.

Olive returned to her spot behind the wheel and Pepper hoisted himself into the passenger seat which was luxuriously spacious after spending an hour and a half in the back. Olive started the truck, reversed, and headed back to the crowded gas station.

Olive stopped behind the last car in line, put the truck in neutral, and pulled the emergency brake. The line was longer than when they passed a few minutes earlier, and didn't appear to be moving at all. The couple sat and listened to the truck idle until Olive turned the key, killing the engine. Pepper didn't realize how loud the engine was until its noise was gone.

In the new, peaceful silence, Olive said, "I'm surprised there is a line. I wonder what's going on."

"Yeah," Pepper agreed. "I heard something about oil shortages on the radio a few days ago. I think OPEC has an oil embargo on the US as a way to try to get aid. They said that Saudi Arabia is in some serious trouble about water. People are probably panic-buying gas because of that."

"Jeez."

"Yeah, I figured we should fill up. Who knows if there will be gas in Plomari, or how much it will cost. I think there are some gas cans in the back we can use also," Pepper said, wondering how long it was going to take to get to the pumps. They still hadn't moved forward and were still a good twenty cars back. "Also," Pepper said after a moment, "I thought the Burdettes might want some privacy."

"Yeah, I'm not sure what I should be doing around them. I feel like Mr. Burdette is embarrassed for us to see him like this."

"I know what you mean. I don't know what we're supposed to do either."

The red taillight of the car in front of them dimmed then glided forward about ten feet. Olive started the truck, inched up, then cut the engine again.

Both Olive and Pepper were deep in thought about Mr. Burdette, worried for his health.

"Maybe I'll go inside and get a treat for while we wait. What do you want?" Pepper asked.

Since Olive lost her job, the couple had been holding onto their money tightly. They never bought non-essential food, so anything other than rice, oil, or flour was a treat. But Pepper figured a snack might lift their moods.

Olive's face perked up without a thought of protest. "You know what I want," Olive responded with a guilty smile. And Pepper did know. Salt and vinegar potato chips.

Pepper hopped out of the truck and walked down the line of idling cars to the gas station. As he opened the door a sharp *ding* announced his entrance, but no one noticed.

The gas station was loud and crowded, filled with the anxious energy of others waiting in the long gas line. Pepper paced the aisles as shelves full of blank spaces stared back at him. He found the chip aisle to be exceptionally bare, and stood for a minute weighing his meager options before finally deciding on a bag of dill pickle flavored chips. He grabbed the bag and walked around to the back of the store to stand in the long line for the register.

In front of Pepper were two young women he assumed were college students. They wore North Face fleece zip ups and jeans with no line designs or rhinestones on the back pockets, as were favored by the locals.

"I heard that they were rationing toilet paper at the grocery store," the woman on the left said. She was tall and blonde and was holding a pint of ice cream.

With a slight pause and eyes fixed to her phone's screen, the other woman asked, "What do you mean?"

"I think they're only letting you buy one thing of toilet paper at a time. People are going crazy and hoarding stuff. I think they will only let you buy like one thing of bread and eggs. And milk too."

"Oh my god," the shorter woman said, distracted and unimpressed. Whatever was on her phone was paramount to toilet paper or milk.

"Yeah," the tall woman continued, unfazed by her friend's disinterest. "I think I'm going to go get some groceries after this, if Shannon will drive me there. I can't believe we got roped into this. I mean, God, I wish I was able to bring my car to school. Relying on Shannon sucks. She's so awkward sometimes. It's like, painful."

"For real," the shorter woman said with fresh engagement, raising her eyes from her phone for the first time since Pepper walked up. "Like, I don't want to be here. Blake invited me to that Friendsgiving mixer, and I need to get ready. I wish more people stayed over break so we didn't have to be driven around by Shannon. It's literally the worst."

"Totally," the tall woman agreed. The shorter woman's attention shifted back to her phone, and the tall woman pulled hers out of her back pocket and fixed her eyes to it.

The line moved forward. The two women took a few steps, and Pepper followed, wondering if Olive was making any progress. Pepper hoped his line would move faster than the one outside. He wanted to be back with Olive.

Once he finally reached the register and paid, Pepper departed the gas station, announced by another unnoticed *ding*. He stood for a moment, searching for Olive's place in line, and soon spotted the truck. To his surprise, it had advanced to where it could almost turn into the gas station.

Pepper hopped back into the truck and greeted Olive. "Looks like you made some progress."

"Yep. Slow and steady," she replied with a half-smile. Then the bag of chips caught her eye. "Really? Dill?" Olive asked in disbelief and disappointment. "I wanted salt and vinegar."

"Pickles are made in vinegar," Pepper teased.

"It's not the same," Olive protested.

"I know. I'm sorry. They didn't have any salt and vinegar. It was crazy in there."

"It's okay," Olive said, accepting her cruel reality. "Chips are chips."

The line creeped forward, so Olive started the truck, pulled up, and cut the engine. Pepper's plan to lighten the mood with a snack worked. Momentarily they pushed their concern for Mr. Burdette to the back of their minds. The couple crunched on the chips, listened to music on the radio, and joked around. On the surface, things were normal. Momentarily Pepper enjoyed a glimpse of carelessness from their past lives, but deep down the stresses of his life loomed. Subconsciously he worried about money, their farm, and of course, Mr. Burdette. But it was nice to pretend, and Pepper was only pulled back to the present when they reached the gas pump.

The couple pumped and paid for the gas, glad they were able to fill up, but worried gas shortages would become normal. The shortages drove the price up, and Pepper and Olive watched with wide eyes as the total on the pump rose and rose. Holding the bag of dill pickle chip crumbs, Pepper felt tension radiating from Olive's presence. Maybe it was imagined, but Pepper swore she was upset at him for wasting money on the chips. Maybe he was projecting, but he knew buying them was frivolous and irresponsible, and made a silent resolution to do better in the future.

Once the truck was all filled up, the couple drove back to the hospital and parked in a dark corner of the lot. They were tired from the long day of driving, worrying, and waiting. Pepper reclined his seat and leaned his head back. He had no idea how long the Burdettes would be. He stared out the window at the outline of the distant mountains illuminated by the moon, and felt comfort. He closed his eyes and slowly and softly the darkness of sleep swept over him.

A light rapping came from the driver side window. Pepper slowly opened his eyes and shivered as the cold had penetrated the cab and his body. Still half asleep, he looked around trying to make sense of what was happening as the light rapping persisted.

First, Pepper saw Olive also being pulled out of her slumber. Then as his senses slowly returned, Pepper looked at the window to determine the source of the noise, but fog on the window hid the identity of the intrusive party.

"I think someone's out there," Pepper said in a raspy voice, encouraging Olive to wake up and see what was going on.

Olive opened her eyes wide to retrieve her senses, then unlatched the door to see who was knocking on the window. They were greeted with darkness outside. Pepper wasn't sure if it was late Thanksgiving night or early the next morning. Standing among the dark was Mrs. Burdette alongside a man Pepper had never seen before.

"Sorry to wake y'all," Mrs. Burdette said with sagging dark circles beneath her eyes.

"Oh, don't apologize," Olive reassured her, still trying to get the situation in focus. "How's everything going in there?"

"It's fine," Mrs. Burdette answered. "They aren't sure what's wrong with Tom and want to transfer him to another hospital."

"Is he okay?" Olive asked.

"I think so. At least right now he is, but they want to get him up to Richmond to run some tests," Mrs. Burdette said slowly, as if still processing the information. "Oh, how rude of me. Pepper and Olive, this is my son, Todd," Mrs. Burdette said, gesturing to the man standing behind her. "He lives up in Richmond and he's going to drive us up there. We are going to stay with him while we sort all this out."

"Hi, nice to meet y'all," Todd said over his mother's shoulder, squatting down a bit to be able to see into the cab. "Thanks for driving my parents, and everything else you've done today."

"Oh, no problem. It was the least we could do," Olive responded with a small smile.

"Well," Mrs. Burdette spoke up again, "Tom is going to be released soon, then we are going to hit the road. So y'all don't have to wait around anymore if you don't want."

"Are you sure? We don't mind," Olive said. Pepper continued to sit in silence in the passenger seat, his mind still partially asleep.

"Oh no. You two have done enough, and there isn't much reason for you to stick around," reassured Mrs. Burdette. "But, if I could ask you one more favor," she paused, waiting for permission.

"Of course, what do you need?"

"If y'all wouldn't mind, could you take care of the dogs, and the goats and sheep until we get back? Hopefully we won't be in Richmond long," Mrs. Burdette said.

"Sure," Olive said. "We can definitely do that."

"Oh thank you so much. I've written down how much food they all get and where to find it," Mrs. Burdette said, handing Olive a folded piece of paper. "But we'd better get back inside. Thank y'all again so much. I really appreciate it, and I know Tom does too."

"Of course, and if there is anything else you need, let us know," Olive said, Pepper a little surprised with her magnanimity. "Have a safe drive."

"Bye bye, you too," Mrs. Burdette said as she and her son turned away.

Olive closed the door and started the engine. "It's cold," she said, turning the temperature dial all the way to the red side. "I guess we should drive back."

"Yeah, I bet Mango thinks we forgot about her. She's probably hungry," Pepper said, looking over at her.

"She's definitely hungry," Olive said with a smile.

"That moonshine wore off a while ago if you want me to drive."

Olive agreed, so Pepper circled around the truck while Olive scooted across the bench seat. Pepper put the truck in gear and pulled away as Olive reclined her seat, settling in for the long drive home.

Pepper drove slower than Olive had driven to the hospital. There was no rush. The moon had set and the night was dark, and Pepper couldn't see anything except the road immediately in front of him.

Anxiety crept over Pepper as he drove down the dark country roads. He worried, not only for the health and safety of the Burdettes, but also for his and Olive's well-being. Pepper tried to wrap his mind around the gas shortages, and rationing at the grocery store, and the implications of both. What would happen if they couldn't buy food? Or gas? How long was he going to have to take care of the Burdettes' property? Was he going to have time to do everything else that needed to be done on his farm?

He drove for a long time with these thoughts, and couldn't help himself from thinking he and Olive weren't ready to be cut off from the outside world. Despite their best efforts, they still had a long way to go before becoming self-sufficient. Pepper tried to focus on the dimly lit road, but his contemplations of worst-case scenarios pushed his mind elsewhere. He couldn't help but worry about his and Olive's future. Eventually, after some time being distracted and struggling to see the sharp curves of the road, Pepper flipped on his brights.

Immediately, he could see a bit more road, and even some of the surrounding woods. Everything was clearer and he was able to focus on the task at hand. With a better outlook, Pepper's anxiety subsided and he more confidently continued to Thirst Hollow.

11

The Hitchhiker

In the days following Thanksgiving, the couple struggled to settle back into their normal routine. They worried about the Burdettes and hadn't heard any news since leaving the hospital. They thought about calling to make sure everything was okay, but decided to give the Burdettes space.

Instead, the couple continued working on the homestead, taking on the new responsibility of managing the Burdettes' sheep and goat herd, and watching the Burdettes' dogs, though they were easy. The dogs, two border collie brothers named Box and Turtle, waited with sad eyes on the Burdettes' porch all day. When dinnertime came around, they reluctantly returned to Pepper and Olive's house to be fed. They missed the Burdettes and saw Olive and Pepper as a poor replacement. The sheep and goats on the other hand were happy enough with the food and being left to their own devices.

As the days passed, Olive and Pepper became more familiar with their new responsibilities. The weather was mild and Pepper and Olive wouldn't have known winter had come if the calendar hadn't said so. The high temperature was regularly in the mid-forties and rarely dropped below freezing. Since the ground never froze, Pepper and Olive were able to dig a holding pond next to the spring, to supplement their well water to irrigate their fields. They constructed two greenhouses, and learned through trial and error about keeping sheep and goats.

Though mild it was still winter, and unable to plant or grow any vegetables, the couple was anxious for spring. Slowly winter yielded, and in early February Olive and Pepper were able to start seedlings in their greenhouses, and in early March, the weather was warm enough to plant them into the ground.

With the early start, the couple hit the ground running, and with the farm in better shape than the previous year, Olive and Pepper were optimistic for a successful season. But their optimism was trailed closely by fear of failure. With life outside of Thirst Hollow declining, the stakes grew increasingly higher. The outside world was growing more chaotic and unreliable, and Pepper worried soon they wouldn't have any other choice besides self-sufficiency.

Olive and Pepper blew through their small stock of canned veggies and root-cellared potatoes faster than anticipated. By the middle of December, they had essentially eaten everything from the previous season, forcing them to regularly buy food in Plomari to sustain them until their first harvests came.

But due to supply chain issues, the grocery store in Plomari was inconsistent in stocking the staples Olive and Pepper needed, and rarely had any fresh produce. The scarcity of food stressed the couple, but with frequent trips to the grocery store, they stayed well fed through the winter and early spring.

The gas station in Plomari also was unreliable. When Pepper and Olive came through town, the gas station often didn't have any fuel, forcing them to carefully conserve their gas.

Bill – the owner of the grocery store who hired Pepper to build a shed – helped the couple plan their trips to save gas. Bill left voicemails on the couple's flip phone informing them of new food shipments, so they wouldn't waste gas driving to Plomari when the shelves were bare. But to Olive's annoyance - of both Bill and Pepper – Bill still hadn't paid Pepper the money owed for his work.

When Pepper meekly confronted Bill at Olive's insistence, Bill insisted he wanted to pay Pepper back, but since he wasn't able to regularly get inventory to his store, he was also struggling financially. The voicemails were a way for Bill to make up for his lack of payment and Pepper appreciated Bill's effort. Pepper wasn't worried about getting repaid. He figured a hundred dollars wouldn't make much of a difference in their lives and wanted to forget the whole thing, but Olive wasn't satisfied.

With food and gas prices soaring, Olive watched with a pit in her stomachs as their bank accounts drained. Olive felt that Pepper's refusal to confront Bill in a meaningful way, equated to him Bill's needs over hers. They were sinking financially, and Pepper refused to get a bit of money that could help them. Pepper was willing to sacrifice for others, but she wasn't.

Whenever Olive thought about Bill, her mind began to swirl. *Why doesn't Pepper stand up to Bill? Why won't he do it just to show he cared about my needs? To show that I'm at least as valuable as some people he barely knows?* Olive thought the voicemails were a weak substitute for money. Afterall, they weren't even especially helpful.

To get enough reception to check their voicemail, the couple had to hike their flip phone all the way to the top of the ridge behind their house – the same place Pepper hiked to seek respite and clarity in times of need.

Early in the winter, Pepper wouldn't waste his energy hiking up the ridge to check for Bill's calls. He only looked when already going to call the Burdettes. So when Pepper heard the messages from Bill, they were usually a few days old and useless. But as the couple's food supplies dwindled, and buying food became more difficult, Pepper began making daily trips to the ridge in hopes of getting the voice mails from Bill in time.

One morning, after days of silence from Bill, Pepper made his daily pilgrimage. Reaching the top of the ridge, Pepper breathed hot, steamy air from into the cold February atmosphere. He pulled the flip phone out of his pocket, powered it on, and dialed *1 to reach his voicemail. The nice, robotic woman informed him he had one new message.

"Hey there Pepper, Bill here. Just giving you a heads-up that I think we'll be getting some flour in today. Probably this morning. Hope to see you later."

Pepper flipped the phone shut. Happy to make a trip to Plomari for a few sacks of flour, he turned and hurried down the slope to tell Olive the good news. As Pepper neared the bottom of the slope, he saw Olive working on the chicken coop and slowed his pace.

"How's it coming?" Pepper asked.

"Good, I'm almost done, but I think I need a little more hardware fabric," she responded. "Hopefully, that will keep the damn rats out."

Rats had been getting into the coop and eating eggs, and Olive had a vendetta against them. But every time she thought the coop was impenetrable, the rats discovered another way to penetrate the fortress. Pepper found it amazing how small of a hole a rat could fit through, and how tenacious they were at finding and exploiting weaknesses. Though Pepper didn't want the rats stealing his and Olive's food, he couldn't blame them. They were just trying to survive, just like him and Olive.

"Dang, I don't think we have any more hardware fabric," Pepper said. "But Bill left a message saying that he was getting some flour today, so I'm going into town. I can stop by the hardware store to see if they have any."

"Oh nice, flour!" Olive said enthusiastically. "Yeah, that'd be great. I'll feed the sourdough starter so we can make some bread." Then with a shift in tone, Olive said, "And ask Bill for the money he owes you. This is starting to get ridiculous."

"Okay," Pepper said, though neither were convinced he would return with any money.

Pepper drove fast toward Plomari. They really needed more flour and if the store ran out before he got there, he would be kicking himself.

In Plomari Pepper was met with a series of disappointments. The gas station was out of regular gas, so Pepper only put a few gallons of expensive premium into the truck, the hardware store didn't have any hardware fabric, so Pepper bought some chicken wire though he knew its holes were likely too big to keep the rats out, and the grocery store only had two bags of flour, not nearly as much as he hoped. Then worst of all was Pepper's interaction with Bill.

On his way to the grocery store, Pepper was dead set on getting the money from Bill. It was what Olive asked for, and he wanted to make her happy. But upon seeing Bill, an anxious pressure rose in his stomach. His thoughts of pleasing Olive were replaced by vague memories of the fire in California, and how his partner and an innocent family died. He no longer thought of what Olive wanted, but only what Bill needed. What if he needed the money more than they did? And what if because Pepper demanded the money from him, something bad happened to him?

Pepper couldn't bear the thought of causing harm to Bill, so he bought the bags of flour and left, not mentioning the money owed. Pepper's memories convinced him that giving Bill the benefit of the doubt was the right thing to do, though as he walked back to the car, his mind returned to Olive's request and he felt guilt wash over his body. He still believed he was right to wait for Bill to pay him back on his own terms, but he didn't want to hurt Olive.

So he drove from Plomari trying to sort out how to reconcile the difference between what he wanted and what Olive wanted. He wanted to make Olive happy. He loved her more than anything and it hurt him to know that he hurt her, but the gap between their beliefs felt unspannable. His mind drifted from driving and he barely noticed the young man on the side of the road sticking his thumb up in hopes of a ride.

As he passed the man, Pepper caught a glimpse of the hitchhiker's face. Firing a neuron somewhere in the back of his brain, he was reminded of Blackwell. Maybe it wasn't that he recognized his face, but the energy he exuded. Desperate, hopeless, disheartened. Pepper knew his story. The man needed help.

Not wanting to make the same mistake as he had in California, there was barely a question in Pepper's mind whether he would give the man a ride. He briefly thought about what Olive would say, but Pepper just couldn't ignore the hitchhiker's look of hopelessness. He had to help, if anything, to atone for past transgressions. So Pepper slammed the brakes, and pulled off the road.

Used to cars passing indifferently, at first the hitchhiker thought Pepper kept driving past. He turned with his head down and continued slowly plodding along, flattening the long grass beside the road one footprint at a time. Pepper lightly tapped his horn to get his attention. The hitchhiker's head jerked up, saw Pepper idling, and broke into a jog to meet him.

Pepper watched in his mirror as he caught up. The hitchhiker had deep brown hair spilling out of a blue knit beanie. He wore canvas work pants, a black hoodie sweatshirt, and a small, overstuffed backpack. Getting a closer look at his face, he didn't resemble Blackwell in the slightest, but something still felt familiar, and that familiarity gave him a stronger urge to help.

Pepper rolled down his window and asked, "Where ya headed?"

"Not sure," the young man responded, pointing down the road in the direction he was walking. "That way, I guess. Just trying to get somewhere I can find work."

"Okay, well I'm only going about another ten miles, and the way I'm headed, there isn't anything else for a long ways. It's probably forty miles to Wyatt in West Virginia, and Wyatt isn't any bigger than Plomari. I don't think you'd have much luck finding work there either."

"That's okay. Ten miles is ten miles farther from here," the young man said.

"Alright, well hop in then," Pepper said with a smile showing that he was happy to help out.

The hitchhiker jogged around the front of the truck, opened the door, and slid into the passenger seat, placing his backpack on the floor between his legs. The hitchhiker didn't say anything as Pepper pulled back onto the road and accelerated towards Thirst Hollow.

After a few seconds of silence, Pepper glanced at the hitchhiker and said, "My name's Pepper." Pepper returned his eyes to the road and waited for the hitchhiker to introduce himself.

The young man hesitated before responding monosyllabically, "My name is Wes."

"Nice to meet you, Wes. Where are you coming from?"

"Up north. Lost my job because of the riots and had to get out."

"Dang. Sorry to hear that," Pepper said, stealing another glance at his passenger.

Wes' face was beaten down. Pepper figured hitchhiking to nowhere can get exhausting, so he chalked it up to that. He looked so tired, but not just his face. There was something deep down in his essence that Pepper picked up on, something that compelled Pepper to help. He needed to. And giving Wes a ride a few miles down the road wasn't enough. Wes needed more. Olive wouldn't like it, but Pepper had to do something. It wasn't fair just to drop this guy off in the middle of nowhere on some country road.

"You know what," Pepper said, again momentarily turning towards Wes, "I wouldn't be able to pay you, but if you come help me put up a deer fence today, we can feed you some lunch this afternoon and some dinner tonight. And we have a couch you could sleep on." Pepper paused, then to let Wes know there was no pressure, followed with, "Just if you want."

"Okay," Wes said after a short pause. Pepper glanced over again, unclear whether Wes' response was affirmation of his desire to come work, or merely acknowledgment of his proposal. Wes' eyes shifted down and unfocused slightly, seemingly weighing pros and cons. Pepper started to slow as the turn to Thirst Hollow was approaching. "Okay," Wes said again. "I'll go."

"Great," Pepper said, easing off the brake and turning the wheel to guide the truck through the turn. As he headed up the Thirst Hollow drainage, Pepper felt good about offering Wes some work. People can get used to not receiving compassion, and small gestures can mean a lot. Pepper's heart went out to Wes. He knew he was going through a hard time. Everyone needs help sometimes, and Pepper was glad to be there at the right time.

Pepper looked again at Wes, but didn't see excitement reflected back at him. Instead, Wes sat dull and emotionless. Pepper knew Wes was tired. Riots had forced him out of his home and he had been traveling ever since, just trying to get by, but Pepper expected to see some gratitude in Wes' face, or at the least some relief. There was nothing.

Wes looked back at Pepper. His eyes conveyed no geniality or compassion, as if Pepper was only a means to an end. Another way to get a meal and a place to sleep. But Pepper wasn't fazed. He barely noticed.

Pleased with himself for helping, Pepper just kept driving to Thirst Hollow, hoping his generosity would soften Wes. And even if it didn't, Pepper knew in his heart it was the right thing to do to help him, even if Wes wasn't appreciative.

12

The Arrival

It was almost noon before Pepper and Wes got back to the house. Olive had made lunch for just two people, herself and Pepper, so she was a little put off at Wes' arrival. Pepper anticipated Olive's apprehension, and made a show of displaying the newly purchased bags of flour on the counter to try to win back some points.

Despite the flour, Pepper could see Olive's restrained annoyance, but she lightened up a little when she found out that Wes was going to help build the deer fence. But Wes was there whether she liked it or not so Olive made another sandwich and redistributed the green beans three ways to accommodate him.

While eating Pepper probed Wes with question after question, attempting to get a dialogue going, but was shut down with many one word or otherwise vague answers. So lunch was eaten over a mostly silent table. Once everyone finished, Olive and Pepper started washing the dishes and, without a word, Wes stood up and walked out the front door onto the porch.

"I don't know about this guy," Olive leaned toward Pepper and whispered as she wiped a soapy rag over her dirty plate.

"Yeah, he is a little weird," Pepper agreed, "but he's been having a hard time. He said he had to leave where he was living because riots destroyed his home and work."

"Oh, dang, I didn't know that," Olive said, handing Pepper a plate to dry. "Where's he coming from?"

"He said from up north," Pepper answered, wiping the plate with a dry rag.

"Hm," Olive hummed disapprovingly. "What was he doing up there?"

"I'm not sure," Pepper said, placing the plate back in the cupboard and avoiding Olive's gaze. He didn't want to justify why he wanted to help Wes. It was the right thing to do. Simple as that. No explanation needed. "Working, I guess. He didn't really say."

"That's exactly why I don't feel good about this guy," Olive said, taking a pause from washing a plate to catch Pepper's eye. "He's sketchy. He doesn't say anything about himself and I feel like he is trying to hide something." Wes' silence reminded her of the way her father acted after a night of big gambling losses. Too embarrassed, or maybe scared of repercussions from Olive, her father would remain quiet, dodging questions and gaslighting her. Olive spent years trying to cut through her father's bullshit and wasn't about to be fooled by this new hitchhiker.

"Yeah, I guess, but I don't know what other choice I had. They guy needed help. He's probably just shy or nervous or something. We can't just judge him without getting to know him. Everyone needs help once in a while, and you never know what would happen if we don't help."

"C'mon Pepper," Olive said with an edge in her voice, "You did have another choice. Not pick him up. Or drop him off somewhere besides here. You didn't have to bring him to our house and offer to feed him. You know that we are low on food."

"You're right," Pepper agreed, though he wasn't convinced. "I guess I could have left him there, but it just breaks my heart to even think about doing that. I'm sorry I brought him here without asking you, but there was no way I could have asked. Also, it's not like we are just feeding him for nothing, Wes is going to help me put up the deer fence, and that will help us protect our fields from deer this summer. We aren't giving up our food for nothing."

Olive paused for a moment and put down the plate she was washing. Pepper saw some of her annoyance flow from her face, and was relieved he chose the right words.

"Okay. I guess it is what it is. I hope you're right about him, but I have a bad feeling."

Pepper took the last plate from Olive, dried it, and stacked it in the cupboard with the others. "I'm sorry. I had to make the decision without you, but I would have included you if I could have." Pepper put his hand on Olive's back. "I'm going to go see how he's doing then get to work. I'll see you out there?"

"Yeah, I'll be out soon. Love you."

"Love you too."

Pepper put his coat on and joined Wes on the front porch. Wes was leaning forward against the railing, bent at the waist with his elbows supporting his weight. Pepper took a similar posture, and looked out across Thirst Hollow. On the edge of the property, the leaves on the trees were just barely emerging, adding a green hue to the drab winter canopy.

As Pepper looked out, the view comforted him. He made the right decision to help out Wes. Everyone is just doing their best to live their life. Living is hard, but making it a little easier for someone else is worthwhile.

After a few minutes of looking and thinking, Pepper turned to Wes and said, "So today I could use your help putting in some fence. It's really easy. I mostly just need you to carry posts and dig holes. I can show you what to do."

During their first summer in Thirst Hollow, Pepper and Olive lost a lot of crops to deer grazing their fields. Pepper didn't blame them for wanting a quick, easy meal, but with food as tight as it was over the winter, the couple made a large investment in deer fencing, hoping to save their tediously grown food.

Wes shifted his weight from one leg to the other and nodded his head. "Okay," he said softly.

The two men walked behind the house to a shed holding the pile of ten-foot galvanized steel poles, and rolls of welded wire fencing Pepper bought a few months prior, but had been too busy to install. Pepper carefully stepped into the shed, locating small patches of bare floor to place his feet, and started passing posts and fencing rolls out to Wes, and once they had enough posts and wire, the two staged them incrementally along the border of the fields. Olive was already out making shallow rows to plant carrot seeds, though she didn't look up when Pepper and Wes came.

"Okay," Pepper said to get Wes' attention. "So we need to dig post holes every sixteen feet." Pepper read to place them fifteen feet apart, but he hoped to squeeze in an extra foot to save posts and money. "How about I start digging, and you mark sixteen feet by taking a scoop full of dirt from the ground," Pepper instructed Wes, handing him a tape measure and a shovel.

Pepper gave Wes the easier job feeling a little guilty that his only payment was a couple meals and a place to sleep. Wes nodded and the two got to work. He marked sixteen-foot increments along one side of the field while Pepper dug the holes, and once he was done marking, Wes helped dig until dinnertime.

Pepper and Wes were silent while they worked. But they were at least sixteen feet away from each other the whole afternoon so any conversation would have been difficult. Olive was in the proximity, but stayed in the field working and made no effort to speak to Wes or Pepper. Soon, the sun's light was fading, and the temperature was dropping. The days were short, but they managed to get a lot of work done. Pepper was pleased.

"Hey Wes…Wes," Pepper shouted at him from a few holes away. Wes looked up and stopped forcing the post hole digger into the ground. "Let's call it quits and get some dinner."

Wes readjusted his grip on the post hole digger to the middle of the handle, flipped it horizontally, and started walking towards Pepper.

When Wes got close, Pepper said, "We got a lot done today. Good work. Thanks for all your help."

Wes responded with a faint mutter and a nod. The two turned and walked together to the shed to drop off tools, then into the glowing, warm house where Olive was squatting in front of the wood-burning stove, feeding kindling into the newly lit fire, slowly building the flames.

"Hey guys," she said without turning. "I was going to make mashed potatoes and some green beans. What do you think?"

"Sounds good!" Pepper called out, a little over the top with enthusiasm to compensate for Wes' lack of it. Turning to Wes, Pepper said, "It'll probably be about an hour before it's ready. Take a seat. Do you want anything to drink? We have water, apple juice, apple cider, I think we have some wine somewhere." Pepper's voice trailed off, trying to think of more options.

"I'm fine," said Wes briefly and quietly. "I think I'll sit on the porch, if that's okay."

"Sure," Pepper said, though he wished he would stay and chat to ease Olive's suspicions.

"We also have hot tea and coffee," Olive said, still feeding the fire and blowing on the embers which ached for the oxygen and sounded more like a jet than a small stove.

"I'm fine," said Wes. "Thanks."

As Wes walked out the front door, Olive decided the fire was sufficient for the moment and walked to the kitchen to start dinner. Pepper followed.

After taking a few jars of potatoes and green beans from the cupboard, Olive asked, "How was working with Wes today?"

Pepper suspected she was probing for something, trying to find another reason not to like Wes. So Pepper tried to talk Wes up. "It was good, he worked hard. We really got a lot of work done. It's hard digging those holes and it'll be hard putting the fence posts in the ground too." Pepper paused, working out the wording in his head. He knew his next suggestion wouldn't be received well.

"I really could use more help getting the fence up, and I know you are busy getting stuff planted. What do you think about asking Wes to stay for a few more days and helping out? I know we are short on food, but getting that fence up will save a lot of food from being eaten by the deer, and also I'll be able to start helping you plant sooner than later." Pepper took a breath after his spiel. He talked quickly so he could make all of his points before Olive responded.

"I don't know." Olive hesitated.

"C'mon," Pepper pleaded as he scrubbed potatoes under the small rope of water trickling from the faucet. "It's not just that he needs our help. We need his help too. I really don't want to be put in a bad position if we don't grow enough food this year. What if we run out and can't buy anymore at the grocery store? And, yeah, Wes is a little strange, but who are we to judge? He is working for just a few meals and a place to stay. I really think we should ask him to stay, even for just a few days."

Olive thought for a second then agreed, "Okay. I don't feel great about him, and I'm not sure why, but I just don't. But you're right, he's probably fine, and we do need the help. Go ahead," Olive nodded. "Ask him if he wants to stay."

Pepper placed the clean potatoes on a wooden cutting board, then started slicing and quartering them into uniform cubes.

"Thanks," Pepper said smiling. "I think it will be a good thing. We all need some help sometimes." He put down the knife and gave Olive a kiss on the cheek. Maybe Olive was softening up and starting to see things from his point of view.

Once he was done cutting the potatoes, Pepper transferred them into the pot of boiling water. Pepper and Olive sat at the kitchen table and waited for them to soften enough to mash, discussing plans for the upcoming spring. Once the potatoes were soft, Pepper drained the water, mashed them, and added salt and pepper. He wished they had some butter to add, but milk from the Burdettes' goats would have to do. Dinner was ready.

Pepper opened the door and called Wes inside. The three shared another quiet meal, this time without questions from Olive attempting to get Wes to open up.

"Hey," Pepper said looking at Wes in an awkward attempt to break the silence after everyone finished eating. "Thanks again for all your help today. It really was a huge help having you here."

Wes nodded, staring somewhere between the table and Pepper's face.

"Olive and I were thinking that, if you want, you can stay here for a few more days and keep helping us out. And we can keep feeding you," Pepper continued. "If you want."

Wes thought for a moment, and without looking directly at Pepper's face he agreed, "Sure. For a few days."

"Great," Pepper said. "Sounds good. I bet we can get all the holes dug tomorrow, then start getting the posts in the ground the next day." Pepper was pleased. They could get a lot of work done depending on how long Wes wanted to stay. "Alright, well, we can get the couch fixed up for you to sleep on. We have an extra pillow and some blankets."

"Actually, I set up my tarp outside."

Pepper took a second to understand what he was getting at, but upon realizing Wes wanted to sleep outside, responded, "Sure, whatever you're more comfortable with. But we really don't mind you staying on the couch. It'd be warmer in here."

"Thanks, but I'll be fine." Wes started to stand up from the table. "I'm going to go to sleep. Thank you for dinner."

"Alright, well we will see you tomorrow then. Feel free to come in if you need anything or you get cold." Pepper offered.

"Goodnight," Olive said as Wes walked out the front door, closing it gently behind.

Olive looked at Pepper with wide eyes, a cocked head, and a raised eyebrow. "Sleeping outside?" she asked.

"Oh c'mon, you like sleeping outside," Pepper responded, defending Wes. "I like sleeping outside."

"I guess so," Olive said, not fully convinced.

"We should sleep outside sometime this summer. Under the stars."

Olive's hard face softened. "Yeah, that would be nice. Snuggling in the moonlight."

Pepper offered to clean up the kitchen to stay in Olive's good graces. He was happy to get help putting up the fence, and hoped that with Wes there he could finish soon and move onto the other tasks nagging in the back of his mind. There was always some chore, some project, that Pepper worried about, and the constant worrying made him tired.

Pepper was tired, not just from worrying, or working all day, but also because he felt he was walking a tightrope.

He was balancing keeping Olive happy, getting the homestead put together, and following the moral code his conscience imposed on him. Squeezed from all sides, he wished he could catch a break. He wished he lived in a different time, when climate change wasn't destabilizing the world. A time when there weren't eight billion people on the planet competing for a limited and insufficient amount of resources. A time when the country wasn't painfully divided, and when corporations and their money didn't rule supreme.

Pepper didn't even know if such a time existed, but he longed for it. He was nostalgic for it. Living in the present day was hard, and Pepper knew it was going to get harder. Pepper knew wishing to time travel was futile, and all he could do was keep moving forward and try to make the best out of the strange, challenging, unsure time he was living in.

13

The Work

When Pepper woke up the next morning, he walked into the living room to look out of the front window to greet the day, and to see if Wes was still sleeping. As Pepper drew the curtains, he saw Wes standing on the front porch, leaning on the railing as he had the day before.

"Mornin'," Pepper said, opening the door. "Why don't you come in while we fix some breakfast?"

Wes turned and walked inside as Pepper held the door.

"Good morning, Wes," greeted Olive as she walked out of the bedroom. "Do you want scrambled eggs or pancakes?"

"Either is fine," said Wes, standing behind a chair pushed under the kitchen table.

"Let's do pancakes," Pepper suggested.

"Sounds good. I'll make them," Olive offered, preferring to have something to do while Wes was in the house.

Pepper went to the kitchen and helped Olive with breakfast. "You can sit down if you'd like," he said over to Wes.

Wes pulled a chair from under the table and it groaned painfully on the wood floor below. Olive and Pepper cooked breakfast and had yet another quiet meal with Wes. Unable to bear the noise of silverware scraping on plates any longer, Olive turned on the radio. She couldn't get any stations to come in clearly, but instead of turning it off, she left the static on at half volume to break up the silence.

Once everyone finished, Olive offered to clean up, and Wes and Pepper left the house to brave the cold morning air. All day the two dug fence post holes surrounding the fields, leaving only a few remaining for the next day. Olive was intentionally distant as she worked on getting more seeds in the ground, and tended to the seedlings in the greenhouses.

The next two days continued in a similar fashion. Pepper and Wes finished digging the holes then moved onto setting the posts. Wes was a hard worker, but kept to himself, rarely speaking unless Olive or Pepper all but forced him to.

Pepper was happy to be so productive, but soon guilt crept up his spine. Wes was breaking his back, working hard every day, and all he was getting was a few meals. It didn't seem fair. Wes deserved more, but Pepper didn't have anything else to give him.

Late afternoon on the fourth day after Pepper and Wes finished setting a post, Pepper told Wes he should call it an early day, go relax, and do as he pleased. Pepper put the tools away and went to go find Olive as Wes headed to his tarp shelter.

Pepper found Olive in one of the greenhouses watering some kale seedlings, many of which were getting big and would soon be ready to go in the ground. She smiled when she saw Pepper walk in. She still wasn't thrilled about having Wes stay with them, but she was happy with how much work was getting done, so she had made peace with the situation.

"How's your day?" Olive asked.

"It's good. We got a lot done. I told Wes to go relax for the rest of the day." Pepper paused. "I'm not sure how I feel about the whole situation."

"Yeah, me too," Olive eagerly agreed. "I hate to talk bad because he hasn't really done anything, but I just don't feel right."

"No, it's not that." Pepper shook his head. "I feel bad working Wes so hard and not being able to pay him. Do you think we're taking advantage of him? I don't know what to do," Pepper's heart sagged in his chest, heavy with guilt.

"I'm sorry," Olive said sympathetically. She rubbed his arm in consolation, but Pepper knew they weren't on the same wavelength. The only reason Olive wanted Wes there was for the cheap labor, and that was exactly what Pepper felt guilty about.

"I think that I'm going to hike up the ridge," Pepper said, "unless you need help here."

"No, you should go," Olive insisted. "I've got these kale plants under control." She smiled, squeezing Pepper's arm to comfort him.

"Okay, thanks. Love you."

Pepper walked out of the greenhouse and headed for the narrow path leading up the ridge, beaten down from many trips. Soon he was breathing hard and his thighs burned, but the pain felt good. As Pepper hiked, his mind was scattered, thinking about Wes, the farm, the Burdettes, his legs, his lungs. He thought about a lot of things, but couldn't focus on any of them.

Eventually, out of breath, Pepper reached the top of the ridge. He turned around, put his hands on his hips, and looked out to the valleys and ridges rolling from beneath his feet. Pepper's back was sweaty, and his chest heaved. The air filling his lungs felt good. Though the view from their house was nice, it didn't compare to the view on the ridge. On top, the world was more open, nothing pressed down on him. On top, there was nothing for him to bear.

While in the valley, Pepper often found himself fixated on his immediate vicinity, only seeing what was directly in front of him. He would forget Thirst Hollow was just a small part of a vast, interconnected network of rolling hills, ridges, and valleys. It was easy for Pepper to lose sight that his farm wasn't the whole world, but from the top of the ridge he remembered.

Pepper's breath slowly returned, and he ambled along the ridge until he found a sandstone boulder large enough to sit on. Permanently recorded in the top of the boulder Pepper could see the ripples of an ancient sea long since drained. That is permanently until – piece by piece, grain by grain – wind, rain, and ice slowly eroded the boulder and moved its constituent elements downhill.

Over countless years sand grains from the boulder would wash down to Pepper's property and into Thirst Run, while others would fall to the other side of the ridge and continue into the creek laying at the bottom of the valley behind him. Just a few inches of separation on top of the ridge could take two sand grains on different journeys. The original distance between the grains was amplified by thousands, simply due to nearly indiscernible variations in their circumstances. And an even greater dichotomy occurred just a few miles west of Pepper, where a ridge separated Virginia from West Virginia.

That ridge was a Continental Divide, separating two of North America's great watersheds. Rain that fell on the Virginia side eventually flowed into the Shenandoah River, north to the Potomac River, and south into the Atlantic Ocean. The rain to the west took a much different route, first to the New River, flowing north to the Ohio, west to the Mississippi, and into the Gulf of Mexico.

Rain just a few miles away could end up thousands of miles from the rain landing where Pepper sat. At that West Virginia-Virginia ridge, a separation of just a few inches would have the same effect. There, something as small as a tiny gust of wind, a seemingly trivial force the drops had no control over, nor could foresee any significance in, could cause an almost incomprehensible difference in their futures.

Pepper turned his body and looked back toward West Virginia. Looming overhead in a dramatic grayscale were threatening storm clouds. Pepper thought about how some of that storm's rain would end up in the Gulf of

Mexico, and some would end up in the Atlantic Ocean. Same storm, same cloud. Raindrops ultimately separated a thousand miles. The only difference between them was timing – when they decided to leave the cloud and fall to the earth. And such a tiny difference in decision leading to two dramatically different outcomes.

Pepper glanced again at the menacing clouds, stood up, and decided he should start hiking down before the rain came. Though Pepper hadn't thought about whether he should ask Wes to keep working, he felt better. Pepper didn't need to think about the problem to know what to do. In fact, he already knew before he hiked up the ridge, he just had to get some clarity and perspective to figure out what he already knew.

Pepper carefully walked down the steep path, back to Thirst Hollow. He watched his feet kick pebbles down the hill, advancing their journey and wondering if they had once been part of the boulder at the top of the ridge.

14

The Departure

That night, dinner with Wes was once again quiet. Pepper's spirits and body were rejuvenated from a short day of work and the hike to the ridge top, but his nerves were in a bundle about telling Wes his decision. Pepper didn't want to come off as ungrateful, or make Wes think he had done something wrong, but Pepper knew it was time for Wes to move on. The silence at the table felt impenetrable, and Pepper wished there was some light conversation so his words wouldn't seem so abrupt, but the only sound was the scraping of silverware.

"So Wes," Pepper finally got the courage to say. Olive and Wes stopped eating, startled by the violation of their silent meal. Food waited patiently on the end of their forks, and both of them looked up at Pepper for an explanation of his phonic intrusion. "We've really appreciated your work the past few days. You've been a huge help." Pepper paused waiting for a reaction from Wes, but got none, so he continued, "I really wish we could pay you, but we just can't." Still nothing from Wes. "So I just don't think it's fair for you to stay here, working for no pay. I think you will be able to find work somewhere. Work that will pay you fairly."

Wes nodded. He understood what Pepper was saying. He had to leave. He looked down at his food, not angry but upset. Beaten down.

"It's not that we don't want you here," Pepper justified, hoping to make his intentions clear. "It's just that it's not fair. For you, that is." He wasn't sure if his point was getting across, but further explanation seemed futile, if not counterproductive. "So how about tomorrow I drive you anywhere you want within, I don't know, an hour from here," Pepper continued. "It's the least we could do."

"Okay," Wes said softly, and finally put the bite of food that had been waiting on his fork into his mouth.

No one responded and the silent dinner continued. Pepper sat lamenting his lack of foresight to wait until the end of dinner to have that conversation. Once everyone finished eating, Wes went outside for the night.

"Do you think he's mad?" Pepper asked Olive.

"I don't know," she shrugged. "He leaves like that every night after dinner."

"Yeah, that's true." Pepper said, but didn't feel any better.

Olive and Pepper cleaned up together, and Olive made an extra effort to help knowing Pepper was feeling down. Pepper went to bed early, upset with himself and hoping the next day would be better.

Pepper woke early the next morning. Chilled, he revived the lonely, dying embers in the wood-burning stove. Once the fire was going, he looked out the window to see if Wes was awake. Every morning, either Olive or Pepper would have to invite him in, despite their insistence for him to make himself at home.

To Pepper's surprise, Wes wasn't standing on the porch leaning against the railing as he usually was. Pepper opened the front door and poked his head out to see if he was still in his tarp shelter, but the shelter was gone.

Pepper stepped out on the porch to get a better view, thinking he may be packing up and out of sight, but Wes was nowhere to be seen.

"Shit," Pepper said under his breath.

He rushed back in the house to get dressed and put his coat and boots on.

"Wes is gone," Pepper said as he walked into the bedroom. Olive looked up as his boots pounded on the wood floor and vibrated through the bed.

"What do you mean?" she asked, still waking up.

"He left, I can't find him anywhere," Pepper answered. "I guess I have to go look for him."

Olive gently protested from the warm bed. "If he's gone, he's gone. It's okay. Let him be." She saw Pepper had tunnel vision, only thinking of how he could help Wes.

Pepper stopped and looked up at her, thinking for a moment. What was he going to do? Search the property? Drive the streets looking for him? And if he found him, what then? Wes wanted to be gone, so he left.

"You're right," Pepper said, accepting the situation and calling off his hunt. "I guess I'll start making breakfast."

Pepper made omelets and had another quiet breakfast with Olive. Unlike their recent meals, that one wasn't quiet because of Wes' presence, but because of his absence. The awkward silence was replaced with a sad silence. Pepper felt guilty. He had wronged Wes and couldn't bear to think he was out there somewhere thinking Pepper treated him poorly. That he had done him harm.

Once breakfast was finished, Olive offered to clean up if Pepper would feed the sheep and goats. Agreeing, Pepper put on his coat, went outside, and walked across the frosty grass towards the Burdettes' property. Instead of slowly evading Pepper, the sheep and goats had learned that when he came into their pasture, it meant food.

Pepper grabbed a bale of hay from the barn, and carried it to the trough where the flock crowded in anticipation of their meal. Breakfast was imminent. Pepper broke apart the bale and spread it evenly across the trough, but when he stepped aside and looked up, Pepper noticed something strange.

The Burdettes' front door was wide open. Pepper stood and stared, wondering why it was open, trying to remember the last time he went into the Burdettes' house. Deciding to investigate, Pepper made his way through the swarm of hungry livestock, across the field, and up the porch steps.

Pepper stood on the porch and peered through the vacant doorway. Inside, the Burdettes' beautiful house was torn apart. Cabinet doors were open, drawers were pulled out, and papers and clothes littered the floor. The gun case was open, but Mr. Burdette's rifle and shotgun still stood proudly.

Pepper walked inside, dumbfounded. He stood, surveying the damage with wide eyes. He walked into the kitchen, then the bedroom and was met with similar scenes of upheaval. Nothing seemed to be damaged, but everything was out of place, rummaged through, violated. Pepper would have heard a car drive up during the night, so he immediately knew Wes had to be the culprit.

Pepper wasn't mad at Wes for what he did. Pepper saw he was desperate and just trying to get by and survive. Pepper even blamed himself for not paying Wes for his work. Maybe if he had been more generous, this wouldn't have happened.

Pepper closed his eyes for a second to recompose himself. He knew Olive was going to be mad at Wes for taking advantage of them and the Burdettes, and mad at him for giving him the opportunity to do it. Eventually, after summoning the courage to tell Olive, Pepper walked out of the Burdettes' gaping door, and back to his house, slowed by his heavy feet dragging behind him. Pepper slowly opened the front door and found Olive at the sink drying dishes.

She looked up to see Pepper's demeanor even more dejected than before, and immediately asked, "What's wrong?

"Wes ransacked the Burdettes' house. It's a mess."

"Are you serious? What the fuck!" Olive said, slamming a plate into the drying rack. Pepper's prediction was right – Olive was pissed. "What'd he take?"

"I don't know," Pepper shook his head, glad the heat was on Wes instead of him, though he knew he wasn't in the clear yet. It was his decision to bring Wes to the farm, and any minute Olive could focus on that. "It's a mess. I'm sure he did, but I don't really know what they had, so I'm not sure what's missing."

"Shit, well I guess we should go to town to call the police, the reception on the ridge sucks," Olive said, pacing around the house with loud steps, gathering her things and her anger displayed in her exaggerated motions.

Olive was steaming, despite everything they had done for Wes, he took advantage of them. Transported back to a time when she lived with her father, Olive couldn't stop thinking about how she always took care of her father, paying the bills and keeping the house nice, only to be repaid with betrayal and hurt.

"Okay," Pepper agreed, going along with Olive's plan not only because it was the right thing to do, but also because if he didn't he worried she may focus her anger on him.

In only a few minutes, Pepper and Olive were on their way to Plomari. Pepper drove, keeping his eyes fixed ahead, the air too tense to make conversation. The drive was slow and windy, and their bodies swayed back and forth as the truck went around the curvy road.

"I guess we should also try to call the Burdettes," Olive said, breaking the silence.

Pepper agreed while cursing himself internally. He hadn't thought about telling them.

"I told you we shouldn't let Wes stay," Olive said accusatively, turning to face Pepper head on. He kept his eyes ahead, cursing himself even further, waiting for Olive's wrath to come down. "Seriously Pepper, you can't keep doing this. What if he had robbed us? What if he had hurt us? You can't go around trusting and helping everyone you see. The world isn't the same as it used to be and something really bad is going to happen to us if you don't change."

"I know, I'm sorry," Pepper responded. And he really was sorry. Wes didn't turn out to be violent, but someone else Pepper might decide to help could be. Pepper imagined himself, or worse, Olive getting hurt. He thought hard about his deep need to help people, and wondered why protecting others came before protecting himself and Olive. Olive didn't have this flaw. She put him and herself before anyone else. Why did he?

Pepper cared more about Olive than he did anyone else in the world, so why didn't he put her before others? Maybe the only way to protect her in the new, changing world was to stop helping others. Pepper glanced from the road to Olive.

"I'm going to try harder. You know it's really hard for me not to help people, but I'm going to try my best to not do anything to hurt us. I'm sorry."

Olive didn't look over or respond. Instead she sat staring ahead without words until they reached Plomari. Though Pepper would have liked some consolation from Olive, he took her silence as a win. At least she wasn't angry enough to keep arguing.

When Pepper pulled into Plomari, a piece of cardboard covered the gas station's sign. "OUT OF GAS" it declared, handwritten in permanent marker. Pepper ignored its implications, refusing to introduce more stress to the day.

"Who should we call first?" Pepper asked meekly, as he pulled the flip phone out of his pocket.

"I guess the police," she answered. "Maybe they know something."

Pepper nodded, grateful that Olive was engaging with him, and dialed the three digits, pausing for a second to collect his thoughts and internally rehearse what he planned to say. Once he hashed it out, Pepper mustered the courage to press the call button, only to hear a busy signal on the other end.

"That's weird," Pepper said to Olive, closing the phone. "It was busy."

Pepper dialed again two more times before hearing an abrupt ring followed by a voice, "911, what's your emergency?"

"Hi, someone broke into my neighbors' house. We think we know who did it."

"When did this happen?"

"Either last night or this morning."

"And what was stolen?"

"I'm not sure, the house is a mess. My neighbors are out of town and we are watching their house for them. We had a man staying with us for a few days who disappeared this morning. I'm pretty sure it was him who did it."

"Okay." The voice on the other end paused, and Pepper could hear the clicking of a keyboard. "I put it in the system, but to be honest with you, we are way understaffed here and we've been getting a ton of calls like this lately. We really don't have the resources to respond, especially if you aren't even sure anything was taken."

"Okay," Pepper said, his voice short with frustration. "Can I at least give you the description of the man?"

"Sure, go ahead," the voice said unenthusiastically.

"His name is Wes. He's about 20 years old, white, five foot ten, with medium length brown hair. He had been hitchhiking with a small, black backpack and I think he was going into West Virginia."

"Okay, I have that down in the file." Pepper could tell the voice ached to get off the phone.

"Well, what are the next steps?" Pepper asked, refusing to give up.

"I guess we can have an officer call you if there is any development, but honestly, we really don't have anyone to look into it. Sorry."

"Okay, thanks. I guess we will wait for a call," Pepper said, closing the phone without waiting for the voice to respond. He looked over at Olive and said, "Well, that didn't go well."

"No?"

"No. They just said they didn't have enough resources and that they'd call me if they found anything out."

"Shit," she said, looking away. "So much for giving the Burdettes a bit of good news."

"Yeah. Do you mind calling them?" Pepper asked, handing the phone out to Olive.

Pepper had enough of the phone and the disappointment that went along with it.

"Sure," Olive said with an edge of annoyance in her voice. Pepper regretted asking her, but it was too late to take it back. Olive dialed the Burdettes' number into the phone and, like Pepper, paused before pressing the call button.

"Hello?" Pepper could faintly hear Mrs. Burdette's voice ring out on the other end.

"Hi Mrs. Burdette, it's Olive."

"Oh, hi!" Mrs. Burdette greeted her warmly. "Is everything alright honey? You sound nervous."

"I have some bad news for you," Olive said, diving in. "Last night, a man that was staying with us broke into your house. We aren't sure what was taken, but it looks like he went through everything. The house is torn apart.

It's a mess. We're so sorry. We were supposed to be looking after your house, and then this happens. We'll do whatever you need to make it right."

A brief silence filled the other end of the line. "It's okay honey," Mrs. Burdette said. "As long as you two are okay, that's all that matters."

"Oh, thank you so much," Olive said, relieved. "We can clean up the mess so when you get back it won't look like a tornado went through there."

"That's so kind of you," thanked Mrs. Burdette, "but don't worry too much. Tom and I probably won't be back for a long while." Mrs. Burdette paused. "I guess I should tell you. The doctors found cancer in Tom's lungs. He's fighting it, and he's being so strong, but we are having more and more trouble finding him treatment. Just last week, the doctor we had been seeing stopped answering his phone. Tom and I drove there yesterday and there was a sign on the door saying the office was closed indefinitely. A lot of people are fleeing the city. It's starting to get violent here with all the protests. It's frustrating, but we don't have much choice besides staying here and trying to find Tom the best care we can."

"Oh my gosh, I'm so sorry," Olive said, readjusting herself on the truck's bench seat.

"It's okay," Mrs. Burdette's sweet voice reassured her. "But we probably won't be coming home anytime soon." She paused, gathering her thoughts. "To be honest with you honey, we probably won't ever make it back there. Tom's time is limited, and once he passes, I think I will stay here with Todd's family. I can't handle the farm on my own."

Olive swallowed. She didn't know what to say.

"So I guess what I'm getting at is if you and Pepper could continue looking after our home and our farm, we would be very grateful."

"Of course," Olive said, nodding emphatically as if Mrs. Burdette could see her.

"Oh, thank you. Tom and I really do appreciate it. And I know you need as much land to farm as you can get, so please use ours. It's the least we can do to repay y'all for watching everything. Also, I know Pepper is a vegetarian, but if you ever want, you can slaughter a sheep or goat for meat. They're yours now. Maybe one day, one of our sons will want to move into the house, but until then, it's all yours.

Pepper's eyebrows rose.

"Okay, wow. Thank you so much," Olive said, having trouble finding words.

"No, thank you for watching after the farm. It's really a load off our minds to know it's in good hands. Anyways honey, I wish I could keep chatting, but I have to go. We are meeting with a new doctor today up in Fredericksburg and need to get going."

"Okay. Good luck with the new doctor."

"Bye bye," Mrs. Burdette said. "Keep in touch."

"Bye," Olive said, closing the phone slowly and turning to Pepper. "It doesn't sound like things are going very well for the Burdettes." Pepper instantly recognized a shift in her tone from before the phone call.

"Yeah, I could hear," Pepper said. "That's awful. I wish we could do something more for them."

"Well, they seem glad we can watch their house."

"One less thing they have to worry about," Pepper agreed.

"Yeah," Olive said flatly.

They sat looking out the window at the scene of an empty gas station surrounded by looming trees. It almost felt like a ghost town. Looking up, Pepper could only see a small patch of sky through the branches crowding his view.

"Let's get out of here," Olive said, shifting in her seat.

Pepper nodded and started the truck. He worried about Mr. Burdette, but was relieved Olive wasn't mad at him anymore. Mrs. Burdette's news overshadowed his responsibility in the Wes situation. As Pepper guided the truck back to Thirst Hollow, he began to digest the new information.

Pepper knew he and Olive needed to grow a lot more food that summer. Their performance was sub-par the year before, and with food becoming harder and harder to buy, their options were limited. The extra acres Mrs. Burdette said he could farm could be the extra boost they needed. With a year of experience under his belt, and more land to farm, Pepper was feeling hopeful.

As Pepper turned the wheel sharply to make a hairpin turn, he started to kick himself. He hated that he was excited about the news. It was terrible Mr. Burdette was sick. Through their weekly dinners, and constant advice, Pepper had grown attached to the Burdettes. They were more than neighbors, or even friends. They were mentors. They were his role models. He really hoped Mr. Burdette would overcome the cancer, so to atone for being selfish, he made himself focus on and feel sad about the Burdettes' situation.

Pepper tried to focus on feeling empathetic for the Burdettes, thinking how hard it would be for him if he found out Olive had cancer. In his brain he knew it would be terrible, but his heart had trouble committing to the hypothetical. Since it wasn't real, it was hard for Pepper to entertain the situation. He had plenty of other problems that were taking up space in his brain. Not least of which was Wes.

If Wes had been a different person, if he had been violent, their day could have gone a lot different. Pepper was grateful that all he had done was rummage through the Burdette's house and maybe stolen some jewelry or other valuables. If Wes was more desperate, he could have easily done a lot worse. Pepper was scared at the way the world was going. Soon, there would be a lot more desperate people, and the more desperate a person is, the more dangerously they will act.

Driving back home felt good. Every mile toward Thirst Hollow was one more away from civilization, and the chaos that festered in it. With the Burdettes gone, he and Olive were the only two inhabitants of Thirst Hollow.

That made Pepper feel safe. Their valley was small and quiet, so he would be able to hear any intruder if or when they came.

Pepper would do anything to protect Olive, and after getting a glimpse of what could happen in the new world they found themselves in, he knew he had to make some changes to protect her.

Pepper was used to being taken advantage of every once in a while, and that had been okay in the past. But now the stakes were higher – literally life and death – he couldn't just go around helping everyone who asked. Driving down the road, Pepper vowed he wouldn't sacrifice his or Olive's welfare anymore. He was going to put their needs first. Maybe he would help someone here or there, but definitely not if it was going to hurt him or Olive.

This wasn't the first time Pepper made the same promise, but before he made it for different reasons. His decision wasn't caused by Olive's disappointment in him, or because he wanted to end a fight. This time, Pepper's resolve to change was to protect Olive. He knew it was going to be hard, that the voice within would try to convince him to help when he shouldn't, but Pepper was determined. He wasn't going to mess up again, because if he did, the consequences could be terrible.

15

The Smoke

Spring soon filled the vacancy Wes left. Warm weather blessed Thirst Hollow, and with it, so did Olive and Pepper's crops. The couple hadn't eaten fresh vegetables in months, so their first harvest of carrots, radishes, and other early vegetables tasted divine. Their crispness was a strong contrast to the spongy softness of the rice and canned vegetables they were used to eating.

Olive and Pepper were also taking full advantage of the Burdettes' offer to utilize their property. The couple tilled and planted almost every square inch of cleared land on the Burdettes' property except the pasture grazed by the sheep and goats.

Pepper tried to make a habit of calling the Burdettes to check on them, but spotty cell service and unanswered calls limited their communication. Every once in a while, Pepper would get through and hear grim news from Mrs. Burdette. When Mr. Burdette was able to see a doctor, they told him his cancer was spreading. Treatment was both ineffective and difficult to get. On top of that, food shortages and civil unrest made Richmond less and less livable. Pepper worried about the Burdettes, but his busy life in Thirst Hollow didn't allow much leeway in his concentration.

In Thirst Hollow, as spring matured, so did the plants. With the extra acreage, Olive and Pepper were stretched thin with the additional work of planting, weeding, watering, and harvesting. Unfortunately, most crops were still immature, and the couple wasn't harvesting enough food to keep them satiated. Their food supply was dwindling, and there wasn't much they could do about it besides hope for early and bountiful harvests.

Shipments to the grocery store had become even less frequent, so Olive and Pepper felt they were backed in a corner. The couple wasn't starving, but they were getting hungry. The urge to eat more lived in the back of their minds, but the pragmatism of their brains forced them to wait – to ration, and to make their food last until they were able to harvest more.

They knew a little hunger now was better than starvation with no options later. Sometimes it was hard for them to justify not eating their fill when they had crops that just weren't quite ripe, but would be shortly. They wanted to take a risk, to fill their stomachs, but tried to keep a cool mind knowing that nothing is a sure thing. The crops might not come in as soon as they wanted, or at all for that matter. The harvest could be pushed back, and if they ate all their food, they wouldn't have anything to bridge the gap.

To keep their minds off their stomachs, Olive and Pepper worked hard to finish the hundred tasks that needed to be done, grinding all day to finish a few and discovering more to add to the list. In addition to the necessary chores, they had side projects to fill any spare seconds. Pepper began making goat cheese and aimed to perfect the art – or just figure out how to make it taste less...goaty.

The fence Wes helped build held up to the onslaught of deer, and by early May Olive and Pepper finally began harvesting a significant amount of food, ending their rationing and hunger. The mild winter, the early spring, and their past year's lessons-learned gave them a better start to their second growing season.

Pea pods were plumping, cucumbers were climbing, garlic was growing, and Olive and Pepper were tired, but happy. Even optimistic. Mango had joined forces with the Burdette's border collies, Box and Turtle, though she didn't understand the appeal of watching livestock all day. Box and Turtle stopped spending long nights on the Burdettes' porch and made themselves at home in Olive and Pepper's cabin. It was small and cozy. There were more dogs than people.

No matter how busy Olive and Pepper were, they always sat down and ate at least two meals together. The couple made a habit to say what they were grateful for before eating, so at least twice a day they were reminded of what they had, instead of only focusing on what they needed. In more dire times when Pepper needed some extra help, he would hike up the ridge to sit with the view.

On the ridge, Pepper was able to think more clearly and problem solve better. The view, the air, the trees, all of it came together to give Pepper what he needed. Perspective. But the ridge was steep, and took time and effort to climb, so Pepper only visited when he needed it the most. Most days, Pepper didn't have the luxury of going there. Instead the day consisted of a regular schedule of chores, breakfast, work, lunch, work, dinner, sleep.

After one ordinary day, Olive and Pepper sat down to a dinner of leftover vegetarian "meat"loaf – where the beef was substituted by lentils.

"It's always better the second day," Pepper said to Olive as he took his first bite.

She smiled and rolled her eyes. Olive heard the same comment every time they ate leftovers. Pepper said it as a joke, but believed it held some truth. Maybe sitting overnight the flavors had time to blend together.

"It is pretty good," Olive agreed.

"Some of the pepper plants were looking a little sad today," Pepper said over his plate of "meat"loaf. "I was thinking and I can't remember the last time we got a good rain. Do you remember?"

Olive thought for a second before answering, "I think it drizzled on Tuesday, but that was barely enough to get the ground wet. We haven't gotten much since that storm which was, what, two weeks ago?"

"Yeah, I think that was about two weeks ago."

Pepper had a hard time keeping track of the days when they did basically the same thing every day, and working through weekends didn't provide a placemark. Trying to think back was like watching a movie in reverse.

"Anyways, I think the well is struggling. It's taking longer and longer to recharge, and I don't think the peppers are getting enough water." Pepper continued. "If the peppers aren't doing well, it won't be long before the other plants get thirsty. I think I'm going to try to get that pump figured out and start irrigating from the holding pond. What do you think?"

"Yeah, might as well. At least use it so we didn't dig that thing for nothing," Olive agreed. "But I think we'll probably get rain soon though. Feels humid outside."

Pepper wasn't sure if the holding pond was big enough, or if there was enough water coming out of the spring to water all of their crops. He hoped for it to be a good supplement, but Pepper knew the plants couldn't survive long without rain.

"It does feel humid," Pepper said, but it always felt humid compared to Utah. His clothes were perpetually damp from sweat, and he missed the dry heat of the west. "I hope it rains soon," Pepper said looking down as he picked at his cuticles.

Pepper started irrigating that day, diverting water into the fields from the small pond he built over the winter. But there wasn't enough to water all the crops every day, so Pepper would empty the dammed spring into one part of the field, let it recharge overnight, and flood another part the next day.

The crops seemed happy with the little boost of water, though Pepper and Olive still hoped for rain. The crops hung on, but rain didn't come, and a week later the couple started to worry about their crops' health.

That week, Olive and Pepper were weeding the bush bean rows when they heard a distant thunder roll across the surrounding hills. Pepper looked at Olive and smiled. Olive hooted back in excitement.

"It's coming!" she shouted.

Ambient electric energy boosted their mood with each successive blast of thunder, and their eyes shot in the direction of the deep sounds each time the thunder announced its presence.

Within minutes the sky darkened as thunderheads hung above Thirst Hollow. Looking up, the couple decided to seek shelter in the house as the storm was imminent. Flashes illuminated dark clouds as they exchanged bolts of lightning, donating electrons from one to the next. Soon, a few jagged beams reached the ground as the lightning sought high points to strike.

The house shook with thunderous vibrations and the dogs panted nervously under the shelter of the kitchen table. Olive and Pepper sat on the front porch and watched the show, waiting for the rain to follow the lightning and thunder. Wind bent the trees back and forth, seemingly past their breaking point, and leaves held on tightly as they rapidly flashed their fragile undersides. The show continued for almost an hour before calm skies entered from the west. Seeing the lighter clouds approach, Pepper grew concerned.

"We might not get any rain from this," he said to Olive, disappointed.

She leaned forward in her chair and squinted up at the sky, looking for clues. "Yeah, it looks like it's clearing up."

They sat for a while, listening to the storm move east, farther and farther away, and with it their hopes for a wetting rain.

"Well, I guess I'm going to get back to work," Pepper said, accepting the dry reality.

The dogs pawed at the screen door, finding new courage to leave the shelter of the kitchen table. Pepper let the dogs out and followed behind. He grabbed the hoe leaning on the side of the house, and took one more glance at the sky to confirm the rain had passed before walking back to the field. Pepper began scraping weeds from the dry soil with his hoe, taking out his frustration on them.

Olive was close behind and began working the row behind Pepper. Though they didn't speak, and couldn't see each other, Pepper was grateful she was there. Her presence quieted his mild frustration.

Slowly, Pepper moved from frustration to gratitude. He was grateful for the spring that provided them with some water to get through the dry spell, and grateful to have Olive working with him. The rest of the afternoon was quiet as the couple slowly made their way up and down the rows, removing weeds that would steal precious moisture from their plants.

Late in the afternoon, in the stifling humid heat, Pepper stopped to take a drink of water. He stood, leaning on his hoe, drenched in unevaporated sweat when something caught his eye. From behind the ridge, a thin line of white slowly drifted into the now blue sky. Pepper leaned harder on his hoe and squinted at the apparition, trying to make sense of it. He thought it could be a cloud, but something was a little off. Scanning his memory, he realized what he was looking at.

"Olive," Pepper said without turning to her, "is that smoke?"

Olive stopped working and looked over.

"Yeah," Olive said. The word left her mouth slowly as her brain processed the information sent from her eyes. "That's definitely smoke, something probably lit from all that lightning. Let's go up to the ridge to see where it's coming from."

"Okay," Pepper nodded. "I'll go get the phone. In case we have to report it."

Pepper walked to the house and stuffed some water bottles, snacks, and the cell phone in a small backpack, then met Olive back in the field where she was still weeding.

"Ready?" he asked.

Olive leaned her tool against the deer fence next to Pepper's, and the couple dashed out the gate and to the path. There was an unspoken urgency between them and they fell into a rhythm, taking large steps to gain elevation quickly. The ridge ahead and the trees above hid the smoke from view.

Within minutes the couple reached the ridge and found a viewpoint through the dense foliage. In the sky, the plume had doubled in thickness and continued to claw its way higher, but it rose from the next valley over so they were unable to see its source.

"The wind is blowing this way," Olive said. "I bet it will jump that ridge soon and once it does, it will climb this one and be in Thirst Hollow. Give me the phone, I'll call it in. Hopefully they can send some firefighters, or maybe a plane to drop some retardant."

Pepper took the phone from his backpack and handed it to Olive. She took the phone and held down the power button. After a short jingle announcing the phone was on, she dialed 911 with three calculated tones followed by a fourth of the send button.

After a few seconds Olive explained into the phone, "Hi, I am calling to report a wildfire two drainages to the north of Thirst Hollow, about twenty miles north of Plomari."

There was a pause but Pepper couldn't hear the voice on the other end.

"Yes, there were dry lightning strikes in the area this afternoon, and there is a visible plume of white smoke coming from a drainage north of our house." Another pause. "No, we can't see any flames." Pause. "Okay, are you going to send anyone?" Silence. "Okay, thanks." Olive closed the phone and turned to Pepper.

"What'd they say?" Pepper asked.

"Not much," she answered, her worried eyebrows tipping inward. "They said that there were other smoke reports, but they would try to send an engine. I don't know though. It didn't really sound like they were going to." Olive shook her head.

"Dang, I guess they are stretched thin. But maybe they will send someone," Pepper said to reassure Olive.

"Yeah, maybe. I don't know. The dispatcher didn't inspire much confidence," Olive said.

"So, what should we do then?" Pepper asked nervously. He hadn't fought fire in years and the smoke coming from behind the ridge brought memories of the fire in California when his partner, Blackwell, and the family they were helping were killed. Pepper didn't want to face the fire. He wanted to stay as far away from it as he could. He didn't want to lose Olive the same way he lost Blackwell and the family.

"We have to take control. No one's coming, and we can't just stand around and watch our lives burn down," Olive said as she surveyed her surroundings. "The best thing would probably be to make a firebreak on this ridge. We can clear all the trees and shrubs so if the fire gets here, it won't be able to burn past and go down into our property."

Pepper paused. He didn't want anything bad to happen to Olive, but maybe attacking the fire was the best thing to do. Pepper swallowed deeply. Fighting fire wasn't something he wanted to do, but he wanted to protect Olive and the farm even more.

"Okay, sounds like a plan," Pepper agreed, sounding more confident than he felt.

"Okay. Let's hike back down to the house and get the chainsaw and some tools," Olive said as she stared at the smoke billow over the ridge and advance towards them.

Pepper nodded, already taking his first steps back down the path and Olive followed close behind. The couple let gravity do the work pulling them down into Thirst Hollow, trying to keep their legs underneath them.

Once down, Olive hustled to the barn to get the chainsaw ready, while Pepper put the dogs inside so they wouldn't follow. He met Olive in the barn as she pulled the chainsaw's starter cord. The saw puttered before slowly coming to life, coughing up some dark smoke. Olive gave it short bursts of gas to encourage it.

"Ready?" asked Olive as she killed the saw's motor and hoisted it on her shoulder to carry, her upper forehead wrinkled in concern.

"Yeah," Pepper said. He took a step toward Olive to give her a hug and kiss for comfort, but Olive didn't see him. She turned, walking from the barn, and Pepper followed a step behind. The two hiked up the steep ridge beneath the growing pillar of smoke, hoping to keep the fire from reaching Thirst Hollow.

16

The Fire

Once back on top of the ridge, Olive and Pepper saw the plume had grown and, like Hydra, sprouted several smaller plumes on either side. The fire was getting bigger.

Olive and Pepper still couldn't see any flames so they weren't sure where exactly the fire was burning, but since fires like to burn uphill, and the wind was blowing their way, they knew it was coming in their direction. After taking a good look at the smoke's behavior, Olive and Pepper walked the ridge until reaching a small drainage leading down the opposite side from Thirst Hollow.

"This looks like a good place to anchor in," Pepper said, looking down at the drainage. To build an effective firebreak on top of the ridge, they needed some sort of feature on either end to contain the fire and keep it from simply burning around.

"Okay, I guess this is as good as we can do right now," agreed Olive and she swung the chainsaw off her shoulder and placed it on the ground. The small drainage was not ideal, since it was barely wide enough to create separation between the crowns of the trees on either side, but the growing plume of smoke drove fear into the couple and pressured them to get to work.

Olive adjusted the choke on the chainsaw, and turned her head to ask, "Do you have your ear protection in?"

Pepper nodded and Olive started the saw. She went to work felling trees on top of the ridge. When she could, Olive felled them toward Thirst Hollow, so as to not create a jackpot of unburned fuel on the side of the approaching fire. She cut up any part of the tree that remained in the firebreak, and Pepper moved those pieces of trunk and branches out of the corridor.

From years in Utah as a firefighter, Olive was fast on the saw, and Pepper had trouble keeping up. However, no matter how fast she moved, it didn't feel fast enough as white smoke poured over from the next drainage. To be effective, the firebreak had to be between a quarter and a half-mile long, which felt more like fifty miles to the couple. After about an hour of cutting, the chainsaw stuttered, then shut off.

"I'm out of gas," Olive yelled, taking her ear protection out.

"I'll go grab more," Pepper yelled back, also taking the orange plugs from his ears.

Their yelling wasn't just a result of the ear protection muffling their hearing, but also the adrenaline running through their blood. Pepper jogged back through the cleared firebreak to where they started. The distance was shorter than Pepper expected, but he grabbed the oil and gas, and as he headed back he thought *this is going to take a long time*.

Pepper continued down the corridor and walked up to Olive as she tapped the air filter against the body of the saw, raining sawdust beneath.

"Do you want to switch?" Pepper asked.

"No, I'll go for another tank, then we can switch," she responded as she clipped the air filter back in place. Olive was faster with the saw than Pepper and she knew it.

"Do you need any water or snacks?" Pepper asked.

"Sure, I'll take some water."

Pepper swung the backpack off his shoulder, took out a water bottle, and gave it to Olive. She gulped down half a liter, before handing it back.

"Are you hungry?" Pepper asked.

"I'm fine for now. I want to keep cutting."

Olive put her ear protection back in, and Pepper did the same. With two mighty pulls of the starter cord, the saw was resurrected and Olive resumed cutting where she left off. Trees around her commenced falling and were divided into small pieces while Pepper continued to carry off the debris.

The couple pushed on for about an hour until the saw stuttered again and shut off. Out of gas. Olive lowered the saw and looked around for the first time since their short break. Pepper did the same. To his surprise, dusk had crept upon them. The sun had set behind the ridges to the west and the smoke column still rose, though without the vigor it had before.

"I think the fire is calming down now that the temperature is dropping," Pepper said to Olive as she used her sleeve to wipe sweat from her head, replacing it with a mixture of sawdust, sweat, and chainsaw grime.

Olive took a drink from a water bottle, while looking across the darkening valley at the smoke.

"Yeah, you're right," she agreed, forcefully exhaling after a long drink of water. "Should we keep cutting, or wait until tomorrow?"

"I don't think the fire is going to do much tonight, and cutting in the dark would be more of a risk than it's worth. Let's go make some food and get some sleep."

"Okay," Olive said as she looked at the ground and nodded.

Pepper repacked the backpack while Olive did a quick clean and sharpening of the chainsaw, then refilled the gas and oil so it would be ready to go in the morning. She swung the saw over her right shoulder, holding the bar in her gloved right hand.

Pepper stood up, took a few steps in the direction of the path, and asked, "You ready?"

Olive nodded her head and let out a small, "Yeah."

The couple bushwhacked down the ridge, back to the trail. Pepper looked behind him the few hundred yards they had cleared. They were making progress, but Pepper was still nervous. They still hadn't seen the fire, which comforted him because it was too far away to see, but also worried him not knowing where exactly it was burning.

As Olive and Pepper walked down into Thirst Hollow, they could barely see their property below. The valley floor was faint, and the opposite side was invisible. Smoke settled at the bottom and its curtain stifled Pepper, making his chest tight as anxiety swept over him. Pepper distracted himself by focusing on his feet plodding downhill, making sure they didn't catch a root or a rock, and soon they were out of the woods and back on their cleared property, but Pepper didn't feel any better. The smoke was thicker lower down, and walking through the hazy farm, he felt smothered, like a hand pressed on him from above.

Olive went to the barn to rest the chainsaw for the night while Pepper headed to the house. As he approached the front door, he could hear the dogs inside pacing and whining in excitement. Pepper swung the door open, and they poured out. The dogs wagged their tails so hard their butts swung with them. Too excited to restrain themselves, they jumped up onto Pepper.

Normally, Pepper would admonish them for jumping, but that night he welcomed the extra love and sat down on the floor of the porch, letting them walk over him and lick his face. Olive walked up a minute later and the dogs scurried off of Pepper to greet her. Olive sat next to Pepper on the welcome mat and leaned against him. They were both exhausted, mentally and physically, and soon the dog's excitement wore off and they laid on the porch, leaning their bodies against their owners.

Hungry, but too tired to make food. Sleepy, but too sore to get up and go to bed. The couple sat on the front porch, resting against the door until

Pepper heard Olive's breath slow and deepen. She was asleep. Pepper let her be for a few minutes before gently shaking her shoulder.

Once her eyes opened, he said, "Hey, why don't you go lay down in bed?"

She nodded her head with no words. They stood up and Pepper led her to the bedroom. She sat on the bed while he helped her untie her heavy leather logging boots, then slipped them off her feet. She lay down on top of the comforter and closed her eyes.

Pepper wanted to do the same, but knew he had to eat or he would pay for it the next day, so he made a quick dinner of bread and goat cheese. When he was finished, he went to lay down, but not before leaving a plate of food on Olive's nightstand in case she woke up hungry. Pepper lay down next to her and felt the cool, soft bed cradle his body. He was exhausted. Pepper needed a lot of things, but what he wished for most was a good night's sleep, enough to rejuvenate him enough to keep fighting the fire the next day. Fighting the fire, and fighting for their home. Enough to fight for their lives.

17

The Spot Fire

When Pepper woke the next day, he heard Olive in the kitchen making breakfast. The clock showed four-thirty and it was still dark outside. Pepper lay in bed for a minute, tightening each muscle one at a time to feel which were sore and which weren't. Once sufficient inventory had been taken, he sat up – to the dismay of his abdominal muscles – and joined Olive in the kitchen.

"Hey," Pepper said to Olive, whose back was turned as she flipped a fried egg on the stove.

"Oh, hey!" She turned to greet him, gave him a kiss, then went back to cooking. "How'd you sleep?"

"Good. I'm pretty sore though. Carrying those logs all day was hard," Pepper responded. "How about you?"

"Like a rock. Until I woke up at four and was starving, so I got up and ate," Olive said watching the eggs sizzle on the frying pan. "I'm making you some breakfast now, and thought we should get an early start on the fire." Olive lifted two fried eggs off the skillet with a metal spatula, put them on a plate to accompany a pancake and cubed, fried potatoes and red peppers. She placed the plate in front of Pepper's seat at the table.

"Wow, what a spread. Thanks," Pepper said sitting down.

"Of course, enjoy," she responded as she consolidated the dirty kitchen utensils and dishes into the sink. "I'm going to make sure the chainsaw is ready to go. I'll see you out there once you're done?"

"Sounds good," Pepper said through a mouth full of potatoes.

Olive walked out the front, and closed the door softly behind. Pepper stood up from the table and poured himself a cup of coffee, then resumed eating and took his time. Though he felt a sense of urgency to start working and protect his property, the weight of the situation slowed him down, knowing that once he finished breakfast and left the house, the fire would become real again. He would have to go back and work all day with a constant reminder of what happened in California and the day of his life he regretted most.

When Pepper finished, he added his plate to the pile in the sink and met Olive outside of the shed where she was refilling spare gas and oil containers, illuminating her work with a headlamp. The eastern sky was just starting to lighten to a dark blue, distinguishing it from the deep black of the rest of the sky.

"You about ready?" Olive asked as Pepper walked up. Before he could answer Olive nodded to the backpack resting upright on the floor and said, "I packed some food and water. If you want to get that, I'll take the saw again."

Before he could think much about the implications of what needed to be accomplished in the day ahead, Pepper was plodding back up to the top of the ridge, closer to the fire, his fears, and the traumatic memories of California. The only sound he could hear was his and Olive's breath, heavy but never overwhelming, and their feet hitting the ground in regular time. The birds hadn't risen yet from their night's sleep and the air was silent.

When Olive and Pepper reached the ridge, it was still too dark to see the smoke so they didn't have a good idea of what the fire had done overnight, but there weren't any visible flames which was promising. They brought headlamps with them, so they didn't have to wait for the sun to start working.

Olive continued to fell trees and cut brush, and Pepper moved the vegetation away from the top of the ridge while keeping a close eye to the north, waiting for enough light to get a view of the smoke.

The sky lightened slowly, so at first Pepper wasn't sure if what he saw really was there, or if his mind was extrapolating patterns from randomness. Slowly as more light filled the sky, the smoke column's shape became clearer and more definite, and Pepper became confident what he saw was real.

As he expected, the smoke column was smaller than the day before. The night's humidity and lower temperatures had reduced the size of the fire. That was good news, but the small column didn't mean they were out of the woods yet. They just had a little more time before the fire blew up again later in the day when the temperature rose. Pepper noticed Olive take a second to assess the smoke before she continued cutting, and he knew they were on the same page.

The work reminded him of his time as a firefighter and of the day Blackwell and the family died in California. Thoughts of his selfish mistake haunted Pepper as he worked. He wanted to clear his mind of that day, but with the monotonous drone of the chainsaw and the mindlessness of carrying logs and brush, the thoughts kept creeping back. He hated himself for what he did, and as the day went on Pepper unsuccessfully fought to purge the thoughts by trying to turn his attention to the task at hand, which was inarguably more important than reliving old traumas.

The couple worked all morning without pausing more than a few minutes to refuel the chainsaw or take a few gulps of water. Olive cut for two gas tanks and Pepper gave her a break by taking over for the third. By noon, the couple had been working for seven hours already and both Olive and Pepper were getting tired.

A few minutes after noon, the saw stuttered again, announcing its thirst for more fuel. Olive put down the saw and slumped to the ground without even trying to find shade under a tree or rock to lean on.

"Let's eat something," Pepper said.

Exhausted, what he really wanted to do was find a nice grassy area under a tree to take a nap, but he worried if he lay down, he wouldn't be able to get back up. With the threat of the fire destroying their lives, a small break with some food was the biggest concession he was willing to make. Pepper found shade under a tree and urged Olive to join him.

Olive didn't move, so he tossed a peanut butter and jelly sandwich in her direction. It fell with a light thud at her feet, and Olive used the heel of her boot to scoot it close enough that her hand could reach. Pepper looked over his shoulder to the smoke – too tired to take the effort to turn his whole body – and assessed it from the corner of his eye.

"The column is growing," Pepper said, not sure if he was talking to Olive or himself, though it didn't matter since neither responded.

After a few bites of his sandwich, Pepper's own words nagged at him, hanging in the back of his mind, so he got up to take a closer look. Pepper found a thick tree stump to stand on and squinted to the north.

There was definitely more smoke than earlier that morning, and it was still blowing in the direction of Thirst Hollow. Pepper stood and watched the billowing smoke slowly move and morph into different shapes. The cerebral wrinkles joined one another then separated, moving up then out, slowly being guided to the south by the wind.

Pepper stood mesmerized, as if watching a lava lamp, until something on the ridge across the drainage caught his eye. At first, Pepper couldn't tell exactly what it was, or even if it truly was there. It blended, almost seamlessly, with the large smoke column behind it. But as it grew larger and more distinct, Pepper became confident it was in fact there, that it did exist. Fear ran down the length of his spine. He slid off the stump and walked to Olive, who lay with her head back and eyes closed.

"There's a spot fire across the drainage," Pepper said, trying to keep his voice steady.

"What?"

"The fire jumped the ridge. There's a small fire on our side now," Pepper repeated, unsure if she hadn't heard him through her sleepy daze, or if she was just confused. "It's only twelve-thirty right now. I think the main fire is going to make a strong push over the ridge once it warms up this afternoon."

Pepper's heart yelled at him to leave. To get Olive and the dogs in the truck and get to safety, fearing a similar outcome as what happened in California. But he had to stay. He knew that they had nowhere else to go, and that there was no other choice but to stay and protect their home.

Olive sat halfway up, still leaning back on her elbows. She squinted at Pepper, but didn't say anything.

"I think I'm going to keep cutting," Pepper continued, "but you should get some more rest. You've been running the saw twice as much as I have and you must be exhausted."

"Okay, just give me five minutes," Olive said as she let her elbows give way and her torso fell back to the ground.

Pepper started the saw and kept cutting. From his experience fighting fire, he knew their time was running out. The fire already jumped the ridge across the drainage, and now all it needed to do was go down, and back up the ridge they were on before reaching Thirst Hollow. Olive and Pepper wouldn't know if their firebreak was sufficient until the fire climbed that final ridge, and if the break didn't hold, they would have little time for contingencies.

If they didn't finish their firebreak and find a good natural feature to connect it to, the fire could simply flank their line and burn down into Thirst Hollow. To Pepper, nothing would be worse than not finishing the line, losing their home, and wondering if they hadn't worked hard enough.

Though his past urged him to run, Pepper couldn't leave anything on the table, or he might never be able to forgive himself.

So Pepper kept cutting, keeping a close watch on the main smoke column and on the growing spot fire. He cut for an entire gas tank before Olive joined him.

"Sorry, I think I fell asleep," Olive said as she walked up, blinking puffy eyes.

"It's okay, but did you see? There's a spot fire," Pepper said, pointing to the opposite ridge, unsure if she had processed the information earlier. "The fire's hopped the ridge."

Olive's sleepy eyes widened and became alert. She walked over to Pepper's side and peered across the drainage, watching the small line of smoke rise from the trees and merge with the larger column that slowly floated in their direction.

"Shit," Olive said. "That slope is pretty steep. Burning debris is going to start rolling downhill and the whole hillside is going to light up."

"Yeah," Pepper agreed, worried they were running out of time. "I'm going to scout ahead a little to see if there is something good to tie our line into." Pepper wanted to continue the firebreak past the far edge of the Burdettes' property and find a wide rocky drainage to connect it with – one the fire wouldn't be able to jump and flank around.

"Sounds good," Olive replied. "I'll start cutting while you go look."

Through a fine layer of dirt and sawdust Pepper gave Olive a kiss then started hiking the ridge, keeping one eye on the growing spot fire. A few hundred yards down, just past the far side of the Burdettes' property, Pepper came to a beautiful rock-filled, moss-covered drainage with a small trickle of cool, clear water tumbling over, under, and around the sandstone cobbles. The high-water mark on the banks was reminiscent of a time of greater rainfall just a few years ago.

Looking at the drainage, Pepper decided it was a perfect place to tie into their firebreak. It was wet and mostly free of vegetation to discourage the fire from jumping over it. Pepper kneeled down and took a few drinks of the cold water from his cupped hands before retracing his steps back to Olive.

The end was in sight, and he was eager to tie in with the drainage so he could spend that evening adding contingency measures around their house in case the fire made it down into Thirst Hollow. The noise from the chainsaw grew louder as Pepper approached Olive, and he had to stop to put in his ear protection. As Pepper squished an orange foam cylinder into his right ear canal, he noticed an inferno to his left.

The fire had summited the ridge and began backing down the slope, meeting and consuming the spot fire. Soon the fire would be at the bottom of the drainage where, hopefully the creek would slow the fire or even stop it. If the fire jumped the creek, it would race upslope with the assistance of the wind to meet Olive and Pepper's firebreak. But Pepper hoped it wouldn't come to that, and if it did, they would have the firebreak completed. Pepper forced the second foam earplug into his left ear and rushed to meet Olive.

As Olive came into view, she briefly looked up from a fallen tree and Pepper saw that her eyes were filled with fear. She must have seen the fire summit the ridge also. Olive gave Pepper a two-finger wave without releasing the chainsaw, then went back to cutting. Pepper smiled in an attempt to comfort her but Olive didn't see, so he passed in haste to clear the cut trees and brush behind.

Pepper's back was wet with sweat from the midday heat, and his muscles ached from rolling, pushing, and carrying large stumps, but he continued on, ignoring the screams from his body to stop. They were close, but so was the fire. Olive cut faster and faster, leaving Pepper with larger and heavier pieces. The fire had reached the bottom of the drainage, but was having trouble crossing the stream. Flames continued to fill in against the stream, one side of the drainage ablaze, while the other patiently awaited its fate.

The chainsaw stuttered off, thirsting for more gasoline, but the absence of its groaning didn't leave the couple with silence as it did before. The air was filled with the sound of hundreds of trees consumed in a single giant flame, roaring like a jet engine preparing for takeoff. Pepper finished dragging the last cut branches from the ridge before approaching Olive who was frantically adjusting the tension of the chain.

"The end is only about fifty yards away," Pepper said optimistically.

Olive's eyes looked up at him in panic as she refueled the saw.

"Why don't you let me finish the rest on the saw?" he asked, hoping to relieve some pressure.

"No, it's okay. I cut faster, and you're stronger carrying the big logs. The fire is stopped at the creek down there, but not for long. We need to get off this ridge as soon as we can. The fire is going to run up here fast."

Pepper knew Olive was right. They were in physical danger on top of the ridge and shouldn't stay any longer than necessary.

"Okay, that sounds good. And I'll keep an eye on the fire so if it starts making a run towards us, we'll get out of here," Pepper said to Olive.

Olive agreed then stood up, gave Pepper a weak smile, and drop-started the chainsaw. Her eyes weren't watering, but Pepper could see she was holding back tears. All his instincts told him to comfort her and make things better, but there wasn't time. They needed to keep going.

As Olive blazed forward, Pepper had trouble keeping up. In addition to clearing the debris, he also closely monitored the stream below, and the fire forcing its way against it. All it would take was one tree to fall, or a single windblown ember to bridge the creek, and Pepper's awareness of when and where that happened could save both their lives.

Within a half hour, as the sun was setting, Olive connected with the small drainage, and their fire line was close to complete. She began to work back towards Pepper, clearing brush and logs out of the corridor, away from the fire.

The couple reunited at a large oak laying where Olive brought it to the ground. It looked almost as it did when it stood, except half was flattened against the ground, and it all was cut into small segments. Piece by piece they hustled to move the century old oak tree twenty feet south, where hopefully its bonded carbon and hydrogen atoms would retain their stored chemical energy.

"We did it," Olive said, lacking excitement, though with a hint of accomplishment as together they rolled the thick base of the oak tree to the side of the ridge. "I'm going to get the saw, then let's get out of here."

"Okay," Pepper agreed.

He walked to the edge of the ridge and looked down on the fire. It was still pushing hard on the stream, and the burnt black and fiery red of one side contrasted heavily with the temperate rainforest green of the other. Pepper watched and listened with a furrowed brow until Olive returned, and stood next to him.

Without words they embraced each other. Holding Olive, Pepper could feel she was safe. Their surroundings continued to darken until the dusk revealed a circle of orange flickering in the twilight on their side of the drainage.

The fire finally crossed the creek, meaning soon, aided by topography and wind, it would race to the top of the ridge Olive and Pepper were standing on, then if their fire break didn't hold, down into Thirst Hollow.

"We should go," Pepper said and turned to Olive, trying to stay calm.

Too tired to talk, they turned together and started back down the ridge, through the fading light, and away from the fire. They walked slowly, their muscles aching from the two long days. The couple did what they set out to do, but not knowing if it was enough kept them from celebrating.

After leaving the saw on the floor in the middle of the shed, the couple went home to frantic dogs, then collapsed in their bed, hoping the cool night would slow the advance of the fire.

18

The Fight

Olive and Pepper were asleep as soon as their bodies hit the bed. Pepper briefly rose, succumbing to the dogs' whining pleas for their dinner, but slept hard through the rest of the night. Somehow Olive and Pepper managed to get under the covers, though surely not through conscious effort.

The next morning when Pepper woke, brightness had already broken through the thin linen curtains and illuminated the bedroom. The dogs waited patiently with restrained excitement watching Pepper's every movement under the blankets, hoping he would rise to feed them breakfast. Pepper sat up and looked across the bed to the clock on Olive's nightstand. It read nine-thirty.

Pepper slowly rotated and placed his socked feet on the floor. His mind was rested, but his body was tired. He wanted nothing more than to lie back down, but it was late, really late, and there was still work to do. He shuffled to the kitchen, and started boiling water for coffee, putting off checking on the fire every second more he could justify. He wanted to pretend, even if for just a moment, that their livelihoods weren't in an existential crisis.

The three dogs watched eagerly as Pepper continued neglecting the outside world and opened the pantry where the dogs' food was kept. He took a scoop and dropped it into one of their bowls, the sound of the kibble ringing against the metal excited them further. Pepper put a scoop of kibble in the remaining two bowls as the dogs waited for him to release them to eat, drool running continuously from their jowls in unbroken streams to growing puddles on the floor.

"Alright," Pepper said. This magic word set them free to eat their meager meal, which they downed as fast as they possibly could.

Without any more chores to procrastinate with, Pepper reluctantly accepted he should poke his head out for possible updates on the fire. He had stalled for long enough, and as much as he didn't want to deal with the fire, he knew he had no other choice, so Pepper slipped on sandals and walked outside.

The air smelled like a campfire as he walked down the porch steps, and smoke lingered in the valley, providing pressure down from above. Turning toward the ridge, Pepper could see thick white smoke billowing over the top, framed on its edges by a lighter translucent haze. No flames had breached the firebreak, but the location and intensity of the smoke told Pepper the fire had gained some ground overnight. He turned, took the porch steps two at a time, and went back in the house to update Olive.

Olive was still sleeping when Pepper entered the bedroom. Her breath was reminiscent of a snore, but lighter, softer, and sweeter. Pepper put his hand on her shoulder and gently rocked it back and forth until her eyes slowly opened, focusing on the warm light surrounding her. He hated to wake her, but addressing the fire held precedence.

"Hey," Pepper said once she was oriented.

"Hey," she smiled. "It's late. Did you check on the fire?" Even in her deep sleep, Olive never stopped worrying.

"Yeah," he said, staring with unfocused eyes at the geometric pattern of the quilt. "There's a lot of smoke. I think it's getting close to our firebreak."

"Dang," Olive said, becoming more awake by the second. "It'd better hold."

"Yeah," Pepper agreed. "If only some firefighters would show up, or if they sent a plane to drop retardant, or something. We could really use some help." Pepper paused. He wished there was someone out there thinking about them, ready to come save the day. But there wasn't. He knew no one was looking after him. No one would do anything, so he and Olive had to. "I was thinking I could get the Burdettes tractor and use the middle buster to scrape another fire line around our property. You know, in case the one on the ridge doesn't hold."

"Yeah. Couldn't hurt." Olive looked up from the quilt into Pepper's eyes and said with a small smile, "And it will be easier than the one on the ridge."

"I sure hope so," Pepper responded with a bigger smile. "I don't know if it's necessary, or if we have enough time, but maybe you can try to figure out how to use water from the pond to wet the property edge in case the fire gets down here."

"Sure, I'll see what I can do," nodded Olive.

"Sounds good. I'm going to get to it," Pepper said, then put on his boots and went outside.

The smoke was even thicker than before. The sky was a sickening yellow and the sun, rising over the ridge, beat through blood red. Pepper stepped back in the house.

"Olive?" he called.

"Yeah?"

"Maybe you should pack some clothes and valuables into the truck in case we need to leave."

"Is everything okay?" Olive asked, poking her head out from the bedroom.

"Yeah, it's just getting smokier. Maybe just get our important stuff, and clothes. And maybe some dog food."

"Okay, I'll do that now," Olive said, but instead of going, she lingered. "How are you doing?"

Pepper paused, not sure how to answer. He hadn't had time to think about himself in days.

"I'm okay. Stressed, for sure, but okay. I just want to make sure we do everything we can. If we don't, and the farm burns, I don't think I'll ever be able to forgive myself."

But Pepper didn't tell her that what he feared most was a replay of what happened in California. That he did an awful thing during the fire in California and now was his chance to learn from his mistakes, even if his actions couldn't change the past.

Pepper took a step back, antsy to get to work, but again stopped. "How about you?"

"I'm okay. Tired, but okay. I'll start packing then meet you outside."

"Okay, thanks Olive. Love you."

"Love you too," Olive said as she disappeared back into the bedroom. Olive was impressed with Pepper. She saw him doing his best to take care of their needs and felt a sense of comfort, even in spite of the stress the fire brought with it. Maybe the ordeal with Wes had changed Pepper. Maybe, she thought, he was done putting other needs before hers. That he was going to start taking care of her first and foremost.

But then Olive shook her head. She was jumping the gun. After all, no one else was in danger from the fire. Maybe if there were other people whose property and lives were at risk Pepper would be off helping them, not working so hard to protect her. Olive shook her head again, shaking off the thought, then opened the dresser drawer to start packing. The fire was getting close and she couldn't afford more distress by thinking in hypotheticals.

Pepper, solely focused on doing everything he could to combat the fire, strode out of the house and to the Burdettes' barn where the tractor lived, then attached the middle buster and drove to the far end of the Burdettes' property. Lowering the plow attachment to the ground, he began driving along the perimeter of the fields and the woods, creating a twelve-inch trench into mineral soil that would hopefully prevent any creeping grass fires from advancing.

Pepper drove slowly to protect the middle buster, and when the view permitted, watched the slope for spot fires. The fire could jump the ridge at any minute and wanted to be aware of when it did. Within forty-five minutes Pepper had circumnavigated the Burdettes' fields. He raised the middle buster, kicked the tractor into high gear, and drove down the Burdettes' long driveway onto the paved road, then up the gravel driveway leading back to his property.

When Pepper came in sight of the house, he saw Olive walking up to the spring fed pond. She finished packing the truck and was on her way to wet the perimeter of the fields. Pepper lowered the middle buster once again and traced the edges of the property with a shallow foot-wide trench. It was almost unbelievable the narrow band of dirt could offer any protection from a fire, but his experience fighting fires taught him that a firebreak, even a foot wide, could prevent ground fires from advancing.

Pepper traced the edge of the fields and soon the line was complete. He felt a little better to have a back up to the firebreak on the ridge. He optimistically told himself that even if the fire got onto their property, the house and fields were surrounded by grass which would burn fast and hot, but would die quickly from the lack of fuel. Pepper tried to convince himself the quick burst of fire probably wouldn't put off enough heat to ignite the house, but even in his most hopeful thinking he couldn't fool himself that the fire wouldn't destroy the vegetable fields and the orchard. Pepper decided to use the tractor to dig another line around the orchard and the house.

He climbed back onto the tractor, swung it around in a wide U-turn, and steered back along the contours of the ridge's slope towards the orchard. As he was driving, Pepper noticed a concentrated column of smoke rising from their side of the ridge. The fire had penetrated Thirst Hollow.

"Shit," Pepper said under his breath.

Pepper knew the fire was coming. It was close enough to the top of the ridge that aeolian embers drifted into Thirst Hollow, one of which landed in a spot with some nice dry tinder, starting a spot fire.

Pepper changed the course of the tractor from the orchard to the driveway. He parked it in the middle of the gravel, away from anything that could burn and cause it damage, then walked with long deliberate strides to Olive, who was still laying irrigation tubing.

"You all done?" she asked optimistically as Pepper approached.

"I guess. I think there's a spot fire," Pepper said, pointing in the direction he had seen it.

They both looked, but couldn't find it. The trees were too close, and the spot fire's smoke blended with the smoke from the main fire.

"Well, if we can't see it, hopefully it's not too big yet," Olive said. "Let's grab some tools, and get up there."

"Okay," Pepper agreed, but thinking of being so close to the fire sent anxiety running down his back. Reminded of Blackwell and the family in California, Pepper hated the thought of putting Olive in a similar situation. But if going meant possibly saving their home, he had to.

Olive laid down the irrigation tubing and the couple hurried to get tools. Time was everything. Catching this spot fire soon could mean the difference between the whole ridge catching or it stopping at the firebreak.

From the shed, Olive and Pepper located the faint line of smoke rising from the forested slope. After making a mental note of where the smoke was, Pepper grabbed a hoe and Olive grabbed a shovel, and they rushed to the ridge.

The couple hustled up the path, and once they thought they were at the same elevation as the smoke, they left the trail to their right. Olive and Pepper's progress slowed as they looked for the spot fire, but only found uneven ground, downed trees, and thick undergrowth. After trudging along for a few minutes, Pepper stopped.

"I feel like we've gone too far," Pepper said to Olive as she walked parallel to him, about fifteen feet down slope.

"You think so?" Olive shouted up to him. "I thought it might be a little farther, or maybe a little uphill."

"Yeah, maybe. Let's keep going a little bit, then circle back uphill."

"Okay," Olive agreed, and resumed fighting her way through the underbrush along the steep slope.

The thick forest made the going slow and navigation difficult, disorienting the couple as downed trees and thick brush forced them one way then the other. As the couple doubled back, Pepper wasn't certain how far away they were from their original path, or whether they had already passed the spot fire. The smoke from the main fire was dense, and became denser the farther the couple went uphill. They kept a constant eye to make sure the fire wasn't advancing onto them. Olive and Pepper searched back and forth, unsure if they had walked too far or not far enough. Eventually, they ended up back at the trail.

"There it is!" Olive shouted.

On the other side of the trail, a small curling stream of smoke rose from a pile of dried leaves at the base of a maple tree. The couple rushed over to the smoke and began using their tools to move dried leaves away from the ember burning deep inside the pile. Once the part that was smoking was isolated, they began mixing the leaves with underlying soil. They mixed and mixed until there was no more smoke, and the mixture was cool enough to touch.

"I think we got it!" Olive said, using her shovel to lean on. Her face was red, sweaty and full of triumph.

Pepper smiled at her, but didn't feel the same sense of accomplishment Olive exuded. One spot fire could mean there were more. The smoke was thickening and Pepper was nervous the fire was getting stronger and bearing down on Thirst Hollow.

"It's weird though," Pepper said, "from down in the fields, I was pretty sure the spot fire was on the other side of the path."

That moment, a mountain laurel bush erupted in flames thirty yards on the opposite side of the path.

Both Pepper and Olive immediately ran to the bush and began pulling fuel away from it. They broke branches of surrounding mountain laurel, and pulled away dried leaves on the ground, but their efforts were futile. The fire raged as it consumed the bush. The couple continued working, shielding their faces from the heat, but the flames spread to a nearby white pine.

The long needles curled and blackened from the flames licking at them, then as they heated enough turned to the color of molten iron and sprouted flames. The flames spread to more needles and in an instant fire engulfed the whole tree, sending flames soaring ten feet into the air. Olive began to pull branches away from the pine but Pepper grabbed her bicep. The flames reminded him too strongly of California. He had to get Olive out of there.

"We have to go," Pepper shouted over the increasing volume of the fire. "If we stay, we're just going to get hurt."

Olive nodded with defeat in her eyes.

The couple turned and ran back to the trail, down to the fields, away from the flames, and into relative safety. The couple looked back up at the slope and saw the flames from many small fires spread out over the entire hill. Burning logs rolled down, expediting the spread of the fire. Pepper looked at Olive, and she looked back in terror.

"What should we do?" Olive asked.

"Let's get the dogs in the truck, ready to go, then I'm going to use the irrigation water to wet the edge of the woods. You should wait in the truck."

"I'm not waiting in the truck," Olive said.

Pepper looked into her eyes and paused. He wanted to protect her. If something happened to her, he could never forgive himself. She was all he really had, and he didn't know what he would do if he lost her.

But he couldn't leave the farm either. It was their home and their livelihood. If he left and the farm burned knowing he could have done more, that guilt would also haunt him.

Seeing the determination and stubbornness in Pepper's eyes, Olive said, "Okay, I'll go load the truck and get the dogs, but after that I'm going to come help you." She wasn't going to let Pepper fight the fire by himself. She didn't need him to protect her. If he was going to be in danger, so was she.

"Are you sure you don't want to wait in the truck?" Pepper pleaded.

"I'm not going to leave you here," Olive said, looking hard into his eyes.

"Okay." Pepper knew he couldn't make her do anything, but wished he could, just so that he could keep her safe.

As Olive walked off Pepper looked back at the slope. He couldn't tell if the spot fires were connecting with each other or just growing in size. Either way, the situation was not getting better. Pepper rushed over to the spring fed pond and looked at the irrigation tubing and pump Olive left earlier.

Pepper connected one end of the tubing to the water pump, placed the intake into the pond, and started it. The motor came to life, adding another noise to the chaotic atmosphere. Pepper walked quickly to the other end of the irrigation tubing where water poured out less urgently than the situation called for.

He picked the tube up and used it to wet a ten-foot swath of grass adjacent to the trench he dug with the tractor. Pepper slowly walked back towards the pond, wetting the grass deeply as the water fell heavily to the ground. The noise from the pump's motor crescendoed as he neared, then gradually softened as he passed.

Pulling the tubing made his tired muscles ache, and his throat and lungs burned from hot smoke pouring down the ridge. Pepper looked up and saw the whole top of the ridge on fire. The firebreak they had worked so hard on for days was nothing more than a minor speed bump for the advancing inferno. Pepper continued wetting the grass until he reached the end of the irrigation tubing. Feeling pressure to get as much done as possible, Pepper walked to the orchard and started spraying down the apple trees and the ground beneath.

As he finished wetting the orchard, Olive walked up from the house.

"Fuck Pepper, did you see the ridge? The whole thing is on fire. We need to leave," she urged.

Pepper looked back and saw the fire raging above. Weakened trees fell, burning debris crashed down the slope, and the roar of the fire pervaded the entirety of Thirst Hollow. Pepper looked down and saw himself standing, holding a measly black tube in his hand with a small stream of water trickling out. He was outmatched. He was defeated. Olive was right, it was time to leave.

"Okay, let's go."

Pepper dropped the irrigation tube and walked to the pond. He shut off the pump and carried it to the middle of the driveway where it was safer. The dogs were tied up in the bed of the truck and Olive pulled herself into the passenger seat. Pepper took one more look around the property.

There was so much more he wished he could have done, so many things he could have put in a safer place, but it was too late. The smoke was thick and screened much of the ridge from view, but the raging fire was clearly visible. It rushed clear up to the edge of the woods, pressing against the small foot wide firebreak.

The fire had wrapped around their property and flames surrounded them. Pepper feared their escape down the road and out of the valley could become impassable by a fallen tree. He wanted to stay but knew he had to go, at the very least to get Olive and the dogs to safety.

Pepper turned his back on the house, the fields, the crops, and walked to the truck. He could feel all their hard work, and their beautiful property begging him for protection, for him to turn and fight, but Pepper knew his life and Olive's were worth more.

He had no choice. Pepper got in the truck, started it and drove down the gravel driveway. He kept his eyes ahead. Pepper couldn't and wouldn't look back in the rear-view mirror, but in his periphery, he could see the orange light of the fire burning. Pepper took a left on the paved road and accelerated down and away from Thirst Hollow.

19

The Return

Olive and Pepper spent the night camped outside of Plomari. Nervous from horror stories of violence heard on the radio, they found a secluded area on Forest Service land where they hoped no desperate people would find them. They slept in the bed of the truck, keeping warm by bundling up in the clothes Olive packed and snuggling with the dogs. For dinner they ate a bag of pretzels scavenged from the near-empty shelves of the gas station.

Plomari was also smoky. The cashier at the gas station said there were two other fires burning in the area, and she didn't think either of them had firefighters dispatched. She apologized for the empty shelves sensing Pepper and Olive were in trouble.

From the bed of the truck, Pepper and Olive could see the smoke above Thirst Hollow illuminated an ominous orange as the fire raged below. They could only imagine what was happening to create such a sight.

At their camp, the night was cold, the truck bed was hard, and Pepper's anxiety was high. He constantly checked his watch, waiting for the sun to rise so they could get up and figure out their next move. Olive stirred through the night, but Pepper could hear her breathing heavily and knew she was getting some sleep. Pepper was grateful at least one of them was resting. He rolled over so his body was against hers, to keep her warm, and to get some comfort through touch.

After an eternity, the sun rose red through the choking smoke and started to warm the air. Pepper got up from the truck bed and went for a walk down the dirt road, leaving Olive and the dogs behind.

Pepper walked to try to clear his head, as if the entire night awake wasn't enough time to sort through his thoughts. Pepper thought about how he wanted to go check on the house and see how it fared. He thought about how it might not be safe or how the road could be blocked with downed trees. He thought about what they would do if their property was ruined. He thought about calling the Burdettes and adding even more problems to their plate. He thought those thoughts and others he had been thinking all night. Eventually, without any conclusion, Pepper's thoughts, and feet, led him back to where Olive and the dogs were rising from the bed of the truck.

"Hey," Pepper said once he was close enough to get her attention.

"Hey," she said with a smile, but dark circles under her eyes from a long night exposed any attempt to create a mask of happiness.

"How are you doing?" Pepper asked, a stupid question but he didn't know what else to say.

"I'm okay," Olive lied. "How about you?"

"I'm okay," he lied back. "Do you want to try to get some breakfast?"

"Sure," Olive nodded.

The couple loaded up and Olive drove down the dirt road back to Plomari and the gas station. The road dipped down into a drainage before circling around a high point with the hillside dropping off to the right. Pepper looked out over the trees below him. Where normally there would be a view of green Shenandoah Valley fields gradually rolling to the faint Blue Ridge Mountains, there was only a yellowish-gray screen of smoke.

Pepper stared out the window and longed for the smoke to be gone, not just because that would mean that fires were quenched, but also so he could see the world. He was stuck in a timeless ether of smoke that he was powerless to escape. He couldn't see anything in the distance and was trapped in his immediate surroundings that shrunk by the minute, smaller and smaller, until Pepper was ultimately trapped inside his own head.

Pepper looked down at the cracked gray vinyl of the glove box and let his head bob back and forth as the truck bounced down the uneven dirt road, trying to exist only in the moment, letting his thoughts go. The movement was mesmerizing and Pepper's eyes relaxed out of focus.

For a moment, he wasn't thinking of anything. His blank mind and the rest of his body had become an extension of the pickup truck, no different than a strut or an axle. He continued along, moving as the truck did, not thinking, only existing as the physical piece of matter he was. The truck rolled onto a smooth paved road and Pepper snapped back into his body and into reality.

Life reentered Pepper, and he was conscious and aware. He looked out the windshield and saw a green tunnel of trees looming from all sides. The road was fairly straight, but turned and rolled enough to prevent a long, unimpeded view. He followed the road with befogged eyes until Olive slowed the truck into the gas station in Plomari.

She killed the engine and asked with forced cheer, "Do you want to go in and see what you can rustle up for breakfast?"

"Sure," Pepper stretched his face muscles into a smile.

Though he was tired, Olive was too. He appreciated her driving, and now it was his turn to be productive. While driving and shopping were normally effortless tasks, that morning the couple was at the threshold of their capabilities. They had to lean on each other to complete the simple tasks, or else they both would crumble.

Pepper's body oozed out of the truck, reentered the gas station, and looked at the same bare shelves and picked over inventory as the night before, and not surprisingly, nothing was any more appealing the second time around. Pepper picked out a can of peaches and a package of strawberry wafers, paid, and went back to eat in the truck's cab with Olive.

Olive inspected the haul and pointed out they didn't have a can opener or spoon to access or eat the peaches with, so Pepper dragged his body back into the gas station, got two plastic spoons, and asked the cashier for help opening the can. After struggling with a multitool can opener, another monumental task in itself, Pepper returned to the truck with the spoons and a can with a ragged opening in the top that only posed a minor lacerative risk.

"Okay, now breakfast is ready," Pepper said, climbing back into the truck. He handed her a spoon, and together they ate directly out of the can. "These peaches really pair well with the strawberry wafers," Pepper joked as he washed off the powdery coating left in his throat by the wafer with a syrupy peach.

Olive smiled but didn't respond. The couple finished eating before Olive spoke again.

"So what do you think we should do?" Olive asked, placing the empty can of peaches on the dashboard. She didn't give Pepper a chance to answer before continuing, "I mean, I guess our options are to try to go back to the house, or wait it out until we think it's safer."

"I don't know, what do you think?" Pepper asked noncommittally. He wanted to go back, to see what had transpired over night, but didn't want to put Olive in unnecessary danger.

"Well, I obviously want to see what happened," Olive said to Pepper's relief. "Do you think it's safe though?"

"I'm not sure, but we can go up there to see how things look and come back if we think it's too dangerous."

"Okay," Olive nodded, and started the truck, wasting no time.

"Do you want me to drive?" Pepper asked.

"No, I'm okay," Olive said, turning her head to look behind her as she backed up.

Olive hurled the truck down the windy roads, plunging into thicker and thicker smoke. As they turned into Thirst Hollow, black remnants of trees stood on the right side of the road. All that remained from the thick woods was a graveyard of ten-foot charred stumps, and maybe a branch or two stubbed outward. A few small fires still smoldered at their bases, consuming fuel remaining from the initial pulse of the fire.

Across Thirst Run, the trees were still green and happy, swaying in the slight breeze. The smoke even seemed less dense under their leaves. The break created by the road and Thirst Run was large enough to stop the fire, at least from what they could see.

Olive slowly rolled the truck forward, making slow, careful progress up the smoky valley. Soon they passed the vacant old stone house on the neighboring property. Before the fire, the house was long neglected, and nature had reclaimed the once manicured lawn. The house had been hard to see through a screen of invading undergrowth, but the fire reduced the lawn into a black plane, and the house was in clear view as the couple drove by, at least what remained of it. The roof was burnt and mostly collapsed, but the singed stone walls still stood upright. Pepper stared at the scorched house and wished Olive would drive faster so he wouldn't have to look any longer.

The glade of trees that separated the couple's house from the road came into view as the truck crested a small incline. The trees were blackened and reduced down to stubs, like those on the neighboring property. Pepper could feel his heart drop to the bottom of his stomach, and looking at Olive, he knew hers did the same.

The truck continued past the burnt glade of trees, and Olive and Pepper squinted into the black mess, trying to get a glimpse of the house that lay beyond, but standing dead trees and lingering smoke prevented Pepper seeing anything.

The truck rolled on toward the driveway entrance. Olive pulled the glossy gray plastic steering wheel to the right and guided the truck off the pavement and onto the gray crushed limestone of their driveway. Olive proceeded slowly and carefully. Pepper could feel the pebbles crunching and shifting beneath the deep tread of the truck's tires.

The driveway curved to the right, and soon they would have a view of their house and fields. Olive sighed and her face was close to tears. Being on the left, she was able to see the house half a second before Pepper. Pepper glanced at her, but quickly returned his eyes forward, knowing the moment of truth had come.

The last tree slid out of the way, and there was their house, standing unburnt, surrounded by green fields of grass and vegetables, swaying branches of apple trees, and a backdrop of black skeletal trees and charcoal soil rising to the smoky horizon.

"It looks okay!" Pepper cried.

He looked over at Olive. Tears streamed down her face as she kept the truck rolling onward. Pepper leaned across the bench seat and took her into his arms. The truck stopped abruptly and they leaned forward, then back together.

"It's okay," Pepper said again, this time softer and into Olive's ear.

She was shaking, crying silently. Pepper held her tighter and they sat in the idling truck until they both calmed down. Olive breathed in hard through her nose to keep it from running more.

"It's okay," she repeated as she started to cry again.

"Yeah, we're going to be okay," Pepper reassured her. "Should we go check it out?"

"Okay," she said, though her voice wasn't working right, and barely a sound came out. She let her foot off the brake, put the shifter into gear, and rolled on slowly to the front of the house. Once stopped, Pepper let the dogs out of the back. Box and Turtle ran to check on the sheep and goats. They probably had been thinking about them since they were forced to leave the day before.

The couple slowly walked around the house checking for any damage. The grass was green, the fields were safe, and if only focused on their property, it was impossible to tell there had been a fire. However, looking past the fireline, it would be hard to imagine anything could have survived. Nothing remained outside. Even the rocks were burnt black.

"We live on an island now," Olive said.

"Yeah, I can't believe it," Pepper agreed. He let it all sink in for another second before remembering the Burdettes' house. "Maybe we should walk over to the Burdettes' to make sure everything is okay over there."

Olive nodded and said, "Let's drive though. In case we have to leave again."

Olive loaded Mango into the back of the truck, and proceeded to their neighbors' property. The scene at the Burdettes' was familiar. Ominous burnt trees surrounded them on all sides and overhead, but once they passed the trench Pepper dug, the grass was green, the plants were alive, and the sheep and goats were happy, herded into a tight group by the two border collies reasserting their dominance.

"Geez, I can't believe that stupid trench saved us," Pepper said. Everything was fine. They didn't lose anything except some firewood not yet collected.

"I know, I can't believe it."

"I guess there is still some fire around though. There's a chance the fire could surge again. All it would take is one ember on a patch of dry grass."

"I guess," Olive said. "It's pretty hard black around us though, not much left to burn."

She was right, but Pepper was still a little worried. "What do you want to do?" he asked.

"Go sleep in our bed." she answered definitively.

She put the idling truck into gear and drove back to the house. They climbed out of the truck and into the front door. The house looked different, like someone had drawn a picture of their living room and kitchen, but missed some details. The same way a house feels strange after coming back from a long vacation, except Olive and Pepper had only been gone for a day, albeit a long one. They pushed past the living room and into the bedroom. Olive collapsed face down on top of the quilt.

"I'm going to stay up, and make sure nothing catches fire, and if it does, I'll be ready to put it out," Pepper said, sitting with his back against the headboard.

"Okay," Olive mumbled, already half asleep.

Pepper watched Olive's breathing slow and deepen as she fell asleep. He leaned back against the headboard and thought of going out to check on the farm. As he sat, his eyes grew dry and heavy. They closed on their own for a few seconds, before Pepper forced them wide open. Despite his best efforts, they slowly closed again, and he was fast asleep. Neither Pepper nor Olive woke until the next morning.

20

The Rain

After the fire, Pepper was surprised at the speed life went back to normal. But there was no other choice, it had to. Pepper and Olive had a lot of work to do and had lost three days of work to the fire. Harvest season was approaching, and they needed to do everything they could to make sure it was successful enough to get them through the winter. So the day following their return, they were out weeding the neglected fields.

As those first few days passed more and more smoke cleared from the valley, and Olive and Pepper were so busy picking and weeding, and irrigating the fields, they started to forget the trauma of the fire.

But when they lifted their heads, the images of burnt trees all around them would bring reality rushing back. The sight of their charred surroundings brought back memories of fighting for their lives, and their close call with destruction, but soon the couple grew accustomed to the new view. They were proving how adaptable humans can be. Though one thing Pepper and Olive weren't acclimating to, and the crops had an even more difficult time, was the lack of rain.

The same drought that dried the forest and allowed it to ignite, continued well into July. The couple irrigated with meager rations from the well and the spring fed pond, and Pepper used the tractor to dig an irrigation ditch from the Burdettes' small stream to divert water to the fields on the Burdettes' property. The supplementation provided enough water to keep the crops alive, but they drooped heavily in the midday heat, and the grass surrounding the fields turned a crispy brown.

Though the plants were holding on, the stress from the lack of water dramatically decreased their yields. The lower productivity created anxiety for the upcoming winter. With the grocery store's shelves completely empty most of the time, Pepper knew if they ran out of food over the winter, buying more would be difficult to impossible. And Olive and Pepper weren't the only ones in the country worrying about food.

The radio told horrible stories of food shortages caused by heat waves and droughts across the world. The protests across the country were no more, but had transformed into violent occupations. People too hungry to be forced into submission drove the National Guard and the police out of city after city across the country. Annexed neighborhoods were run by either Net Zero or We the People gangs, putting themselves in positions of power by hoarding food and resources.

People were hungry and the government was losing control. Pepper and Olive worried, not only about themselves, but also about the Burdettes who lived in one of the cities affected by the conflict. The couple tried their best to keep in touch with the Burdettes, but it was difficult. Olive and Pepper were busy, and hiking to the ridge was often more effort than they had energy for, especially when there was only a small chance to get a hold of the Burdettes.

Then one day, a voice on the other end of the phone said the Burdettes phone had been disconnected. Olive and Pepper knew that could mean a hundred different things, but they chose to tell themselves the cell phone towers in Richmond had been destroyed. They preferred that explanation over the other more grim scenarios crossing their minds, but never their tongues, fearing that once they were spoken, they would be proven true.

Luckily, the violence was just a story on the news for Olive and Pepper. People in Plomari, while very suspicious of any stranger passing through, didn't turn on each other. Their lives more or less went on without problem besides the lack of resources coming into the town. It was a rural community set up well for taking care of itself.

The couple was welcomed in town, but still avoided going at all costs. Plomari was isolated, but Thirst Hollow was remote, providing an extra layer of protection from the outside world. Olive and Pepper enjoyed the comfort of their own little farm, in their own little valley, and preferred not having to see or think about anything else.

Life was serene and beautiful in Thirst Hollow. Going into town reminded them of the troubles happening elsewhere, which frightened Olive and Pepper. Since they rarely went into town, tending the fields and hoping for rain consumed the couple's lives. One day in late July, their hope for rain was finally granted.

Olive and Pepper were picking tomatoes, chatting and laughing. Mango laid in the thin, constantly shifting line of shade cast by a burnt trunk of a once mighty oak. She watched the couple work with drooping eyes when a long, deep wave of thunder rolled in from the distance.

Pepper immediately stopped moving, cherry tomato in hand, and looked over at Olive who was also frozen. Both of them stood crouched in silence, waiting to hear the sound again, filled with a mixture of fear and hope.

Fear caused by the memories of the last thunder they heard; the dry lightning storm which kick-started a multiple day struggle to save the land they loved and relied upon. Hope of a wetting rain to quench the thirst of their poor plants and saturate the soil for days or even weeks to come. So the couple silently stood conflicted, not knowing how to feel, afraid if they acknowledged the thunder, it would disappear.

Another wave of thunder pulsed through Thirst Hollow and they knew the sound was real.

Olive and Pepper continued picking tomatoes and dropping them lightly into five-gallon buckets. Each time thunder sounded it was followed by electric quiet. The longer the silence lasted, the more doubt grew in Olive and Pepper's hearts. But every few minutes a new wave of thunder rolled across the valley, restoring their hope.

Clouds crowded overhead, turning the sky a miserable gray. The couple continued working in silent optimism, until Pepper finally heard a few raindrops hitting the ridge behind. He looked up at Olive and smiled. The rain picked up and soon their shirts were plastered to their backs with the cool summer rain.

"Do you want to go inside?" Pepper shouted, only then realizing the enormous noise of the rain falling around him.

Together the couple ran to the safety and shelter of their front porch, Mango beating them to it. Under the porch their clothes dripped water into small puddles underneath them, and the rain clanged onto the tin roof above.

"It's beautiful," Olive shouted over the rain, leaning forward on the railing to be a little closer to the miraculous water.

They stood and watched the raindrops streak across the gray backdrop until they began to shiver in their wet clothes.

"I'm going to go change," Olive said, turning to Pepper.

"Okay, me too."

They peeled their wet clothes off on the porch and scampered to the bathroom to dry off. Through a storm of giggles, the couple put on warm pajamas even though it was the middle of the afternoon. A new wave of thicker rain collided with the metal roof, letting them know what they were missing by going inside, and the couple ran back to the front door to provide witness to the revitalizing precipitation.

On her way, Olive snatched the radio off of the kitchen counter and met Pepper on the porch, gently slipping her hand into his as he looked over the railing into the rain. Pepper smiled at her as she clicked on the radio and scrolled through staticky stations until Louis Armstrong's La Vie En Rose rang sweet and clear through the small speaker.

She put the radio down on the railing, then pulled Pepper's hand and brought him close to her body. Pepper wrapped his arms around the small of her back, feeling her damp hair on his cheek. Almost unconsciously, as if the music guided them, the couple swayed back and forth, feeling the warmth of each other's bodies as the deluge of rain persisted all around them. Sheltered in safety from the cold and wet, they easily mistook each other's body heat for a feeling of safety.

They held their intimate embrace for a few songs before the radio went to commercial and the couple relaxed into the wooden Adirondack chairs, still connected by interlocking fingers spanning the gap between the arms of the chairs. They looked out across Thirst Hollow. The opposite ridge was green and lush, untouched by the fire, but Olive and Pepper could barely see it through the millions and millions of raindrops. Each only blocking an insignificant portion of the ridge, but all together, obscuring the ridge until it was fuzzy and distant. Pepper turned off the radio so they could listen to the music made by the rain.

The couple sat for a while longer, watching the storm slowly grow more intense. The humidity was high and the temperature was dropping.

"It's getting cold," Olive said. "I think I'm going to go in."

"Okay, I think I'm going to stay out for a bit."

Olive squeezed his hand, released it, and walked inside. Mango, Box, and Turtle followed, hoping to beg their way to an early dinner. Pepper shifted forward in his chair, sitting on the tilted edge, and leaned his elbows on his knees. Looking to his left, Pepper noticed a little stream of water forming a small channel on the side of the driveway.

He went back out into the rain to take a closer look, letting the rain fall onto his warm, dry pajamas. The water was opaquely black, choked with ash and soot, and carried small pieces of charred wood on its surface. A tiny river had formed, rushing down its self-created sinuous channel, crashing into and around the larger pieces of limestone gravel too large to be swept away.

An imitation of a grand river Pepper hadn't had the opportunity to lay eyes on, it had everything a large river did – rapids, calms, ripples, banks – only scaled down a thousand times. Someone could take a picture and claim it was an aerial picture of the Colorado, or some other ferocious river, and no one would know the difference. Without context it looked like a river roaring towards the ocean, and the more Pepper thought about it the more he realized that's exactly what it was.

That mini river was roaring down to Thirst Run, which would in time flow all the way to the ocean. Though the little river had less water, and moved less sediment than the Shenandoah or the Potomac, it was in many ways their equal. Once the tiny river at Pepper's feet reached Thirst Run, it would be connected uninterrupted all the way to the ocean. Pepper had thought the little river as separate from Thirst Run or the Shenandoah River, but where was the boundary? How could he say they were separate, when they were one in the same?

Pepper looked up to the ridge, the catchment basin and headwaters of the newly formed river. Thick black water rilled into the steep slope, cutting through the dark layer of ash and charcoal into the lighter underlying rocky soil. The fire had burnt the vegetation that held the ridge's rocks and soil in place, so the deluge of rain washed the unrestrained sediment down with it. The water rushed off the slope to more level ground, where it slowed, spread out, and dropped its load of rocks and burnt wood.

The whole system was dynamic – fighting to find a new equilibrium without regard for what Pepper considered permanent. Pepper always felt the ridge was stable. It was an unmoving landmark. But one fire and one thunderstorm were enough to destabilize it. Pepper saw the impermanence of the world, how one event could have rippling, unexpected consequences.

He watched until he was soaked once again, amazed, but also a little frightened by what was happening before his eyes.

He knew the changing baseline probably wasn't a good thing, but he was powerless to the incredible forces of nature. How could he stop the rain or the erosion? He couldn't. Nature was going to do what it would do. He was powerless, and there was no point in trying to go up against something he couldn't change.

So Pepper looked away from the ridge, and walked back to the house where he took off his soaked pajamas, and piled them next to his other wet clothes.

When Pepper reentered the house, Olive had started cooking dinner, and the smell of sautéed onions and garlic filled the house. Pepper put on a cheery face. He couldn't do anything about the erosion, so he didn't want it to bring him down. He wanted to act like everything was normal, and inside the house, it was.

"Mmm, smells good!" Pepper said enthusiastically.

Olive turned from her preparations and smiled at him.

"You say that every time I fry onions and garlic. One day I'm going to serve you a plate of just onions and garlic and I think you would be happy," Olive joked.

"Well, maybe you should," Pepper teased. "I'm going to change, then I'll help cook."

Pepper went into the bedroom to change into some soft sweatpants and a sweatshirt, comfy clothes, not expecting to go in the rain again. Pepper went back into the kitchen and helped Olive make a simple, but delicious meal of beans, rice and vegetables. They finished eating much earlier than usual since they normally worked until sunset, so they put some music on the radio, pulled out a deck of cards, and played until it was time for bed. Pepper enjoyed the time with Olive.

Pepper and Olive were always together, but rarely had time to simply enjoy each other's company. Spending intentional time with Olive was one thing Pepper missed most about Utah. There, days were freer and less stressful. The weight of surviving wasn't hanging over their heads. Pepper was nostalgic for their lives in Utah, but knew even if they never left things wouldn't be any better. They would probably be worse.

Aridification of the west continued. People were hungry, thirsty, and desperate. Riots plagued the streets, and people looted the few remaining resources. People couldn't stay there, but many had no other place to go. So Pepper was happy to be in Virginia, even if he was usually too busy to spend much time with Olive. And he was especially grateful to have the rare, rainy evening with Olive.

The storm persisted in pounding on their metal roof. After their last game of cards, Olive put them back in their tattered cardboard sleeve and said, "I can't believe it's still raining. Should be good for the crops."

"Yeah, I hope so," Pepper responded as he turned off the radio. "Oh, I forgot to tell you, the rain was eroding quite a bit of material off the ridge. It was bringing dirt and debris down toward the valley."

"Really?" Olive asked. "Should we go check on it?"

"If you want to. I don't think it was really a problem, and if it is, I don't think there's anything we can do to stop it."

"Okay, let's just check in the morning then."

Olive and Pepper finished cleaning up, brushed their teeth, and went to bed. The pattering on the tin roof put Pepper to sleep almost instantly and he slept hard until three in the morning when both he and Olive were jarred awake by a huge crash of thunder.

Half asleep, Pepper rolled over and through his eyelids saw what seemed to be daylight enter the room. The light disappeared as quickly as it came, and was immediately followed by a crash of thunder, this one not only heard, but also felt by vibrations running through the foundation of the house, through the floor, into the bed, and rattling bones deep in their bodies.

Pepper rolled over and put his arms around Olive. As soon as he closed his eyes, the pattering of raindrops on the roof intensified to a roar, as if someone diverted Thirst Run to flow onto the roof of their house.

Pepper lay awake, and rain crashed down until five in the morning. Pepper only gave up on trying to sleep once the noise of the rain subsided. Frustrated by his pluvial insomnia, Pepper quietly slipped out from under the quilt in an effort to not wake Olive. Pepper wasn't sure if she was sleeping or just lying in a delusional state as he had been. He walked to the kitchen, rubbing his head, and began to make coffee, then eventually breakfast as he waited for either Olive or the sun to rise.

The sun rose first, so Pepper put on his raincoat and muck boots to go outside for a walk, and maybe get a few chores done. The dogs sprung up and bolted out as Pepper held the door, and followed after the last one scampered away. The rain had slowed to a mist and the dawn barely snuck a faint glow through the thick cover of clouds above. A soft, dull light flooded every nook of the valley and somehow did not create any shadows.

Pepper stood on the porch and watched the dogs sniff the ground, investigating the night's events they missed, a sacrifice they were willing to make for a night of dry comfort. The dogs' noses led them to the back of the house, so Pepper walked down the porch steps and followed them. As he rounded the house, Pepper was shocked as he was met with an entirely new landscape.

Three large gullies slashed the ridge above, each scouring more than five feet into the earth. The walls of the gullies expose large cobbles of white sandstone lodged in a soil matrix, and horizontal fins of sandstone bedrock on the bottom. An arterial network of small canals joined larger ones, eventually accumulating into the main gullies.

At the base of the slope, where the steep ridge met more level terrain, fans of dirt, pebbles, cobbles, and burnt woody debris radiated from the gullies. The sediment fans were thick against the ridge, and thinned as they spread out. Their surfaces were near horizontal flat planes sloping towards the house, marred with interruptions of cobbles and burnt logs rising above their surroundings. The fans flowed up to and bulged against the outbuildings.

Pepper walked over to the chickens. Fortunately, the coop was built on stilts and had enough room below to accommodate the sediment fan, because if built flush to the ground, the flock wouldn't have survived the storm. Pepper watched the chickens inspect their new landscape, elevated a foot and a half higher than they stood the day before.

Relieved the chickens were alive, Pepper walked across the new barren moonscape towards the Burdette's house to check on the status of the sheep, goats, and the vegetable fields tilled and planted earlier that year.

Pepper left deep footprints in the soft, wet sediment as he walked, and once close to the property line, Box and Turtle came to greet him. They had beaten him to check on the herd. Pepper hopped the fence and saw the sheep and goats huddled together in a small corner of grass on the south side of the field – the only bit not covered by the invasive sediment fans.

The downpour had also incised the ridge above the Burdettes' property. Like on Pepper's land, deep gullies fed sediment fans covering much of the landscape, though since the fields Pepper and Olive tilled on the Burdettes' property were close to the slope, Pepper sensed destruction. After making sure the herd was okay, he hurried over to the fields behind the Burdettes' house to see how they fared.

As Pepper rounded the house, he confirmed his suspicions were correct. The deer fence surrounding the fields were choked with woody debris and large rocks, straining the metal mesh inward between the fence posts. Inside, dirt, ash, and small rocks passed through unimpeded, covering the fields, filling the trenches between the rows, and smothering the plants. In the southern part of the fields, some potato plants had a few leaves periscoping above the new ground level, but the closer the crops were to the ridge, the more they were buried. All of the plants were at least partly covered by sediment.

Pepper stood and looked at the destruction. So much work, time, and sweat, destroyed in a single night. The food they were counting on to get them through the winter, gone. Pepper felt a croquet ball weighing down his stomach with the thought of telling Olive what happened. He hated being the bearer of bad news.

Pepper made his way back to the house, the new landscape compressing under his feet as he walked. In some places, the sediment was saturated with water and Pepper's boots sank, coating them with dark, black, ash-filled slurry. Pepper looked at the mess. That's how he felt inside.

As he walked around the front of the house the sediment fan yielded to grass, and black muddy footprints recorded his path behind. Pepper got to the bottom of the porch, stopped, and looked at his boots, over at his footprints, and up to the fresh surface of the sediment fan, eroded ridge, and burn scar. Pepper looked back down at his boots and saw them start moving, not up the steps into the house, but back to the sediment fan and up the steep, muddy, barren ridge looming over the valley.

Pepper struggled up the slope. His feet slipped in the mud, and on loose rocks and woody debris as he fought to make uphill progress. Eventually, Pepper reached the top of the ridge. Stumps of trees Olive and Pepper felled to make the firebreak were charred, but visible, indicating that the fire didn't burn as hot in their firebreak, a small success.

The backside of the ridge was unrecognizable. All vegetation was gone. The lush forest reduced to a barren bowl of ashy grays and blacks. Deep gullies cut through the landscape feeding to the creek at the bottom, now better described as a small canyon. Parts of the hillsides were stripped down to bedrock, and their sediment had been swept far downstream – the finest silt and clay particles would maybe make it all the way to the Chesapeake Bay and even the Atlantic Ocean.

Walking across the ridge, Pepper found a sandstone boulder to sit on. He sat with his feet dangling, and stared at the space between his legs and thought about his losses. The debris flow covered about a third of his crops. A third gone. On top of that, most of the sheep and goats' pasture was also covered.

Moving that sediment off the field would be impossible, even with the tractor. The fields at the Burdettes' were done. The couple was back to the same amount of cropland as they had the year before, and with that much room to farm, they hadn't produced nearly enough food to sustain themselves. They relied on the grocery store to get them through the winter, but Pepper knew the store would offer little support in the coming winter.

They would only have the crops they grew, and the lack of rain wasn't conducive for a strong crop. Though he was able to irrigate and give the plants a little bit of water when they needed it most, they weren't getting enough. The crops were stressed. Pepper was stressed. It seemed no matter how hard he tried, no matter how much he planned, something always came up. Something was always wrong. Something was always difficult. Nothing was ever easy.

Drought, wildfires, landslides. Pepper was used to these in Utah. They were the effects of climate change he was trying to escape. He packed his whole life and moved thousands of miles to get away, but they managed to follow him.

It was supposed to be safe in Thirst Hollow. It was supposed to be easier. He felt foolish to try to run from climate change. Of course it wouldn't only affect the west. It was changing things everywhere. No where was safe. He couldn't run.

A tear fell from his face. For a second it was suspended, unmoving in the void between his legs, floating in the ether. Finally, it started falling again, and hit the bare ground with a small splash. Pepper looked up.

For the first time, he saw the panoramic view the fire-cleared ridge revealed, free of obstructing vegetation. Sunlight radiated at him, warming his face and chest, and illuminating the tops of the clouds a deep golden yellow, the same color as an autumn aspen grove. The billowing textured clouds blocked some of the sunlight in the distance, tattooing dark shadows onto the valley far away – the sun reducing the clouds to two dimensions and projecting their silhouettes on the land below.

Pepper imagined the people in the valley, some enjoying the sunlight, others buried under the clouds' shade. Both were having different experiences, though ultimately shared the same existence. The shadows slowly migrated across the valley floor. In some places they moved to reveal brilliant sunlight, while others just occupied by light were consumed by the penumbra.

Just then, a cloud moved over the sun, blocking the light that warmed Pepper's body, casting a shadow over him and Thirst Hollow. A chill ran through him, but he didn't move. He didn't fret or panic. He knew the sunlight would soon return, so he waited.

21

The Line

The storm kicked off something of a monsoon season. More storms came in the following days and weeks, bringing more water to the barren landscape, though none brought as much as the first one. Subsequent storms stripped more dirt, rocks, and burnt vegetation off the ridge and brought them down into the valley below, but not in volumes capable of destroying any more crops. The fields on the Burdettes' property couldn't be salvaged from the thousands of pounds of overlying debris, so the couple decided to focus their time tending to their other crops, trying to make them as productive as possible.

The sediment fans also covered most of the sheep and goat's pastureland, leaving them little room to graze. Olive had the idea of moving them to the other side of Thirst Run in the lawyer's property. They hadn't seen the owner since moving in, and with the state of the country they thought it unlikely they would in the future. Olive argued that forgiveness is easier to ask for than permission, so Pepper agreed and moved the herd to the other side of the valley.

For a while the herd was happy on the other side of Thirst Run. The vegetation was unburned and ample, and they had plenty to eat. But soon the coyotes found them. After that, every once in a while when Pepper would go check, he found one or two reduced to a bloody mess. Their deaths upset the couple – Pepper because of the loss of life, and Olive because of the loss of resources – but there wasn't much they could do.

They couldn't bring the herd back to their side of Thirst Hollow since there wasn't anything for them to eat, and they couldn't stay up all night watching them. Even Box and Turtle didn't want to be that far away from home at night. So the slaughter was slow and persistent, and the herd's numbers dwindled.

Soon summer turned to fall, the rains became lighter and less frequent, but the crops were still well watered. That year's harvest was greater than the previous year's, though not as bountiful as they hoped. Olive and Pepper were on track to grow as much food as they hoped until the debris flow destroyed a third of their crop. They could only hope they would have enough food for the upcoming winter, because they knew they wouldn't be able to buy much in town. Olive and Pepper didn't express their concerns to each other, but both of them were quietly calculating rations in their heads.

The canning process was exhausting, constantly preparing vegetables, filling jars, and boiling them. The weather cooled outside, but the inside of their house was always hot from the stoves. The couple doubled up, using both the kitchen stove and the wood-burning stove for the process. After taking a batch of jars out of the boiling water, Pepper and Olive would hear each jar's lid pop – a satisfying indication it was properly sealed. The pantry filled with vegetables, and soon everything was canned and preserved so the couple shifted their attention to firewood.

Gathering wood that year was more difficult than the previous fall. The fire burned all the wood on their side of Thirst Hollow, so the couple had to venture farther to find any. Also, due to the gas shortage, they used the truck as little as possible, fearing they would not be able to refill it. Buying gas was nearly impossible, and when it was available, the price was astronomical.

Once a week, when Pepper checked for voicemails from Bill – the grocery store owner who still owed Pepper a hundred dollars and called him when food shipments were scheduled – he also began calling the gas station in Plomari to see if they had gas. On Mondays, Pepper would make his weekly pilgrimage to the top of the ridge in search of service and good news.

"I'm going to check the phone," Pepper said to Olive who was busy chopping wood. "Want to come with?"

"No, I'm okay," Olive said without breaking concentration on a log in front of her. She forcefully swung the ax at half of a log standing on an old stump, splitting it into two smaller wedges, which fell into piles on either side.

"Okay, I'll be back soon," Pepper said as he walked off, double-checking his pocket for the flip phone. Pepper wasn't sure, but he thought he detected a hint of annoyance in Olive's voice. The stress of their fragile situation had been getting to her, and Pepper noticed she was on edge lately.

Pepper began walking to the top of the ridge. After the fire, a new trail was hard to establish because each time rain came it would wash out. But since the rains slowed, a faint trail formed from his weekly trips. Once on top of the ridge, Pepper faced south, in what had become a habit. Looking north at the burnt drainage was a painful reminder of what happened, so he always faced south where the view was green, untouched, and pristine.

Pepper turned on the phone, and with no new voicemails from Bill, Pepper dialed the gas station's number.

"Fill Up Eat Up, how can I help you?" a voice asked after a few rings.

"Hi," Pepper greeted the voice, "I was just wondering if you have gas today."

"We sure do," the voice answered cheerfully, surrounded by the chatter and movement of other people, "but you'd better hurry, a line is already forming. And bring cash, we don't take cards anymore."

"Okay, great, thanks so much," Pepper said as he started closing the flip phone.

"Uh huh, buh bye," he heard the voice say as he snapped the phone shut.

Pepper slipped the phone back into his front pocket and started descending the hill in a gentle trot. Pepper continued over the debris flow deposits and to Olive, who was still chopping wood.

"Hey," Pepper said to Olive, who turned and lowered the ax head to the ground. "They have gas, so I'm going to go into town. Do you want to come?"

Olive shook her head and answered, "No, I'm good."

But she wasn't good, Pepper could tell by her tone.

"Okay, I'll see you when I get back then." He started walking off, but before he got far he heard Olive's ax fall to the ground.

"While you're at it, why don't you go ask Bill for that money he owes you? It's been over a year now for Christ's sake."

"Okay, I'll see what I can do," Pepper said meekly, hoping that her frustration was with Bill, but knew it was probably with him.

"No, don't *see what you can do*. Just do it. Go into the grocery store and ask him. Be assertive. We're running out of money and probably don't have enough food for the winter. We need everything we can get. You gotta stand up for yourself, Pepper." She paused, a little out of breath, partly from chopping wood, partly from her rant, then said a little softer than before, "You gotta stand up for us."

"Okay, okay," Pepper said reluctantly as his eyes darted to the ground. "I'll go to the grocery store after I get gas."

The stress was getting to Olive. Pepper knew she wasn't trying to be rude; she was just trying to get him to make sure they would be okay. As he turned and walked to the truck, he heard Olive's ax come down again with inordinate force, cracking hard into the stump and sending splinters of wood flying.

Pepper loaded all of their empty gas cans in the back of the truck with optimism. He would be lucky to get a few gallons for the truck, but he'd rather have extra cans than be kicking himself wishing he did. Lastly, he loaded the dogs in the back who followed him closely in hopes of going for a ride.

Pepper drove down the driveway debating if and how to ask Bill for the money. Pepper didn't really want to confront Bill. Not only would it be awkward, but he figured that if Bill wasn't paying him, he must have a good reason. Maybe Bill was also struggling and couldn't afford to give up the money.

He didn't want to, but Pepper had to find a way to ask Bill. He couldn't go back to Olive without at least trying, and trying to figure out a solution, Pepper realized his best-case scenario was that Bill wouldn't be at the grocery store so he would have a good excuse for not asking.

After the short drive down winding roads, Pepper and the dogs arrived in Plomari. The gas station attendant wasn't lying about a line forming. Plomari's entire main street was backed up with people in their cars waiting for gas, so Pepper drove down a side road to get in line from the other direction, hoping the line on the other side would be shorter.

It wasn't, but he stayed put, and without the slight distraction of driving, Pepper couldn't stop his mind from analyzing every possible interaction with Bill, and the subsequent conversation with Olive. To distract himself, Pepper flipped the radio on.

"Live from NPR news in Washington, I'm Linny Elpert. Violence continues throughout Los Angeles as several divisions of the US Marine Corps from the nearby base in Twentynine Palms have defected to join the far-right group We the People. Many parts of the city have been under control of the opposition group Net Zero, but with the influx of soldiers and weapons, We the People have…"

Pepper forcefully turned the plastic knob, changing the radio to a classic rock station. He couldn't add more fodder to his overstimulated mind. Instead, he hoped music would calm him down a bit, or at the very least, not contribute to his anxiety.

Looking ahead, Pepper sighed at the long, slow line. Unlike when he and Olive waited for gas when they took the Burdettes' to the hospital, Pepper didn't even consider buying a snack. He didn't have any money to spare even if the gas station had any food to buy, which he doubted it did.

When the line inched forward, Pepper didn't turn on the truck. Instead, he put it in neutral, got out, and pushed. Anything to save a little money or gas. Once the line stopped moving, he hopped back in and hit the brakes to avoid a very low speed fender bender with the car in front of him. At least with the line's slow pace Pepper was afforded some rest between jumping in and out and pushing the truck.

The line moved slowly, and there were many cars in front of him. Pepper worried he wasn't going to be able to get gas, and if he didn't, he wasn't sure he had enough to get back to Thirst Hollow.

As he sat, Pepper became curious who all the people were waiting in line. He didn't by any stretch know everyone who lived in Plomari, but Pepper thought he would know more faces based on the amount of people. But he didn't recognize anyone. The line was full of out of state license plates from places like Oklahoma and Kansas, which Pepper thought was odd. *Who were all these people, and why were they in Plomari?*

The line crawled, and after over an hour Pepper finally pushed his truck in front of a pump. As Pepper pulled out his wallet to pay the extortionate gas prices, shouts erupted from two men at a nearby pump.

"What do you think you're doing?"

"Getting gas. What the hell does it look like?"

"There's a line. Everyone else is waiting, you can't just walk up here."

"Fuck you. What are you going to do about it?"

A man standing beside his car at the pump was arguing with another man trying to fill a five-gallon gas can. The second man had cut the line and defaulted to aggression to get his way. Without thinking, and maybe fueled by a misinterpretation of Olive's demands to take action, Pepper rushed over.

"What the fuck is going on?" Pepper shouted, inserting himself between the two men, puffing his chest at the man with the gas can.

"Go back to your car, buddy. It's none of your business," the aggressive man retorted, posturing large.

A few curious people pumping their gas idled in the periphery, straining their necks to glimpse the drama. They shuffled close enough for a good view, but far enough to avoid any risk of becoming involved. Pepper glanced around for back up, but didn't recognize any of the bystanders. He considered turning away. After all, the man was right. It wasn't any of his business.

But I always fold to people, he thought, *and Olive thinks I'm weak because of that. It's not true though. I can be assertive. I can be strong, and this is my chance to prove it. I can stop this guy, then when I go home, I'll tell Olive about it and she'll see that I'm not weak. She'll see that I am assertive, and can stand up to people who mean harm. I can do it.* So Pepper took another step, this time large and toward the aggressive man.

"Seriously," Pepper roared. A deep voice rose from his chest that even surprised himself. "Get the fuck out of here."

Pepper put his hand on the gas pump to block the man and took another step forward. Inspired by Pepper's confidence, the first man stood shoulder to shoulder with Pepper, forming a wall between the aggressive man and the gas pump. With his confident demeanor fading, the aggressive man took a step back, and before he could find words for rebuttal a shout came from one of the peripheral onlookers.

"Yeah, get out of here!"

A small mob had formed, composed of bored people who left their cars for what was turning out to be the most entertaining part of their day. More of its members started jeering at the man, though they maintained their distance.

As the volume of the crowd's disapproval increased, the aggressive man took another step back. He looked once more at Pepper, then at the surrounding mob. Accepting but not expressing his defeat, the man stormed out with a farewell "fuck you," weaving through the sea of cars to the taunts and laughs of bystanders'.

With no further spectacle to be seen, the crowd dissolved and made their way back to the cars, perhaps worried they too may be the victim of line cutting. After many thanks and handshakes from the first man, Pepper rode a high all the way back to his truck, adrenaline running through his veins.

He was amped, not just from the excitement of the argument, but because he thought he did something Olive would approve of. He was assertive, and stood up to an aggressor. Granted Pepper didn't stand up for himself, but at least he stood up for somebody, and it felt good.

Pepper pumped his gas then left the gas station slowly, but with purpose. He no longer had any doubt whether he should ask Bill for the money. He no longer wished for Bill's absence from the store. He wanted to confront him. Pepper wanted to get his money.

Pepper stopped the truck outside of the grocery store. The parking lot was full of cars, most of them with out of state plates, and people milling about them, rummaging through their piled belongings and setting up tents in the adjacent grass. But blind with self-empowerment, Pepper didn't pay them any attention. Instead, leaving the dogs in the back of the truck, he stormed into the grocery store. Within three steps of the automatic glass doors scurrying out of his way, Pepper saw Bill smiling and waving at him from the checkout counter, blissfully unaware of Pepper's newfound indignation soon to crash down on him.

"Hey Pepper, how's it going? Did you get some gas? I saw the line out there. Looks like a pain." Bill asked cheerfully as Pepper walked up.

"Yeah," Pepper answered sharply, approaching the checkout counter feeling the confidence in his steps. "Look Bill, we need to talk. I need that money you owe me. Or food. Either one works, but I need it soon. Actually Bill, I need it now. I'm sorry to come in here like this, but enough is enough."

"What do you mean?" Bill asked, confused.

"The money Bill, from when I helped you build that shed. The hundred dollars, Bill. I need it. C'mon, don't make me get upset, we both know what I'm talking about."

Bill sighed. "Okay, okay. I get it," he said, defeat in his voice and cheer leaving his body. "Let me go in the back and open the safe."

Bill turned and walked to a door leading to the office in a sectioned-off corner of the grocery store. Bill disappeared for a few minutes, then came out with one arm rubbing the back of his neck nervously.

"Here you go," Bill said as he offered Pepper a pile of crumpled bills and a few rolls of quarters. "A hundred dollars. Sorry it took me so long, it's just been really hard around here."

Pepper snatched the clump of money from Bill's hands, and jammed it into his jeans' tight pocket. Though fueled with a new conviction, Pepper was still trusting enough not to count the money.

"Thanks, Bill," Pepper said, calming down as he felt the money in his hands. "I'm sorry to come in here like that, but Olive and I really need it."

"Hey, I get it. I owed you, and you said it. Enough is enough. Thanks for being patient, and I'll still give you a call when we have a food shipment coming in."

Pepper thanked Bill then left the store, not bothering to look around since he knew the shelves didn't have anything he needed. Pepper felt the money in his pocket and slid the bills past each other. *Damn* he thought. *It feels good to get what is mine. Olive's going to be happy. And not just happy, she'll be proud.*

Replaying the scene in his head, feeling proud of himself, and working out how he would describe it to Olive, Pepper glided through the parking lot barely aware of the world around him. Olive was right. It felt good to put himself first. Pepper would never see what good the money would do for

Bill, but it would help him and Olive. It would put some gas in their car, some flour in their pantry, some food in their stomach.

He and Olive were struggling, but now, because he stood up for himself and kept his and Olive's best interest at heart, they would struggle a little less. Pepper was on a cloud, happy and accomplished. But as he neared the truck, he was ripped from his thoughts back to the grocery store parking lot.

Standing at the back of his truck, there was a man wearing dirty blue jeans and a black hoodie reaching into the bed and rummaging around. The dogs were nowhere to be seen, and Pepper's heart dropped. Grasping the money tight in his pocket, Pepper ran over to the truck to confront the man. Pepper was done being taken advantage of. He was ready to take action.

22

The Family

"Hey!" Pepper shouted as his feet pounded on the cracked, black asphalt of the parking lot. "What are you doing?"

The man looked up in surprise. He was tall, much larger than Pepper, with dark hair and a dark beard. "Is this your truck?"

The man's tone wasn't confrontational, which took Pepper aback, but he was set on not letting anything stop him from standing up for himself, so he ignored the dissonance. "Yeah, it's my truck," Pepper snapped at the man.

"It's okay man. Your dogs got out, I was just checking if there were leashes back here," he said. "Sorry," he added, addressing Pepper's defensiveness.

"Oh," Pepper's voice softened with his shoulder muscles, realizing the man was helping, not hurting. Pepper was on edge from his earlier confrontation, and felt bad he had come at the man so aggressively. He would have never done something like that if he wasn't following Olive's insistence on being more assertive. "Where are they?"

"They're playing with my kids over there," the man answered. "I just wanted to get leashes so they didn't run off."

"Yeah, I know, thanks," Pepper said, feeling embarrassed. "I'll get them, sorry about that."

"Hey, no worries. The kids are loving playing with them. We had to leave our dogs in Kansas and the kids really miss them." His eyes softened and he looked down as if he was ashamed. Both of the men stood for a second. Pepper didn't know what to say, but the man broke the silence. "Well, your dogs are over here," he said, taking a step toward a plum-colored minivan.

Pepper followed across the lot to the other side of the van. As he walked, Pepper noticed quite a few other cars parked similarly. Their owners aimlessly milled around them, seemingly not in a rush to get anywhere fast.

The man led Pepper around his van where two little kids played, a boy about five years old, and a girl probably closer to ten. The girl was rubbing Mango's belly, who was upside down and in heaven. The boy was chasing one of the border collies while the other pranced behind.

Sitting on the floor of the van with the sliding door open was a slumped woman, watching the kids play with the dogs. The inside of the van was completely packed with things: clothes, bags, suitcases, stools, and pots. Things. Pepper was surprised they managed to fit the kids back there with the rest of it. Even the roof of the van had bags and a cooler secured tenuous with ratchet straps and rope.

"Hi honey," the man said to the woman. She smiled at him, but looked at Pepper with a hint of suspicion. "I found the dogs' owner," he explained.

"Hi," Pepper greeted her, "I'm Pepper." He reached out his hand for her to shake.

"Hi," she responded, tentatively taking his hand. "Joleen."

"And I'm Oscar," the man said, grasping Pepper's hand once his wife released it.

"Nice to meet you," Pepper said, with a polite smile. Then seeing their license plate, he asked, "Y'all are from Kansas?"

"Sure are," she affirmed. "Born and raised. Actually, this is the furthest I've ever been away from home."

"What are y'all doing out here then?" Pepper asked. Gauging their reactions, he instantly felt he had broached a sensitive subject.

"Well," Oscar started, then stopped. "With all the droughts and crop failures, I lost my job. I was a heavy equipment operator on a farm, but the wheat dried up, and so did all the jobs. We thought there might be some work out this way since there seems to be more rain than Kansas, so we packed up and headed out."

Pepper nodded his head. "Where are you going?"

"Well, we're not exactly sure," Oscar said, with sunken eyes. "We're out of gas, money, and food. We were even lucky to make it here. Our van ran out of gas about thirty minutes out and a man gave us enough gas to get here."

"An angel," Joleen corrected.

"Yeah, an angel," Oscar agreed. "I'm actually pretty surprised there's gas here. Most places we've been through are out, if not closed down completely. I wish we had money to buy some, because otherwise, we are stuck. No food to eat, no gas to get anywhere, and no work to get money."

Pepper felt a twinge of guilt – a Pavlovian response to help Oscar and his family – but he bit his tongue and fought it back. After the close call with Wes and his empowering morning, he was determined to put himself and Olive first. Seeing the family in need pulled deep on his gut, but Pepper remained firm in his resolve. He wanted to make Olive proud. He had to stay strong.

"I like your dog," a meek voice said from behind Pepper.

He looked over and saw the little girl rubbing Mango's belly. Her skinny, little arms looked like they were ready to snap, and dark crescents lay beneath her eyes.

"Thanks, she sure seems to like you too," Pepper said back with a forced smile. He could feel his throat tighten at the suggestion of the girl's struggles. She didn't deserve what was happening. She didn't deserve what the world had come to, just like the children in California during the wildfire didn't deserve what happened to them. Pepper swallowed hard, trying to loosen up his throat. "She loooves belly rubs."

The girl giggled. "What's her name?"

"Her name is Mango."

The little girl let out a small, sweet laugh. "That's a silly name for a dog."

She went back to petting Mango. From a short distance away, her brother saw the attention his sister was getting so he ran over, Box and Turtle close behind.

"My name is Brandon," the boy declared.

"Hi Brandon, my name's Pepper."

"Yesterday, we saw a fighter jet. It was so loud!"

"Wow, that sounds awesome," Pepper said, kneeling next to him and petting one of the border collies.

"Have you ever seen a fighter jet?"

"I have. They are really loud!"

Pepper's heart ached for the small boy. He was too young to understand what was going on. Sure, he could sense his parents' stress, and already knew a hunger most Americans couldn't have imagined only a couple years prior, but he was still just a kid. He was still enthralled with dogs and fighter jets. He didn't understand how close his family was to perishing. He needed help, and Pepper could see the boy's parents weren't able to provide any for him or his sister.

Oscar shooed away the children and began describing their journey to Virginia. It was harrowing, but Pepper wasn't listening. He couldn't get the poor children out of his mind.

The kids, as well as their clothes, were dirty. And not just the type of dirty kids get while playing. Their clothes had a surficial layer of dirt that had accumulated in the last day or two – normal kid stuff – but there was also dirt embedded deep in the fibers. Dirt that was seeped into the essence of the clothes. Dirt that hadn't been washed out for so long, it was integral to the garments. Their hair was greasy, cowlicked, and messy from the night before.

On the hood of the car was a wet tent drying in the sun. It was damp and though Pepper wasn't close enough to smell it, he knew it reeked of mildew. With the humidity, Pepper figured they battled daily to keep it dry.

In the van lay a gas camping stove among blackened pots and pans, charred from cooking over a fire because the family couldn't find, or afford, gas for the stove. The children were playing, but they were tired. Their eyes were sunken from following their parents who were chasing hope. And they were skinny. So skinny.

Playing with the dogs, the kids' erratic movements made Pepper worried for their safety. Most children he had known could bounce right back from a skinned knee or a fat lip, but these two looked fragile. Their pale skin and protruding bones made Pepper nervous that even a small accident could do serious damage. He wanted to call the dogs over to prevent any unnecessary injuries, but didn't have the heart to deprive the children of the small amount of joy derived from playing with them. So he let them be as his heart dropped in his stomach.

The kids needed help. As Pepper looked at their dirty clothes and boney arms and legs, he forgot about how good it felt earlier to stand up for himself. He didn't think about Olive, or the delicate situation they were in. The only thing on Pepper's mind was how if he didn't help those poor kids, they would go hungry, and something bad could happen to them.

If it had just been Oscar and Joleen, Pepper would probably be okay without helping. His day of standing up for himself and self-empowerment would have continued, and he would have gone home to impress Olive. But the little boy and girl reminded him of the kids who died in California during the wildfire. Pepper could have helped those kids, but he didn't and they died because of his inaction. He couldn't bear the thought of anything bad happening to more children because of him. Pepper couldn't ignore the kids. He had to do something. He had to help.

"Anyways," Oscar's voice rose above Pepper's internal dialogue, "folks just don't seem friendly these days. Everyone only looks out for themselves, but I guess I can't blame them. It's been hell trying to keep these kids fed, and I don't know what we are going to do now that we don't have money for gas to get anywhere. We were hoping to get towards Charlottesville. My brother knows a guy who has a farm there and he doesn't need help, but my brother said if I show up, maybe he'll know somebody that does."

"Are y'all hungry?" Pepper choked up, immediately feeling Olive's disapproval of his proposition.

Oscar looked at Joleen, and Joleen back at Oscar as they had a nonverbal conversation in which Pepper didn't speak the language. Their pride prevented them from answering right away, but their hunger and concern for their children precluded them from turning down any help.

"Yeah," Oscar said sheepishly. "We could use a bite."

"Well, will you all still be here in about an hour?" Pepper felt embarrassed asking another question they all knew the answer to.

"Yeah, I suppose we will." Oscar said.

"Alright, well I'll be passing through here again in about an hour," Pepper said as if he was already planning on coming back to Plomari, which he wasn't, "and I'll have a few jars of vegetables if y'all would like." He tried to make the offer seem as little like charity as possible, but couldn't think of a good reason he would need to give them food.

"Wow, yeah of course," Joleen said enthusiastically. "That's really kind of you."

"Yeah, thanks so much, Pepper," Oscar said, shaking Pepper's hand aggressively in appreciation.

"Oh, it's no problem at all," Pepper responded, trying to squeeze Oscar's hand as hard as Oscar was squeezing his, though wishing he could just let go.

Pepper took his hand back and said, "I'd better get going though. I'll be back through in about an hour."

"Sounds good," Oscar said, taking a step back towards his wife and putting his arm around her.

As Pepper drove off, he knew Joleen and Oscar were watching the truck. He could feel their stares, and in them their hope he would return with food, as well as their fears he wouldn't.

Pepper kicked himself for agreeing to help. He knew this would overshadow any good he did earlier in the day. Olive would be angry. Pepper considered not going back to the family, and simply not mentioning them to Olive, but couldn't bear to think of the children waiting for his return, their stomachs empty and their hopes high, waiting for Pepper until their parents called them into their moldy tent for the night. He had to lay in the bed he made. Maybe one day, Pepper would be strong enough to put him and Olive first, but that wasn't the day. His past wouldn't let it be. Instead he was driving home, getting closer and closer to upsetting Olive.

23

The Truth

As Pepper crept up the driveway, Olive was nowhere to be seen. Pepper got out of the truck, looking where Olive had been chopping wood, and around the house, but she wasn't anywhere to be seen. Pepper figured she was across Thirst Run on the lawyer's property tending to the goats and sheep. Every few weeks, coyotes had been injuring or killing the sheep and goats, so checking on the herd and addressing any injuries had become a regular task.

Pepper gave up looking and went to the house to get the family the food he promised. As he walked through the house, his footsteps were loud on the wood floor. He felt he was intruding in his own house. Pepper put a cloth bag of the pantry, and began hastily filling it with whatever vegetables looked like there were the most of. Once the bag was full, Pepper lifted it from the long cloth handles and was surprised at the weight of it.

There were a lot of jars in the bag. A lot of weight representing a lot of work and effort. The bag was heavy with his and Olive's sweat. It was heavy from the hunger they were sure to experience over winter from the lack of food, and made heavier because Pepper was giving some of it away.

Pepper slung the long cloth handles over his shoulder so the bag didn't feel so heavy, and hurried out of the house before he could think more about the implications of what he was doing. He looked around once more for Olive, then loaded the dogs into the truck, and started driving back to Plomari, glad to have gotten away without having to confront her. He knew he was just prolonging the fight, but at least this way he was able to help the family before Olive tried to convince him otherwise.

The drive felt longer the second time that day. He turned on the radio to distract himself, but escaping thoughts of the imminent fight with Olive was impossible.

Pepper pulled onto the main street in Plomari and noticed it was empty. The line of cars was gone, and the cardboard "Out of Gas" sign hung askew over the station's sign. The town was quiet once again, but the family and their minivan, along with several other cars, were still sitting in the grocery store parking lot. The family's tent must have dried some because it was set up, and the two little kids were carrying their sleeping bags inside.

Pepper had unreasonably hoped someone would have given the family a few gallons of gas by the time he returned and the family would be gone, but nobody did, and they were still there. As soon as his truck was in sight, Oscar and Joleen's eager eyes locked onto it and Oscar said something hopeful to Joleen.

Pepper turned into the parking lot and stopped next to the van. He let the dogs out of the bed, and they ran right back to their kids to play and get more belly rubs. Dropping their sleeping bags, the kids squealed with excitement. Close behind, Pepper lifted the heavy bag of food off the passenger seat and walked around the van to meet Oscar and Joleen.

"Hey Pepper," Oscar said standing up. "Glad you could make it back through." He grabbed Pepper's hand and gave it another good shake.

"Of course, I'm glad to see y'all again." Pepper said, trying to put his reservations to the back of his mind. It was too late to change his mind, and he accepted he would have to deal with Olive's frustration later. "Looks like it emptied out around here pretty good."

"Yeah, once they ran out of gas, everyone left. At least everyone who could," Joleen said, glancing at the other cars in the parking lot. "We were really hoping to get some. Who knows when this little town will get more."

Pepper wasn't sure how she was expecting to pay for the gas, but then noticed a cardboard sign claiming the old platitude that "anything helps."

"Both you and me hope that they start having gas more often," Pepper paused and sensed their anticipation. Peripherally their eyes burned a hole in the cloth bag hanging from his shoulder. "Well, I didn't bring too much, but I got some carrots, green beans, peppers, I don't know, just some veggies."

As he pulled the items out of the cloth bag, he realized how difficult it would be to make anything resembling a meal from the mismatched ingredients.

"Oh my gosh, thank you so much," Joleen said emphatically, seeming not to notice the clashing food types.

"Yes. Thank you," echoed Oscar, holding a jar of green beans in his hand, looking at it intently.

"No problem. I'm happy to help," Pepper said, feeling both genuine and dishonest at the same time as he thought about what Olive would say if she was there.

"Seriously, thank you so much," Oscar said looking up from the food. "You don't know how big this is for us. It's been really hard since we left Kansas. Just knowing someone cares enough to do something like this means a lot."

"It's really no problem," Pepper repeated, itching to leave. Guilt began to settle in as he saw the food leave his possession. He knew Olive was going to be angry, and he dreaded going back home. He wondered if there was something he could do, however small, to show Olive he did care about their needs.

Maybe if he brought the mason jars back, that would be something – maybe not enough, but something – to show Olive. It would show that at least he was thinking about their needs. Afterall, jars might be hard to come by in the future, and Joleen and Oscar didn't need them, just the food.

"If you don't mind, can I have the jars back?"

The couple looked confused for a second, thinking Pepper wanted the contents of the jars back as well. Their faces showed a story of hardship and mistrust.

"Maybe we can pour the veggies into a pot or something?" Pepper asked to clarify.

"Oh, sure," Joleen said, looking relieved and opening the back of the van. She rummaged through the jumble of possessions before eventually pulling out two pots and pouring each jar into them, creating an unappealing hodgepodge of a soup. "Thank you so much," Joleen said again, handing the jars back to Pepper one by one.

"Happy to help. I hope you guys find some work soon," Pepper said as a segue to leave.

"Okay, thanks again," said Oscar. "Hope to see you soon." He took Pepper's hand once again and gave it a final firm shake.

"Have a safe drive back," Joleen said, taking a step toward Pepper and leaning in for a hug.

He gave her a short unenthusiastic hug, then said, "Alright, y'all have a good night."

Pepper walked to the truck and called the dogs over, who reluctantly came. He sat in the truck and released a long sigh. It was done. The food was gone. Now he had to go back to confront Olive.

When Pepper returned home, amber light illuminated the house from the inside and thick white smoke billowed out of the chimney. He didn't see her, but knew Olive must be inside. Unsure if she already noticed the missing food, Pepper cautiously opened the front door. If he was a dog, his ear would have been back and his tail between his legs.

As Pepper entered, he saw Olive on the other side of the house, stirring something on the stove with her back turned.

"What happened?" Olive asked without turning around.

With a million answers running through his head, Pepper was petrified, trying to figure out what question Olive was really asking, and the best answer to that question.

"I heard you come home then leave again, is everything okay?" Olive asked before Pepper decided on a response.

"Yeah, everything's fine."

Olive hadn't noticed the missing food yet. She would have been much angrier if she had. Pepper debated whether he should tell her of his self-interested victory at the grocery store, or if he led with that he would only be setting her up for a higher fall.

"I went back because I met this family in Plomari."

Pepper paused and Olive turned from the stove to face him. A look of disappointment and rage seared in her eyes causing Pepper's stomach to drop. "What do you mean? What family?"

"Well, they left their home in Kansas to look for work but hadn't found any. They didn't have any money left for gas or food so they were stuck in Plomari," Pepper said. "They have two little kids and they're so skinny. They're hungry. I just couldn't leave them without doing something." Pepper's voice trailed off as he could see anger building in Olive's face.

"So, what'd you do?" Olive asked, trying to restrain her frustration, but doing a poor job.

Pepper's eyes darted to the pantry, and Olive turned her head to see what he was looking at.

"You didn't," she said, tearing over to the pantry. Pepper stood motionless, helplessly watching it all unfold, a pit sinker deeper and deeper into his stomach. Olive swung the door open and glared in disbelief at the empty spaces on the shelves. "You gave them our food?" she cried.

"They were hungry, Olive. There were kids. I couldn't just leave them."

"What do you mean 'you couldn't leave them?' You always say, 'you couldn't'. You *could* leave them, Pepper. You said that they're hungry. Well, we are going to be hungry! What you can't do is put *us* in a bad situation. You're hurting *us* just to help these people that you don't even know. Maybe if we knew them, and cared about them, I would understand, but we don't. For all you know they are lying and taking advantage of us. Remember the hitchhiker? I feel like you never learn. 'You couldn't do that to them.' Well, you can't do that to us! We're going to starve Pepper, and then what? How are you going to save everyone else if you can't even save yourself?" Olive was tearing up.

Pepper knew Olive was fed up. He knew she didn't think he was considering her wellbeing. That he disregarded her, only focusing on other's needs, opening up old wounds first inflicted by her father.

But the truth was that he was trying. He wanted to make her happy. That's why he demanded the money from Bill. That's why the whole drive home he dreaded telling Olive about the family. Caring for others and caring for her weren't mutually exclusive. He always considered her needs, but he was also condemned by his past to help others. Pepper tried to explain this to Olive.

"I'm sorry. I know that I *could* ignore them. I know that it's physically possible, but my mind, or my heart, won't let me. Every time I try to ignore someone in need, I think back to that fire in California and the pang of guilt so strong, nothing stops it besides helping, and sometimes even that doesn't make me feel better."

"Pepper, you've got to get over that. It wasn't your fault. Fires are unpredictable. You did everything you could, and you can't live the rest of your life trying to make up for something that was out of your control!"

Pepper's eyes dropped to the floor and he felt a lump growing in the back of his throat. "It was my fault. I could have done something," he said softly.

Olive, upon seeing Pepper's distress, softened her demeanor and took a step toward him. "What do you mean?"

"Never mind," Pepper said, shaking his head. He didn't want to go into it. He hadn't told Olive the truth about that day for years and didn't want to tell her now. He feared Olive's judgment of the terrible thing he did, even if she would be justified in doing so. "I'm sorry about the food. I won't let it happen again."

"No, tell me what happened," Olive persisted. She always had suspected something more happened that day in California, that whatever it was carried the responsibility of Pepper's generosity, and his incessant need to help others regardless of what it cost him.

Pepper looked up at her, worried wrinkles creasing his forehead. Pepper didn't want to tell her. He feared if she found out what he had done that day, what kind of person he really was, she would be disgusted. She would leave. But he had hurt Olive more than anyone from his reaction to that day. She deserved to know, so Pepper began.

"Well, you were there. We were on that assignment in California getting into position when the wind picked up and the fire made a run. We all split up into pairs to warn the residents to get out of there.

"Well, me and Blackwell got to this one house and there was this family there, a mom and her two kids, a boy and a girl. They came out into their driveway and were asking us a bunch of questions. We tried to answer them and get them out of there, but no matter what me and Blackwell said, they just didn't understand how close the fire was or the danger they were in. They didn't want to leave.

"After what felt like an eternity pleading with the mom, she finally agreed to leave as long as we helped their take her suitcases to her car. I was already frustrated so I refused to help. I knew the fire was getting close and wanted to get us out of there. But Blackwell agreed to help. He was always so patient."

"Yeah, he was," Olive said, much calmer than before. Pepper's story was already drawing some empathy from her.

"Well, while Blackwell took his line gear off and left it on the ground as he went into the house, I stormed off, annoyed we were spending even more time there. I got about a hundred yards away from the house, and that's when I heard the fire behind me.

"It came like a freight train. I knew it was there before I had time to turn around and see it, and when I did turn I saw a wall of fire, spanning from the ground to the tops of the trees. With the wind blowing behind it, I barely had time to react as it raged toward me.

"I started running to the house, with flames licking my back. I needed to warn Blackwell and the family, but by the time I reached the front of the house the flames had encompassed me. I shouted but I didn't have time for them. I had to save myself. So I yanked my fire shelter from the bottom of my line pack, shook it open, pulled it over myself, and laid down on the ground.

"And you know from training how those shelters are. They're hot and small, and you feel like you can't breathe. But being in one during training was nothing like it was in the fire. I felt like I was suffocating in a plastic garbage bag. The hot air burned my lungs, and soon my back felt like it was blistering from the burning heat. For what felt like an eternity I tried to endure. I figured the heat was normal, but the pain intensified until I finally rolled over to see what was going on.

"As I looked up, I saw a long tear along the entire length of my shelter and the fire blazing through it. It must have torn when I took it out of my bag, but whatever happened, I knew that with the fire already surrounding me and growing hotter by the second, my shelter wasn't going to protect me. I was going to be burned alive unless I did something.

"So I ripped it off and stood up, only to be met with a burst of scorching air down my lungs and flames in my face. I looked around but there was no way out. Fire was everywhere. But then I looked down and saw Blackwell's line pack on the ground next to me."

"So what'd you do?" Olive asked, her face wrinkled with concern and terror, as if she was alongside Pepper in the fire.

Pepper paused. "I took Blackwell's shelter out of his pack," he finally said, the words barely audible as they left his mouth. "I don't know what I was thinking. I guess I wasn't. Maybe I figured he was safe in the house. Or maybe I didn't think at all and it was just instinct, but either way, I took his shelter." Pepper stopped and buried his face in his hands.

"Oh my god Pepper, I'm so sorry," Olive said, reaching out and putting her hand on his arm. "It's not your fault though. You just reacted. No one can blame you for that. Blackwell would probably be happy that you used his shelter. It saved your life."

Pepper shook his head, pulling his arm away from Olive's. He didn't deserve her sympathy. At least not until she knew the whole story.

"I'm not done. There's more," Pepper said. Olive withdrew her hand and placed it on her lap, confused about why Pepper was acting so strangely. "So, I took his shelter and got under it. The fire was still hot, and I could barely breathe, but it was better than before. At least barely.

"And I stayed under there for what felt like a long time. The fire grew louder and louder. It felt like forever, but it probably was only a minute or two. Then, through all the noise I heard something human through the noise of the fire. It was Blackwell and the family rushing out of the house."

"Oh my god, were they okay?" Olive asked, as if she forgot they didn't make it out of the fire.

"Yeah, I guess. I was barely surviving underneath the shelter. I have no idea how they made it to me, but they did. Blackwell, the mom, even the two little kids.

"Blackwell was the first one to reach me. He grabbed the shelter and shook it, trying to get me to let them in. Then the mom started screaming, begging me to at least let her kids in. But I didn't. I put my arms through the shelter's straps and dug in, holding on as tightly as I could to save myself. I didn't even respond to them. I just laid there, trying to keep as tight of a seal with the ground to keep out the heat and the smoke.

"Soon their screams for help shifted to screams of agony, as their battle against the fire came to a close. And I just laid there in the safety of my shelter, listening to them burn alive."

Pepper hung his head, but no tears came from. He was numb, but also a little relieved. After replaying the scene in his head thousands of times before, letting it haunt him, and steer his life in the direction it took, it felt good to get it out. It was no longer a secret, and the relief almost overshadowed his concern over how Olive would respond.

At first Olive looked at Pepper in horror, almost in disgust, trying to comprehend how someone could be so selfish as to listen to his partner, and an entire family burn to their deaths only feet away. But then Olive softened.

That person was not the same as the one she knew now. Pepper used to be selfish, self-serving, and egotistical. Though she didn't like the idea of Pepper listening to his partner and a family burn to death, he wasn't that person anymore. In fact that incident created the Pepper she knew and loved, even if sometimes he went overboard on helping people.

Olive couldn't even imagine the type of guilt Pepper had been carrying with him. She figured he already paid the price of his decisions, and what he needed was some love and understanding.

And how could she judge? Pepper was only looking out for his own safety. His actions were probably instinctual. And after all, those shelters are only designed for one person. Pepper would have probably died alongside the rest of them if he had done anything differently.

She put her hand back on his arm, then drew him close and embraced him. Pepper rested his head on Olive's shoulder.

"I've never been able to forget their screams," Pepper said, his voice muffled on Olive's shoulder. "It was terrible. I wish I could go back. I wish I could have put all four of them under that shelter and that it was me who died, but I can't. I have to live with it, and all I can do to try to make it better is to help people.

"Every time someone asks me for something, I think of their screams. I hear them in my head, and I have to do something, because if I don't something else bad could happen.

"That's why I agreed to help the family today. What if they didn't get any other food? What if they die? Their deaths would be on me, and I couldn't live with that.

"And I know it's hard on you. It's hard on me too. You're not wrong when you say we need to watch out for ourselves first. You're right, but I just can't not help. I'm sorry."

Olive didn't respond at first. She just stroked Pepper's back. But after collecting her thoughts, she said, "I'm so sorry. Why haven't you told me any of that before?"

"I don't know. I guess I just want to forget. I just want to move on, but I can't," Pepper said.

"I'm so sorry that happened to you," she said, pulling him in tight. She knew nothing she said would help, but maybe holding him would show that she still loved him. So they stood in silence for a few moments until Pepper leaned away.

"It's okay," Pepper said in a low, sad voice. "Thanks for listening and I'm sorry about giving our food to that family. I'll try not to let it happen again."

"It's okay," Olive answered. "I think I understand a little better. Do you want some dinner? I think it should almost be ready."

"Sure, but I think I'm going to go outside for a second. I need to clear my head."

"Okay. Come inside when you're ready. I'll get everything ready."

"Thanks," Pepper said, then slid out of his seat, walked out the front door, and closed it quietly behind him.

Pepper leaned against the porch railing and looked across Thirst Hollow. He was glad the day was over, but was emotionally drained. Driving back, Pepper couldn't stop debating if helping the family was the right thing to do. Though Olive softened when he told her about what happened in California, Pepper knew she was right.

He couldn't keep indiscriminately helping everyone who asked. He let Olive down by giving away their food. The fact that he was doing so well earlier that day made the shame even harder to swallow.

After confronting the man at the gas station, then demanding Bill pay what he owed, Pepper was having a great day. If he had just gone home, Olive would have been proud. Pepper would have finally done what she wanted – put their needs first – but instead he ran into the family and ruined the day.

Sure, the family was happy. They got help, and they got it when they truly needed it, but what about Pepper? He came out last. He hurt Olive and gave away food they would need later that winter. The family's good fortune and gratitude was little consolation to him. He wished he had never seen the family, and even more, he wished he didn't have to help everyone who asked.

Across Thirst Hollow, the sun was low in the sky, and Pepper watched it closely in his periphery, only daring to glance briefly near the retina-damaging corona.

But even in his perimetric observations, Pepper could see the movement of the sun. It creeped behind the tops of the trees on the ridge, making its way across the sky.

On an intellectual level, Pepper knew the sun moved, but had never thought to observe its migration in real time. From his porch, Pepper watched the sun skim the tops of the trees. Then dipping lower in the sky, it moved through the trees' silhouettes, toward the opaque boundary of the ridge top.

The sun sailed much faster than Pepper expected. It flew across the sky, and Pepper was shocked he never noticed it before. Either he hadn't paid enough attention, or simply never had a point of reference like the trees on the ridge to observe the movement. But that evening Pepper watched the sun's arc relative to the treetops, and realized it always zoomed across the sky at an incredible speed.

Pepper tracked its descent, lower and lower. Not until the sun was partially behind the ridge did he recognize that what he saw wasn't the sun moving at all, but what he witnessed was actually the rotation of the earth. From his humble home in Thirst Hollow, Pepper stared in wonder and observed the earth spinning on its axis, amazed that all he needed to see it was a bit of awareness and a point of reference.

Pepper watched the sun fall until the ridge eclipsed the last speck of light. Pepper wished the thoughts of the California fire would also disappear. He wished they would slide behind the ridge as easily as the sun had, out of sight and out of mind. But Pepper wasn't optimistic that would happen. He feared some things couldn't set as easily as the sun did.

But just a few minutes earlier before taking a closer look at the sun, Pepper had never realized how the sun set. Only after looking carefully was he able to recognize its behavior. Maybe that's what he needed to free himself from the bonds of his past mistakes, to look at the situation with a new perspective. To gauge his behavior from a reference point to better understand its patterns. Still in contemplation, Pepper pushed away from the porch railing, took one last look across Thirst Hollow, and went inside for dinner.

24

The Escape

Over the next few days, the voids left from the donated food haunted the shelves, nagging Pepper every time he went in the pantry. They would need that food over winter, and there was no getting it back. He let Olive down, and he felt terrible.

Soon, tired of being reminded, Pepper slid the rows of jars to the front of the shelves, visually erasing his misdeed. Everything in the pantry looked almost as they had before, the rows were just a few jars shallower than before. But the damage was done even if he tried to hide it, and the lesson was learned. At least so he hoped.

Fall progressed and apples ripened, filling the house with autumn smells as they processed their harvest. The couple hustled to squeeze in any last efforts to ensure their brumal survival. It was a fast, hard time, almost too busy to worry, and almost too busy to do the mental math on how much food they had and how long it needed to last. They worked well into the cold weather and their first day off was when the snow finally arrived.

Until the middle of January winter was mild, and Olive and Pepper were able to have a fairly productive garden in the greenhouse, adding a meager amount of lettuce and other greens to their supply. But even with the extra bump, their food was running low, and their chances of making it until the first harvest in spring were dropping.

Together, they calculated the first day they could expect to harvest more food, and made a rationing plan. The small meals rarely satiated their stomachs, but the plan made them feel more secure. At least they had some food every day.

The first snowstorm wasn't shy. In the evening, the accumulation didn't even prevent blades of grass from poking out through the snow's smooth surface, but by morning the snow created an uninterrupted plane from the top of the front porch over the fields. The deep snow created such a seamless transition from the ground to the porch, one wouldn't even know there were stairs leading down to the ground if not for the railing suspiciously plunging into the snow.

Pepper woke first and slid out of bed to check the window. He knew snow had been forecasted that night, but as he glanced out, he was shocked with the view. Their little valley had transformed into a blistering tundra. Powdery ice crystals swirled across the perfectly smooth rolling surface.

The whole valley was white. The ground, the sky, and almost everything between. Only the trunks and some branches of the trees were too vertical to grasp and hold the snow. These burnt, black wooden pillars contrasted harshly, a reminder of what lay below the new imposing, but ephemeral surface.

The dogs, which had been snuggling to conserve heat, were awake and pacing in front of the door in anticipation.

"You guys want out?" Pepper asked rhetorically, though they gave their answer by crowding even closer to the door with unrestrained anticipation.

Pepper opened the door for them and watched as they scrambled over each other to get outside. But as soon as their warm furry faces met the frosty, ice laden wind, the leader slammed the brakes and the two followers threw themselves in reverse.

"Nuh uh," Pepper said, blocking their regress with his foot. "Y'all need to go pee." The dogs looked at him in sad protest, leaning against his foot in hopes of getting back inside. "Go on," Pepper urged, pushing their rears harder until they reluctantly went to brave the cold.

Pepper regretted letting them out so soon. As they plodded through the perfect snow, Pepper wished he waited for Olive to wake up so she could provide witness to the snow's virgin beauty.

Pepper turned and went to the wood-burning stove to add a few wedges of wood. With barely any live coals from the night before, he had to bargain and plead with the fire for its resurrection. Despite the wintery scene outside, the house stayed very warm overnight, probably thanks to the three feet of snowy insulation on the roof.

Once the fire was hot, Pepper boiled some water and made two cups of coffee, one for each of them. The coffee was only half coffee beans. The other half was dried dandelion roots – a coffee substitute the couple sourced while weeding their fields. The grocery store hadn't had coffee in months, so the couple was conserving their precious supply. Soon, coffee would only be a memory, and dandelion root tea would be the norm.

They rarely went into town anymore, mainly because there wasn't anything to buy. No gas at the gas station, no hardware at the hardware store, and no groceries at the grocery store. Once, Bill set aside food for Pepper, but after that either Bill didn't receive any more shipments, or he neglected to call.

Olive never brought it up, but as their food supply dwindled and they got hungrier, Pepper worried she held onto some resentment over him giving away their food.

Although the couple never experienced the violence firsthand, like the rest of the country, Plomari had become dangerous. The last time Pepper was in town getting gas, the cashier told him he had been robbed twice in the past month for money and gas the station didn't have.

He also told Pepper about a few houses in Plomari robbed by thieves knocking on the front door and forcing their way inside. They stole food, money, anything they could use or sell. He said that maybe some of the robberies were from locals, but he thought most of the crime, especially the violence, was from people passing through. *Desperate people*, Pepper thought. People who were tired of looking for work, tired of starving, and willing to do whatever to get by.

There wasn't much left for them outside of Thirst Hollow, so the couple isolated themselves. Olive brought up the idea of destroying the road leading into Thirst Hollow so no one would be tempted to drive down it, but either the couple hadn't gotten around to it, or the implications of complete isolation scared them more than the chance of being robbed.

It was easy for Olive and Pepper to live in their little bubble and pretend the outside world didn't exist, or at least it wasn't so terrible. And that's exactly what they were doing. Pretending.

They both knew what was happening in the rest of the world, and the significance of their work in Thirst Hollow. They knew the importance of success. It was literally life and death. That idea pervaded their minds and never fully left, no matter what they were doing. It was ever present and permeative, but at least they could pretend. And it was easy for them to pretend when they had a beautiful distraction like the huge snowstorm that covered their valley the night before.

"Holy crap, it snowed!" Olive cried as she rushed out of the bedroom.

"Yeah, it's crazy," Pepper said, smiling and trying to match her energy.

"The dogs are loving it out there," she laughed. "I saw them from the bedroom chasing each other and taking bites of snow as they ran around." She walked to the window and pressed her nose against the foggy glass, looking out of a small window within the window she created with the swipe of her sleeve.

Pepper fried an egg for Olive and put it between two pieces of sourdough toast. That was another thing they would eventually run out of: flour. They tried to make it last by cutting it with cornmeal and ground acorns, but that made the bread dry and heavy, and soon the sad day was inevitable when they would only have the latter.

"Wow, it looks great," Olive said as Pepper placed the plate in front of her. "And it feels so cozy in here. The snow is so beautiful."

"Yeah, I was kind of thinking of taking the day off," Pepper said hopefully. "Maybe get a few things done around the house, but we can't really get much done outside today."

"That sounds nice," smiled Olive.

They sat and ate their breakfasts until Pepper heard the dogs scratching at the door. The excitement of the snow had worn off and they wanted back in to warm their paws. The dogs tore into the house, excited to see their owners. They paced back and forth, played with each other, and came up to Olive and Pepper to be petted, only momentarily stopping to shake off the melted snow that had sunk into their coats. Slowly, the excitement wore off and they lay down, soaking up the heat from the fire and from each other.

Olive and Pepper spent the morning sitting at the kitchen table, talking and laughing. They played cards and pretended to get mad when the other won. Lunchtime came and they made more egg sandwiches, too lazy to cook anything else. In the afternoon, melting snow began dripping outside, and every once in a while it avalanched off the slick metal roof and crashed to the ground.

"It looks like it's warming up out there," Pepper said. "Do you want to go sit on the porch for a while?"

"Sure! I guess I should change out of my pajamas though," Olive laughed.

They layered on coats and hats, then stepped onto the porch with the dogs close behind, sitting on the cold Adirondack chairs and looking out at the new world around them. The snowy silence from earlier had been replaced. Melted snow from the house and trees smacked onto cold slush below, and birds sensing the rising temperatures emerged from their hideouts and sang songs of excitement. The smooth snow surface covering the fields was broken by lines of dog tracks, but was still beautiful nonetheless.

Pepper and Olive sat on the deck enjoying the views and light conversation for almost two hours before Olive shifted forward in her chair and said, "I think I'm going to deep clean the kitchen. It needs it."

"Okay. I think I'm going to stay out here for a bit," Pepper said, not wanting the day to end.

Olive was right. Cleaning the house often took a back seat to other chores with more immediate consequences, so taking advantage of the day to catch up on overlooked tasks was smart. But Pepper didn't want to.

His stagnation wasn't from laziness or tiredness, but because he didn't want to go back to the worrying, back to the hunger, back to reality. The snow day had not only been a break from working, but it was also a break from the crushing pressure of trying to survive. Pepper was physically tired from working every day, but even more than that, he was mentally tired from constantly trying to keep their heads above water. That day could have been productive. He could have done a thousand things to better their situation, but making the decision to not do anything had taken a little weight off Pepper's back.

He didn't want to go back to worrying but Olive was inside being productive, and the weight began to bear down on him. And he knew once he went inside, it would crush him.

So Pepper sat on the front porch alone. He sat and thought. Every once in a while, feelings of guilt snuck into his head, but he did his best to let those go as easily as they came. He let his mind wander and relax. Pepper sat on the porch until the midday warmth retreated, and the water dripping off the roof recrystallized into long, undulating icicles, growing longer and longer, stretching toward the ground.

The melted snow started to refreeze, as did the tip of Pepper's nose. He pulled off his glove and touched it with his fingers. On his nose he felt the warmth of his fingers, and on his fingers he felt the cold of his nose. Pepper's toes, lacking blood circulation, had been numb for a while. He debated with himself about going inside to warm up but continued to sit, staring off at the strange new landscape, and the light that was fading by the minute.

Pepper couldn't go back in. His legs wouldn't let him. Pepper knew once he went back, he would not only return to the house, but also to reality and all the trouble and worries that go along with it. So instead he sat.

25

The Sheep

The snowstorm marked the end of the mild winter. More snow continued to inundate Thirst Hollow, and whenever it began to melt – giving Pepper and Olive hope spring was on its way – another storm would rebury the valley.

The ground remained covered until the first weeks of April. Cold weather stunted or killed most of the plants in the greenhouses, and prevented the couple from getting seedlings into the ground. Each day they couldn't plant their fields, the first harvest was delayed, and their food supplies further dwindled.

Their rations were constantly diluted by the delay of the spring harvests, stretching their meals thinner and thinner. The couple still had a reasonable amount of canned vegetables, but they were getting dangerously low on staples like beans, corn, potatoes and flour. They were running out of calories.

Due to short winter days, and their difficulty foraging for food in the snow, the chickens laid fewer and fewer eggs. Pepper and Olive reluctantly dipped into their own corn supplies to keep the flock alive. If all the chickens died, replacing them would be difficult, so the corn was an investment they hoped would pay dividends in the future.

Pepper and Olive ate less every day. After every meal hunger lingered, and Pepper's empty stomach constantly reminded him of the food he gave away to the family in Plomari. Olive was right, he should have put their needs first and he kicked himself every day for being such a pushover.

Though Pepper's stomach never stopped reminding him of his mistake, the sight of Olive's thinning body troubled Pepper the most. Both of them were constantly buried under layers of clothes to ward off persistent chills – no matter how much they stoked the fireplace, how much tea they drank, how many clothes they wore, they were always cold – so it was hard for Pepper to know how much weight Olive had lost, but Pepper caught glimpses.

Boney elbows, thin fingers, sunken cheeks, Olive was wasting away. They simply didn't have enough food, and were hopeless to get more until spring harvests came.

Pepper was reminded of a survival tip he heard while fighting fires in Utah. Many people who die of dehydration are found with undrunk water. Determined to ration, the victims perished conserving the very thing that could save them, so the rule for survival was to drink when thirsty. Pepper wasn't sure if the same applied to starvation.

Pepper and Olive's hunger slowed them down. Even the most basic chores like bringing firewood inside felt extremely laborious and required rest afterwards. They struggled to keep their farm running but just didn't have any more energy to give.

While Pepper and Olive rested their weak bodies, they often listened to the radio, too tired to even attempt to converse with each other. When they did, they heard stories of lawlessness, armed conflict, and looting.

Clashes between We the People, Net Zero, and the military created chaos. Nothing was stable, and control of cities constantly shifted between the groups. Goods were unable to enter cities, food and water were scarce, roads were destroyed, and cell towers were sabotaged. Olive and Pepper were unable to call the Burdettes or anyone else to check on their well-being.

They worried about the rest of the world, but were too scared to leave the safety of Thirst Hollow to do anything about it.

The couple withdrew all their money, and just in time before all the banks collapsed. They tried to spend their cash on things like food and seeds, but no one else trusted in the government or its money so their wads of bills became all but useless.

As the country's institutions failed, the couple stopped engaging with them. They stopped paying their bills, then taxes, then insurance as their faith in anything besides their farm failed.

The stories on the radio flooded in until suddenly they stopped. One morning, the radio didn't get a signal which wasn't unusual, but then there was another day of static, then another, and another. Eventually, the couple chalked the lack of reception up to a destroyed radio tower, and accepted their total isolation.

Without contact with the rest of the world, the couple focused entirely on maintaining the farm, unaware of what was happening elsewhere. But in their case, ignorance wasn't bliss. Not knowing what was happening outside of Thirst Hollow made the couple uneasy. The fear of the unknown haunted them and they could only assume the country's situation was deteriorating. They didn't think they could trust anyone, and their best chance of survival was to remain separated from the rest of the world.

Food always remained at the forefront of their minds, or more accurately, their lack of it. Olive and Pepper tried not to complain about the shortage, as talking about it only made their hunger more apparent, but somehow the topic always came up. One morning Olive shifted her focus from the lack of food to its acquisition. Olive was in the kitchen frying eggs when she brought up her thoughts.

"So, the other day I saw a book at the Burdettes' about slaughtering livestock," Olive said, keeping her eyes down on the eggs.

Pepper looked up from his dandelion-coffee concoction. "Yeah?" he asked, pausing to see where she was going with her statement.

"Yeah," she echoed. "I was thinking maybe we could supplement our food with some mutton."

Pepper noticed Olive avoided using the word *kill* or *slaughter*, but that's what she was getting at. She also used the word *mutton* instead of *sheep*, maybe to distance the thought of tasty food from the thought of a cute fluffy animal.

"You mean, like killing it?" Pepper asked, feigning confusion. He wanted her to come out and say it, not because he didn't know what she was talking about, but so she was forced to face the reality of what *supplementing their food with mutton* actually meant.

"Yeah," Olive said. She didn't have a problem with killing the sheep.

After the debris flow covered the Burdettes' pastures, and the couple moved the sheep and goats across Thirst Run, coyotes ravaged the herd, and the flock had dwindled to one. Olive had been thinking of slaughtering a sheep or goat for weeks but she wanted to be considerate of Pepper's beliefs, and her hunger hadn't been quite strong enough.

"We're running out of food," she continued. "I don't think we're going to make it until spring unless we do something." With thoughts of food in her head and nothing in her stomach, Olive became frantic. Her speech quickened as she went on. "We can't just sit here and wait for the coyotes to eat the last sheep. I'm fucking hungry Pepper, and I know you are too.

What's going to happen when we run out of food? Are we going to eat the dogs? We have to do something now. We can't wait any longer."

Pepper closed his eyes and slumped his shoulders. She was right. They were hungry and losing weight by the day. He could feel his elbows poking out more, and when he banged them on something, the pain rang sharper.

Working on the farm burned far more calories than he took in, and he knew he would keep losing weight until they were able to harvest food.

But Pepper would have been willing to endure if it weren't for Olive. The thought of killing the sheep left him with an uneasiness that overwhelmed his hunger. He hated the idea of killing something just to eat it. But Olive couldn't keep going for much longer without more food. He hated to see her wasting away, and since Olive proposed a solution, Pepper couldn't bring himself to say no, even if it went against his morals.

Though maybe, he thought as he tried to justify his decision, *it's not against my morals. Whenever someone asks me why I don't eat meat, I reply that if I can eat something else besides an animal, I'll just do that. But there isn't anything else to eat. At least not enough of it. There's not enough vegetables or bread or anything else. We have to eat the sheep.*

"Okay," Pepper said quietly, knowing he was doing the right thing, but still not feeling good about it. "You're right. It's probably best to…get some mutton."

Pepper decided that if he was going to eat the sheep, he should be the one to kill it. Otherwise he would be shirking responsibility. Over the next few days he read and reread the section of the book outlining how to slaughter and butcher sheep. In a nervous attempt to learn as much as possible, he also searched the rest of the Burdettes' books to find any information that could be remotely useful.

Early in his life, before becoming vegetarian, Pepper learned to gut a fish, but he wasn't confident those skills would translate. Pepper was nervous about doing something wrong and spoiling the meat. Killing the sheep in vain would not only be upsetting for the waste of life, but also for the loss of food they dearly needed. With only one sheep left, there wasn't any room for error, but after a few days of research and procrastination, Pepper convinced himself it was time.

The day of the slaughter, Pepper woke up early, skipping breakfast due to an uneasy stomach, and left the house before Olive rose. Pepper gathered the butchering accouterments from the Burdettes' barn: block and tackle, a gambrel, two meat hooks, a sharp six-inch knife, and a butcher's saw. Pepper double checked his tools before wrapping them into a piece of canvas, placed the roll on the tractor, and drove over to the sheep that was standing in a makeshift corral on the barren sediment fan.

Pepper parked the tractor and lowered the bucket attachment over the fence and into the corral. He stepped down from the machine and looked at the poor sheep. Pepper read that the sheep's stomach should be empty for slaughtering, so the night before he only left a pale of water.

The hungry sheep walked over to Pepper, the one she trusted to feed her, in hopes of a meal. But feeling he was acting as a betrayer, Pepper turned away to avoid more guilt and walked to the Burdettes' house to get the last tool he needed.

Before entering, Pepper wiped his feet on the welcome mat out of habit and respect for the Burdettes, though dirty shoes wouldn't change the state of the house much. The Burdettes hadn't lived in it for over a year and it was slowly falling into disrepair. A thick layer of dust blanketed everything in the house except for the few items Olive and Pepper used. Mouse droppings littered the floor as they had claimed the house as a winter refuge.

Sadness draped over Pepper as he walked through the house. He wished he could take better care of it, but he just didn't have the time or the energy to do much more than lay mouse traps every once in a while.

The heels of Pepper's boots knocked loudly on the wood floor, echoing through the house as if it was empty. And it was empty. Not empty of things, but empty of people, empty of life. Pepper felt out of place. He felt like he was intruding.

Pepper walked to the gun case, and carefully opened the glass door to remove the shotgun. In the few days prior, Pepper familiarized himself with the gun, and quickly found the shells he been practicing with. Pepper put one of the red plastic cylinders in his pocket, then reconsidering, added two more just in case.

With the shotgun's stock in his hand and the barrel leaning on his shoulder, Pepper left the house listening to the knocking of his boots. His steps quieted some as he stepped onto the deck, then more on the gravel between the house and the corral.

The hungry sheep greeted Pepper again with expecting eyes, and he granted her wish by placing a small tin of feed on the ground. The sheep was familiar with Pepper, so without hesitation she put her head down and began eating. While the sheep enjoyed her meal, which was her last, Pepper opened the action of the shotgun, and put a shell into the chamber. As he closed the slide, the sudden metal on metal sound startled the sheep, momentarily drawing her attention to the gun.

But the animal couldn't comprehend the lethality of the object, so she eagerly went back to her meal. From his pocket, Pepper produced two small foam cylinders, which he scrunched up and placed in each of his ears for protection.

Looking back to the sheep, he saw its forehead exposed and facing him. Pepper put the stock of the shotgun against his shoulder, positioned the barrel six inches from the sheep's forehead, and with a small contraction of his finger, a firm blow to his shoulder, and a loud, echoing bang, the sheep dropped to the ground leaving but a few bits of feed in the tin.

Pepper felt a stab of remorse as the sheep fell, but with no time for anything besides urgency, he unfurled the canvas bundle and got to work. He selected the six-inch sharp knife and approached the slain sheep, making a deep cut through the thick wool surrounding her neck, severing all major blood vessels. He needed to bleed the sheep immediately or the meat could go bad.

He attached the sheep's hind legs to the tractor's front attachment and raised the carcass into the air, letting the blood drain onto the bare ground. Viscous red fluid streamed from the sheep's cut neck into a shallow puddle.

Pepper turned and walked to the back of the tractor. He faced away to avoid watching the dripping blood, though he couldn't escape the smacking noise the blood made as it struck the ground.

As he waited for the noise to stop, Pepper looked out to a familiar view of Thirst Hollow, though something about it felt a little off. Instead of looking out from his own property as he normally did, Pepper saw Thirst Hollow from the Burdettes', viewing it from a slightly different angle than usual.

Once the smacking slowed to a drizzle, and the drizzle slowed to a drip, Pepper returned to the corral and began skinning the hanging sheep. Slowly, he separated the skin and wool from the marbled pink, red, and white remainder beneath. He flinched at every cut, but as he progressed the sheep began to cease looking like an animal that would be walking around the field, but more like a labeled illustration in a biology textbook and his guilt began to wane.

Pepper continued peeling off the skin, using the knife to cut stubborn connecting tissue until he reached the head, then he paused. It was time to behead the sheep. Time to remove the last vestige giving it personality. The last bit separating the animal from being food. From being mere calories.

Cutting through the throat's flesh until he hit the hard bone of the spine, Pepper let the knife find its way between two vertebrae and cut as far as the bones would allow. He signed deeply then closed his eyes, twisted the head, and listened to the remaining connections pop and snap until the sheep's head was separate from its body.

231

Pepper had to look away. The noise of tendons and sinew breaking was too much. His eyes drifted up and were met with a view of Thirst Hollow. The ridge, the trees, the rocks, the burn scar, the sky, all the elements were there, but everything felt a little off. Pepper had looked at that view hundreds, if not thousands of times before, but this time it felt foreign and unfamiliar. Everything was the same, but with a slightly distorted form, and slightly warped proportions. The differences were hard to identify, but their subtleness made them more unnerving.

Pepper looked away from the uncanny view and back to the sheep's head dangling from his hand. He carried the head outside of the corral and placed it onto a patch of grass, planning to bury it later out of respect and not wanting to get it dirty in the meantime. He walked back to the corral. His next step was disembowelment.

The beheaded and skinned sheep no longer looked like any animal Pepper had seen. His work sped up as he dissociated the carcass from the animal. Pepper used his knife to open the abdomen, revealing the sheep's innards. Once open, Pepper carefully removed the organs, nervous about tearing or breaking any of them and contaminating the meat. He placed the organs in a pile on a black plastic bag, separating the liver, kidneys, and heart for him and Olive, and the lungs for the dogs.

After rinsing the carcass of any rogue wool and dirt, Pepper was almost done. He got back onto the tractor and placed the shotgun behind the seat, feeling maybe it would be better to keep at their house instead of leaving it at the Burdettes'. Pepper pulled on a control lever and raised the sheep enough to clear the corral's fence. The meat would be best if aged for about a week outside in the cool air, so Pepper wanted to hang it on a tree near their house where it would be safe from wild coyotes and their own dogs looking for a free meal.

Pepper kept the carcass high so he could see in front of the tractor, and it swung back and forth as he slowly drove down the Burdettes' driveway and back to the house. Though no one was around to watch, Pepper felt he was parading his kill for the world to see, as if he was proud of it.

But Pepper wasn't proud, he was ashamed. Ashamed he couldn't take care of himself and Olive, and ashamed he killed an animal to make up for his shortcomings. The sheep would keep them fed for a while, but then what? There were no more sheep. Even if the meat lasted until spring harvest, what about next winter? Would they be able to grow enough food to get them through next year? And if not, what would they do without more sheep to bail them out?

Without answers and only anxiety, Pepper drove the carcass to a tree outside of their house and hung it up by its rear legs. He covered it with a canvas sack to protect it from the elements, and to protect himself from being reminded of his failings, hoping the sheep would provide them enough food to last until spring. But the sheep wasn't very large, and spring was a long time away.

26

The Noise

Olive enjoyed the sheep's meat, but Pepper enjoyed it even more. Of all Pepper's reasons for abstention, none of them were gustatory in nature. After the first few days of omnivory the dietary change normalized and Pepper's guilt waned as he embraced the long-missed taste. The new sensory pleasure paired with their hunger made rationing difficult, though they did the best they could. But even with meager portions, the mutton ran out by late March.

The snow was mostly melted, but the cold weather lingered and the ground remained frozen. Weeks remained before the couple would have a chance to plant anything, and months until they harvested. The couple was back to eating tiny rations of rice, flour, and canned vegetables, with portions not even close to satiating them. They were hungry. Day by day Pepper saw weight melt off himself and Olive. They had no more fat, so their bodies consumed the small amount of flesh clinging to their bones.

Food was running so low Pepper and Olive decided to stop feeding the dogs. It was a choice Pepper would like to think was hard, but their hunger was so intense, it was barely a conversation. They justified their decision by quietly deluding themselves into thinking the dogs were somehow scavenging enough food, but they were barely hanging on.

Mango's ribs showed through her black coat, and Box and Turtle's hip bones jutted out sharply. Pepper and Olive gave the dogs anything they couldn't eat. The sheep bones while they lasted, then after that, the chicken's eggshells. At first the dogs ignored the shells, but as their hunger grew, they learned to eat them for the calories in the residual egg whites. The dogs had a rough time, but they didn't realize they were lucky to not share the same fate as the sheep, for in times of their worst hunger pains, the thought crossed both Olive and Pepper's minds.

To distract from their hunger, the couple doubled down on their day-to-day chores, trying to accomplish as much as they were physically capable of. But no matter how hard they worked, they couldn't keep up. They were exhausted from their hunger and something always needed their immediate attention on the farm. They scrambled to keep their lives moving forward, though their accomplishments were overshadowed by their shortcomings.

One day, the most pressing need was firewood. The piles had shrunk beyond avoidance, so Olive and Pepper had to venture out to find more as the fire burned all sources close to the house.

The previous year, the couple drove their truck to look for wood, but with the scarcity of gas, and their devalued money, Pepper jerry-rigged a handcart out of some bicycle wheels and scrap lumber to haul the wood.

So the couple hiked up the Thirst Hollow valley into the woods of the surrounding National Forest. In the cart lay the chainsaw, a handsaw, and an ax to cut logs into pieces small enough to fit in the cart. The couple followed the road past the Burdettes' house, pulling the cart into the forested mountains. The dogs scampered behind, excited for a change of scenery, though lagging a little more than they used to.

Pulling the cart and walking uphill was exhausting. Neither Pepper nor Olive were eating enough calories to sustain themselves, much less to exert that amount of effort. Hiking into the mountains would be an exhausting day, but they needed more wood and there was no other way to get it.

"It's nice out today," Pepper said, breathing heavily as he pulled the empty cart. The spring sun shone bright, and tried its hardest to warm the cool, foggy air lingering in the trees' shadows.

"Yeah," Olive agreed. "Maybe winter's finally over."

The couple slowed as they gained elevation and walked in silence. Plodding along, they tried to muster energy while scanning the forest floor for wood. Soon Olive spotted a few logs worth taking, so they stopped. Back when the couple drove the truck to get wood, they would end up much farther down the road. Pepper wasn't sure if they developed a keener eye, or on foot they were just less picky in their emaciated state.

Olive and Pepper worked together to cut up the logs, and placed the pieces on the side of the road. Not enough to fill the cart or replenish their stores at home, they left the wood behind and continued their search. There was no point in lugging it farther since they could get it on their way back. Though walking uphill was hard, Pepper was grateful gravity would be on his side when they returned with a full cart.

Olive and Pepper continued until early afternoon, finding wood and placing it on the side of the road for later collection. After breaking up and stacking a sizable pile, they stopped.

"Are you hungry?" Pepper asked Olive, already knowing the answer. Upon hearing the *h* word, Mango's ears perked up and she sat as politely as she could, remembering a time of regular meals and full stomachs. She watched attentively hoping to find some dropped food, or at least get a few sniffs of it.

"Yeah. Should we eat lunch?"

"Sure," Pepper said, grabbing their lunches from the handcart. "It looks like it's sunny over there," he gestured to a grassy clearing, just past where they collected the wood.

The couple walked over and sat on the damp ground, and Pepper pulled out their lunch of a boiled egg and a thin slice of sourdough bread each. The other dogs appeared and sat next to Mango, watching resolutely. Pepper hated their eyes following his every move, but didn't have the heart to tell them to go away.

They sat peeling the eggs, littering white shells on the dark, organic rich soil. Once the dogs saw the shells, all three rushed to reap the bounty, snarling at each other as Box was first to snatch a piece off of the ground. Pepper raised his voice to snap them out of their tunnel vision, and made them sit to calm down.

Olive and Pepper peeled the eggs, placing the shells into three piles and gave them to the dogs separately. They ate their small piles in a single bite, then licked up the underlying dirt, hoping to ingest any bits they missed.

Though the sun was warm, the air filtering through the leafless branches was cool, and it chilled Pepper's malnourished body. He put on his jacket and felt a slight reprieve under its weight.

"I think we probably have enough wood for a trip back to the house," Pepper said with a mouth full of bread and egg.

"Yeah, I think so too," Olive agreed, nodding her head as she finished chewing the last bite of her inadequate lunch. She forced a small burp out. With so little to eat, her stomach had shrunken, and food almost always upset it. "It's cold up here." She stood up to get off the heat sucking ground and get her blood moving a little. "I'm ready to get going whenever you're finished."

Pepper stood up and brushed the dirt and leaves off his butt as they walked back to the handcart. The couple started piling the wood into the cart, but were stopped short by a noise.

Olive and Pepper had grown accustomed only hearing the sounds of the forest, of each other, and the dogs, so anything foreign caught their attention. With thoughts of chaos and violence at the forefront of their minds any outside noise was alarming, so both Olive and Pepper stopped moving and listened intently.

The noise was quiet, barely noticeable at first, but grew louder and louder. Pepper recognized it as a vehicle driving up Thirst Hollow. It wasn't a loud vehicle like a diesel truck, but sounded more like a small, practical car. The noise lasted for a couple minutes, and when it cut out Olive and Pepper looked at each other.

"It stopped," Olive said, almost posing it as a question.

"Yeah," he agreed. "That means they're at the Burdettes' house. Or ours."

Olive looked at Pepper and he saw perturbation in her eyes. Memories of the hitchhiker came rushing back, and visions of looters and anarchy flashed through their minds.

"What should we do?" Olive asked.

"Let's stash the handcart here, then go to try to see what's going on. Maybe it's nothing," Pepper said optimistically.

"Okay," Olive agreed with a little more confidence in her voice.

The couple pulled the cart about fifteen yards off the road, behind a tree and some bushes. Before they left Pepper and Olive cut the rope used to tie down the wood, and fashioned it into leashes for the dogs. They didn't want to take any chances by putting the dogs in danger, or worse, have the dogs put them in danger.

Olive and Pepper began down the dirt road, back to Thirst Hollow. They walked swiftly and quietly so they could hear any new noises. Part of them hoped to hear the car leave so they wouldn't have to confront the intruders, but they also hoped to get down in time to defend their property. They walked for about a half an hour before coming to where the dirt road met the pavement, then stopped to decide their plan of action.

"Let's follow the side of the ridge to the burn scar," Pepper said to Olive, out of breath from burning so many calories. "From there we will have a pretty good view of the Burdettes' house and maybe ours."

The couple hiked halfway up the ridge and followed a contour to the edge of the burn scar where no trees blocked their view. Standing on the edge of the clearing, Pepper and Olive could see the Burdettes' house and driveway. Parked was a dark blue sedan, and walking from the house to the car's open trunk was a man carrying a large cardboard box.

"What the fuck is going on?" Olive asked, grasping Pepper's arm and squinting at the man.

"I'm not sure," Pepper responded.

"We need to get back to the house," Olive said decidedly.

"And do what?"

"We have to protect our property," Olive said, as if her previous statement was self-evident. "We need to get the gun."

"What? Are you crazy?" Pepper asked, astonished. "What if that guy has a gun too? He probably does if he's bold enough just to walk into that house and rob it. We should just wait here and let him have what he wants. Our stuff isn't worth our lives."

"Yes, it is. Our stuff *is* our lives," Olive pleaded. "We can't just go buy new tools or more food. What we have is all we have, and we aren't going to be able to get more. If we let that guy take what he wants, we will starve. It will be either soon because he took our food, or later because we won't be able to farm. Either way, we have to go now and defend ourselves."

Pepper looked down at the man, who was going back into the Burdettes' house. The man's demeanor wasn't menacing, but his presence in the Burdettes' house was disturbing. Pepper didn't want to confront him. He didn't want to go anywhere near him, but if doing so meant saving himself and Olive, he would do what he had to.

"Okay," Pepper caved. "You're right. How are we going to get to the house? We can't go down the road since he'll be able to see us."

"Yeah," Olive said, formulating a plan in her head. "You're right. We shouldn't go on the road, but we also can't cross the burn scar here. We'd be too exposed. Let's hike up to the top of the ridge and follow it behind our house. Then we can drop down to our property from there."

Pepper took Olive's hand and squeezed it. "Okay, let's go."

The couple tore up to the top of the ridge, fighting through brush and trees. Their malnourished bodies momentarily forgot their exhaustion. Pepper glanced down, and the man was making another trip into the house.

The couple hurried. Running across the ridge, they no longer had a vantage on the man, and could only hope they would reach the house before he made it there first.

27

The Shotgun

Olive and Pepper tore down the open burn scar behind their house. They ran, still leading the dogs, to their front door and busted in, closing the door swiftly but quietly behind them. Pepper took hurried strides into the bedroom and grabbed the shotgun from under the bed. Just minutes before, he was shocked at the suggestion of using the gun, but being in his house and seeing all he had to lose, Pepper knew it was the only option.

From under the bed he pulled out a box of shells, which lightly jostled against each other as they were disturbed from their slumber. Pepper took the shotgun in his hands, and turned it so the barrel pointed at the floor. One by one, he clicked the dull red shells into place, each one pushing the previous farther down into the magazine. Once full, Pepper pulled the pump action back, then pushed it forward so one shell was forced into the chamber, ready to be fired.

Pepper double checked that the safety was on before walking back into the living room. Olive stood by the window with the curtain pulled back just enough to peek out. Before Pepper could say anything, they heard the car start at the Burdettes' property. An adrenaline filled look was shared between them, which intensified as they heard the car start moving.

"Is he coming here?" Olive asked, the whites of her eyes showing the terror within.

"I don't know," Pepper responded, his heart racing. "Why don't you go into the bedroom? It will be safer in there."

"No," Olive said definitively. "I'll stay out here with you."

They could hear the vehicle driving on the paved road. In a few seconds, it would either continue down Thirst Hollow, and hopefully out of their lives, or turn down their driveway, forcing them to confront the man.

The room was still as the couple listened closely. The car slowed and the noise of the quiet pavement turned to grumbling gravel. The intruder was coming to their house.

Panicked, Pepper unlocked the deadbolt to walk outside, but reconsidered, relocked it, and opened one of the front windows just enough to slide the barrel of the shotgun through.

"Why don't you go to the bedroom?" Pepper asked again.

"No, I'm going to stay," Olive's shaky voice responded.

The car's noise grew louder and louder as it neared. Pepper turned to the window, and Olive took a step forward to stand behind him. He pulled the curtains back an inch and saw the intruding vehicle. The sky reflected off the windshield, and Pepper couldn't see more than a silhouette of the driver.

The car steered to its right and parked about fifty feet away with the driver's side facing the house. The door swung open and the man pulled himself out as the car sat idling. He looked at the house and adjusted his blue jeans without the sense of urgency or nervousness Pepper expected from a thief.

The man didn't appear to think anyone was home as he began to walk with long, intentional strides to the porch. Pepper stood looking out the window, frozen with a lump in his throat. He knew he had to do something, but his body wasn't working. His voice was paralyzed.

Pepper took a deep swallow to lubricate his throat with saliva. He yelled with what was intended to be a deep, intimidating voice, but it came out cracked and shaky. "What do you want? We're armed in here."

This stopped the man in his tracks. He looked around at the house, unsure of where the voice was coming from.

"Sorry?" the man asked into his surroundings.

"What are you doing here?" Pepper shouted again, this time deeper and more confident.

"I'm sorry," he said, lifting his hands out from his sides with fingers wide open, in an attempt to show he wasn't armed. "Do Pepper and Olive live here?"

The question caught Pepper off guard. He turned to look at Olive who was also surprised. Pepper wasn't sure how to answer. He worried the man was up to something and answering honestly would be a mistake.

"Who are you?" Pepper asked, avoiding the man's question.

"I'm Barry," the man answered. "Barry Burdette."

Pepper's tense shoulder muscles relaxed and his brow furrowed.

"You're Barb and Tom's son?" Pepper called out, less loud and less deep than before.

"Yeah," he responded. Pepper noticed that the man's voice was a little shaky. Maybe his deep voice had worked.

"What are you doing here?" Pepper asked, pulling the curtains back farther, revealing a little more of his face through the window.

"We came to get some of my parents' stuff," Barry explained. "We're headed down to Tennessee."

"Is Mrs. Burdette in the car?" Olive whispered behind Pepper.

"Is Mrs. Burdette in the car?" Pepper called through the window, relaying Olive's question.

"Yeah. She's sick though. She's too tired to get out."

"Oh my god, I think she's really out there," Olive whispered in excitement behind Pepper. "Put down the gun. Let's go talk to them."

Pepper slid the barrel of the shotgun off of the windowsill and leaned it next to the door as Olive rushed out, no longer scared of the man. The dogs ran outside and Pepper jogged to catch up.

"Hi, I'm Barry, Barb's son," the man said to Olive, first gently shaking her hand, then bending over to pet Box and Turtle. The dogs recognized Barry from years ago, and whined in excitement as they pushed their bodies against him, rolling over to be petted.

"Sorry about that," Pepper said, walking up. "We thought you were robbing your parents' house. It's happened before." Then reaching his hand out, he introduced himself, "Pepper, nice to meet you."

"Not a problem. I completely understand. You can't be too careful these days," Barry said, relieved. "Barry, nice to meet you." He reached and firmly grasped Pepper's hand. He was warm and friendly, and Pepper thought he took after his mother more than his father.

Olive leaned in the direction of the car and Mrs. Burdette, antsy to greet her old friend, but not wanting to be impolite. Barry noticed her eagerness and urged the couple to greet his mother. Like when the dogs were released for their dinner, back when they had enough food, Pepper and Olive rushed to the passenger side of the car and opened the door. Inside sat a small, weak Mrs. Burdette, almost unrecognizable from the strong, able woman who left Thirst Hollow just over a year ago.

Her skin was translucent, revealing blue blood vessels and the outline of bones beneath. Her hands rested on her lap, a good thing Pepper thought, because her wrists didn't look strong enough to support the weight of her hands. As Barry opened the car door, Mrs. Burdette slowly looked over, the act of turning her head a monumental task in itself.

"Hiii," Olive said in a long, drawn-out voice, an octave higher than normal. "How are you doing? It's been such a long time. It's so great to see you."

"Oh, hi dear," Mrs. Burdette smiled. "I'm doing fine. How about y'all?"

"We're getting along," Olive responded, thinking about all their hardships but choosing not to burden Mrs. Burdette with them.

"Hi Mrs. Burdette," Pepper piped in from behind Olive. He wanted nothing more than to give her a hug, but was scared her frail body couldn't handle such an impact.

"Hi dear. My lord, it has been so long. It's really nice to see you two."

"It really has been a long time. We miss you and Mr. Burdette so much," Olive replied. "Do you want to come inside for some tea and to catch up?"

Pepper noticed Olive offered tea but not dinner, though it was about the time they normally started cooking.

"Oh, that would be nice. Yes," Mrs. Burdette answered. Like before, her voice was sweet, but now smaller and tired.

Barry stepped in from the periphery to help his mother out of the car. She held his arm as he guided her across the driveway and into the front door held open by Pepper. Olive walked ahead to start boiling water.

"This used to be your house, didn't it?" Pepper asked once Barry got his mother settled in a chair and took a seat himself.

"Sure did," Barry affirmed. "We built this place, me and my wife. I like what you've done in here though. Also, my parents said you've been working the fields more than I ever had the time or motivation to."

"Yeah, it's been a lot of work, but I think we are starting to get the hang of it," Pepper responded, hoping what he said was true.

"What are y'all doing back in Thirst Hollow?" Olive asked from the kitchen as she pulled a jar each of dandelion and mint leaf from the shelf. The couple had run out of store-bought tea months ago, so they only had herbs grown or collected to offer.

"Well, when Dad got real sick, I drove up to see him and Mom," Barry nodded toward Mrs. Burdette. "When I first got up there, things weren't great, but they seemed okay, food shortages, electricity blackouts, but at least no violence. I was only up there for about two months to get everything sorted out, but in that time things escalated fast.

"That damned We the People group started taking over the streets, hoarding all the food at the grocery stores and selling it back for crazy prices. Soon, the Army came and that's when the fighting started. After a few weeks of gunshots and tear gas, We the People forced the Army out and there was peace for a bit. We were hungry, but at least we were safe.

"We tried to get Dad some medical help, but there just weren't any doctors left so all we could do was sit in that little apartment and watch him waste away. Then once he was gone, as if that wasn't hard enough, we had to figure out what to do with his body. With no other options we ended up leaving it in the park across the street. We tried to find a nice place, but with all the violence, we couldn't even dig a grave. We just left him there. It was terrible. I wanted to get Mom out then, but soon the leftist resistance groups sprung up and the fighting started making it impossible for us to leave.

"Every night we heard their battles in the streets. They learned how to make bombs, and several rocked the building we were in. Shrapnel broke our windows and we covered them with furniture and cardboard. We never left the apartment unless it was absolutely necessary. There was no food, no electricity, and no running water. I couldn't leave Mom there like that. I tried everything I could think of to get a little gas and food, and once I did, we left. Things aren't great by any means in Tennessee, but I live out in the country and at least there aren't people shooting at each other. Yet, I guess."

"Oh my gosh. That sounds terrible." Olive said, truly distraught as she brought over four mugs of hot tea, setting one in front of each person at the table.

"Yeah," Barry confirmed. "Before I went, I heard about things like that happening, but I guess seeing them in person made it real."

"Jeez, I'm so sorry to hear that. And what about your other son, Todd? Is he going to Tennessee also?" Pepper asked Mrs. Burdette, holding his mug, absorbing its heat through his hands. The warmth felt good on his palms and fingers, but his body's core was still cold. He hadn't been warm since the beginning of winter when there was enough food to eat.

"Oh no, he can't," Mrs. Burdette spoke up in a small voice. "Barry asked him, and I begged him, but he wouldn't. His wife has family in Richmond, and he said she couldn't leave them."

"Well at least you got to spend some time with him," Olive said.

"Yes, it was really nice staying with him and his family," Mrs. Burdette nodded. "I'm not sure if I will make it up there again to see him."

The table quietly reflected on the meaning of Mrs. Burdette's comment. Pepper couldn't bear to think about Mrs. Burdette's death any longer, so he broke the silence, "Things are better in Tennessee then?"

"Well, better than Richmond for sure, but it's not great," Barry answered. "I don't really think it's good anywhere. When I left Tennessee, we could barely buy anything besides rice at the grocery store, but at least it was safe. I've had trouble getting through to my wife since the militia groups have been destroying all the cell phone towers, but I heard from her a few days ago, and everything was still safe. She and the kids are getting by, but they are running through our food storage.

"When the protests started, my wife was smart enough to buy a ton of canned veggies and nonperishable food, but they're running low. That's one reason we stopped here, was to see if there was any food left at the house. We really could use some extra for our trip. Mom is weak. She needs food. And also gas. We don't have enough to get to Tennessee, and I'm not sure where we're going to be able to get any along the way."

An awkward silence followed as Olive and Pepper tried to understand the intention behind his statement. Was he asking for food and gas? Were they expecting it? Pepper looked up from his cup of tea and saw Olive, Barry, and Mrs. Burdette all staring deeply into their cups of tea. Pepper took a deeper look at Barry's face.

He saw similarities to both parents. His laugh lines matched his mom's, but his gray eyes and sharp nose matched his dad's. The thick beard distracted from sunken cheekbones. His face was bony. Where once had probably been full cheeks, the skin was pulled tight against his skull, hinting at his mortality. Pepper didn't know Barry before that day, but as he looked, Pepper felt a connection to him – both through Barry's humanity and through his parents that Pepper knew so well.

Pepper shifted his focus on Mrs. Burdette's face. Though it had only been one year since he last saw her, she looked as if she aged thirty. Much thinner than before, Pepper wasn't sure if her condition was a product of watching her husband die, living in a literal war zone, or the lack of a regular food supply, but he figured it was the sum of her circumstances. Pepper saw they were struggling and he felt bad for them. The Burdettes were asking for help, but were too proud to outright say it. Pepper saw Barry's eyes lift, and embarrassed, Pepper dropped his eyes quickly back to his cup of tea.

"Well, I guess it's getting late so we'd better get going. I think we're going to try to hit the road early," Barry said, sensing the tension stemming from his unspoken request.

Not even five o'clock, it was anything but late. Pepper thought if Barry was anything like his dad, he couldn't bear to impose on him and Olive. He was already out of his comfort zone by sharing that he and his mother needed food and gas, and only felt it was polite to leave Pepper and Olive alone to discuss his implicit appeal.

"Okay, well it was really nice catching up with you two. Stop by before you leave tomorrow," Pepper said, standing up.

A round of awkward goodbyes was exchanged, then a round of sad goodbyes were said from Barry and Mrs. Burdette to their former dogs. Pepper wished their visit had gone better. He dearly missed Mrs. Burdette, and wished they could have talked more, but the mood of the evening had shifted and there was no bringing it back. The Burdettes left, on their way to sleep in their former house for what would likely be their last time.

Without them, the house felt quiet. Olive and Pepper stood in place for a moment, not knowing what to say to each other.

"So what do you think we should do?" Olive asked.

Though always advocating for taking care of themselves first, Olive had a soft spot for the Burdettes. Without their help, she didn't know where her and Pepper, or their farm would be. It definitely wouldn't be as successful without the Burdettes, and they were barely hanging on as they were. Without the Burdettes' help, she and Pepper would be much hungrier than they were, if they were even able to stay in Thirst Hollow. Maybe without the Burdette's, they would have been forced out into the dangerous world and who knows what would have happened to them out there.

Olive always told Pepper to take care of themselves first, so she didn't understand why part of her wanted to help Mrs. Burdette and her son. Maybe, after all their help, she considered the Burdettes part of her "in" group. Maybe they were part of the people who she wanted to protect before helping everyone else.

But they couldn't afford to lose any more food. She and Pepper were walking a tight line, and any disturbance could send them falling.

"Well, it's probably too late to go back up and get the firewood and handcart." Pepper said, avoiding Olive's real question.

"Okay, maybe I'll just start dinner then," Olive said. She understood that Pepper didn't want to talk about it, though surprised Pepper didn't immediately want to help the Burdettes. Maybe giving away food to the family in Plomari and their hunger really had changed him.

"I think I'm going to go up to the ridge to see if there is cell service. Maybe Barry can use our phone tomorrow to call his wife," Pepper said, putting his coat and boots on.

"Okay," nodded Olive. They both knew it was just an excuse to have some time to get away and think.

Pepper gave Olive a kiss. "I'll be back for dinner. I love you." He appreciated Olive's understanding, and wondered if she had a little extra sympathy for him after learning what happened during the fire in California.

"Okay, love you too," Olive said with a tight-lipped smile that only turned up the very corners of her mouth.

Pepper walked out the front door into the cold, and started hiking up the steep slope to his place of refuge, his place of contemplation. He needed space to think. Pepper didn't know what to do, and there didn't seem to be any good options. But he had to make a decision one way or another, so he hiked harder, hoping to find some clarity on the ridge.

28

The Decision

When Pepper reached the top of the ridge, the setting sun ignited the clouds with fluorescent orange and pink fire. Pepper's breath escaped his lungs as steam, mushrooming into the cold air. His shirt, damp from sweat, clung to him, and when he stopped moving it immediately chilled his body.

Pepper put on his coat to block the wind, and felt it hug his cold torso. He sat down on a sandstone boulder, but instead of looking at the sunset, Pepper's gaze fixed on his boots dangling beneath him. The brown leather was smudged and streaked black by burnt soil. The fire only happened a few months before, but the amount of work, struggle, and worry Pepper experienced since made him feel like it happened years ago.

Considering the extent and severity of the fire, Pepper still had trouble believing that literally nothing of theirs – not their crops or their possessions – burned. Devastation encompassed their house and fields, but somehow, the fiery destruction spared them.

He was so grateful they were able to continue to provide for themselves, but the fire showed him that the foundation they built their lives upon was delicate. It was a house of cards ready to tumble. The subsequent debris flows also blew wind at their house of cards, and even knocked a few down. They destroyed an entire field, and reduced their food supply for the winter. If

Pepper and Olive didn't have the sheep to kill, they would be in the same boat as Barry and Mrs. Burdette, starving and desperate.

Well, more than he and Olive already were. And though they did have some food to eat, who knew what was going to happen the next day. Who knew if their plants would grow that summer. Who knew if another fire would rage through their property. Who knew if someone would come violently take what he and Olive worked so hard to create. Wes already gave them a taste for what people were capable of, but luckily that lesson was learned at a low cost. No one was hurt, but Pepper knew the next person could be more desperate in their attempts.

The world wasn't the same as it was when they first moved to Virginia. When they didn't grow enough food that first winter, they were able to go to the grocery store and get more. If their house burned down last year, they could have gotten money from the insurance company. If one of them had gotten hurt or sick, they could have gone to the hospital.

But in the times of extremist groups controlling cities, grocery stores without food, gas stations without gas, and people willing to hurt others to survive, the couple's safety nets were gone. Pepper didn't trust anyone. Not people, not gas stations or grocery stores, no one. Survival was solely on their shoulders. No one could, or would, help them.

So, Pepper thought, why should he help anyone else? Even if they were in need. Even if it was someone they knew. Even if it was Mrs. Burdette, who was critical in many of their successes, and he owed so much to.

Pepper looked up from his boots and back to the sunset. The intense oranges had relaxed to pinks, and the pinks had faded to dusty purples. The sky, a deep, pelagic blue, framed the clouds' calming colors. Pepper's mind drifted to the Burdettes.

Since the first day he and Olive moved into Thirst Hollow, the Burdettes were always incredibly generous to them. From answering their hundreds of questions, to having them over for Thanksgiving dinner, they were always there to help, and Pepper wanted to help them back. Mrs. Burdette and Barry were struggling, and deep in his heart, Pepper felt the urge to make things right, to give them some food.

He thought of Blackwell and the family. They needed help, just like Mrs. Burdette and Barry, but Pepper didn't respond. Instead he listened to their screams and let them die. He could have saved them, but he didn't. And as a result, they died.

And Mrs. Burdette and Barry could easily share the same fate if Pepper didn't do something. The road to Tennessee was long, and food and gas were scarce. The outside world was dangerous. They could get stuck somewhere and end up in serious trouble. Pepper couldn't let anyone else die because of his inaction. It would be a sacrifice to give them food, but it could mean the difference between success and failure. Life and death. Pepper knew helping the Burdettes was the right thing to do. It's what he should do.

Pepper shifted on the rock. His butt was cold and sore, and his legs were falling asleep. The clouds' last colors faded, leaving only a remnant glow where the Earth's edge obscured the sun's final light. Stars and planets would have been emerging from the night sky, if not for the cloudy overcast. There were no stars, only darkness.

Soon, the last light dissolved into the night sky and Pepper sat, looking out at a black canopy with no view at all. Pepper knew the trees were there. He knew Thirst Hollow was there. Shenandoah Valley was there. Pepper knew it was all there, he just couldn't see any of it. Nothing remained outwards, so his mind fell inwards.

And when it did, Pepper knew what to do. Looking out at the black curtain, Pepper knew he couldn't let Olive and himself go hungry. They had to take care of themselves before taking care of the Burdettes. Helping anyone else would be harmful to them, so refusing help to Mrs. Burdette would be the same as helping themselves. He couldn't ignore Olive's call for help anymore, nor his own. He had to protect his life and Olive's. They needed to come first.

Pepper hopped off the rock and walked down the trail through the encompassing darkness. He couldn't see where he was, or where he was placing his feet, but he knew where he was going. He was going to have dinner with Olive.

29

The End

The first crops came in late April, relieving Olive and Pepper of their hunger. Though through careful rationing, they still had a few jars of vegetables and some rice left in their pantry. Maybe they could have spared a little for the Burdette's, but neither regretted their decision. After Mrs. Burdette and Barry left, Olive and Pepper never talked about them again, and tried their best not to think about them. Neither were proud of their decision, but they did what they thought they had to do, and on some level were okay with that. They had to be, and neither of them regretted it.

Pepper and Olive survived, and after all, wasn't that the goal? Whether they actually needed to keep that food for themselves or if they could have spared some, it didn't matter. The decision was made, and they made it to see another winter.

Both Pepper and Olive worked hard to make that growing season more productive than the last. The farm was set up better than before, and they had two years of knowledge and experience under their belts.

But the couple still expected complications. They didn't know what would happen, but they knew something was likely to come and ruin their careful planning. A fire, a drought, a flood. They weren't sure what it would be, but they wouldn't be surprised when it showed up. Though, they weren't expecting any problems from one source. Other people.

Once the weather warmed that spring, the couple used the tractor to destroy the road at the entrance of Thirst Hollow. They tore up the road making it impassable, preventing any vehicle, friendly or not, from entering their valley. The couple wanted to be left alone. They couldn't keep out natural disasters, but at least they could keep other people out.

The world was full of people trying to prevent the couple from surviving. It didn't have anything for them. Humans changed the climate, and the climate changed the world. There was nothing left for them to give or take, so they cut all ties.

Pepper hoped one day the world would change. Maybe not back to the way it was before, but to a world that was safe, to something better. He hoped in the future he would again be able to help others. That desire wasn't lost, but he accepted he couldn't help if it hurt him and Olive. So until the world improved, if ever, it was just them and Thirst Hollow.

And their existence in Thirst Hollow was ephemeral. It was fragile. They didn't know how long they could survive in that world, after all, it was changing, and maybe too fast for them to adapt.

But they had no choice. Pepper and Olive would continue living there, season after season, crop after crop. All they could do was try to persevere. Persevere and prepare for the next winter. They would go until one day, they didn't. They might be able to live in Thirst Hollow for fifty more years, or maybe only five more. Or maybe they would perish the next winter. The next day.

www.ingramcontent.com/pod-product-compliance
Lightning Source LLC
Chambersburg PA
CBHW031942010726
47493CB00007B/2031